THE LAST ATLANTEANS

by Katrina Ryan

Twitter: @LastAtlanteans
Facebook.com/TheLastAtlanteans
Instagram: @LastAtlanteans
#TheLastAtlanteans

To my mom and dad. Thank you for everything.

CONTENTS

PROLOGUE

Atlantis was the most dangerous civilization the world would ever see.

In the beginning, after the gods left, generations of Atlanteans prospered under the reign of King Atlas. He celebrated education, fair laws, and righteousness. The Atlanteans did not tolerate violence or inequality. The paradise endured for a thousand years after Atlas's death, until vanity and a thirst for power corrupted royal blood. Princes killed princes, and the Atlanteans were cursed for generations. Elite Atlanteans faced no punishment when they abused their powers, and common Atlanteans were too indifferent and too complacent to demand justice.

In the end, on the evening before the gods destroyed Atlantis, the sweet scent of tropical flowers and fruits lingered in the humid air, as it had every night for thousands of years. At sunset, a fleet of ships appeared on the horizon, and Atlanteans flooded the streets. The military had returned at last, victorious from a war that had ruined generations. Fireworks illuminated the night, music filled the streets, and the most expensive wines flowed. Most Atlanteans believed that a new era had finally begun.

Only a small group of scholars realized Atlantis was facing its destruction. They begged their neighbors, families, and friends to evacuate, and some Atlanteans listened. But when the sun rose again, nobody who remained on the islands was worried that this day would be their last.

That morning passed in a hungover silence as the night's rain grew heavier. A sense of restlessness replaced the euphoria of the previous night, and even the most reluctant Atlanteans had to admit that something felt wrong. In the afternoon, strong winds howled through city as the canals began to flood the streets. The water rose at an alarming rate. The Atlanteans stayed in their homes, watching their neighbors for a signal to return to their celebrations and praying that the storm wouldn't damage their homes.

At one of the military towers on the great Mount Theus, a young Atlantean Guard was watching over the city. Hungover and tense, he had the same sensation of impatience that often overcame him before battle. He could sense the lethargy of the city and tried to remember if he had ever seen the streets so quiet. Even the ocean was an unremarkable shade of gray, growing more violent as the day progressed. More ships filled the harbor than he had seen in years, now swaying in the gales and waves. Another Guard had tied the masts away for the storm, and the ships were unprepared to go anywhere, especially now the war was over.

The Guard stared at the black words that had been on his wrist since birth. Just as he thought he would have nothing to report at the end of his shift, the stone watchtower trembled under his feet. *Earthquake*, he thought, bracing himself from falling on his sleeping companion. But as the tremors intensified, he looked to the horizon. There, barely distinguishable through the rain, was the unmistakable cause of the disturbance.

Enormous waves were approaching Atlantis.

Swearing, he shook the other Guard on duty. The waves were approaching Atlantis with speed that his hangover could not comprehend. The men lit their beacons, issuing a preliminary warning to the island, before they rang the emergency bells. Atlanteans flooded the saturated city streets, rushing to the shelters, as the bells drowned their cries of terror.

At the same time, the princess of Atlantis raced through the Eternal Forest at the base of Mount Theus. This had always been one of her favorite places on the main island because other Atlanteans rarely came here, and today had been no exception. She loved how the trees here had leaves like glass, so translucent that they reflected rainbows of light like diamonds, but she didn't have time to admire the forest now. She sprinted along a crude, dirt path, feeling like she had been drugged. Her black dress clung unhelpfully to her slender body, and her infant child slept peacefully in her arms.

"We're almost at the shelter," the princess breathed, though she wasn't sure who she was reassuring. She was sure the Guards had sounded the alarm because of the storm, but it was impossible to tell. "It'll be okay."

In her heart, she knew Atlantis was bound for destruction. The bells pounding in the distance confirmed her deepest fear that the prophecies had been right.

Her muddy path finally broke through the forest and became paved with ancient, translucent stone. In the corner of her vision, she noticed that the beautiful beach was deserted, apart from the shipwreck that had been there for generations. She had never seen such large waves, and they would reach her home, the Isle of the Gods, in minutes. Feeling sick at the thought, she ran even faster, determined to save her baby.

She was nearly at the ancient castle at the middle of the island when her vision seemed to dim. Affording one glance behind her, she found that the fault was not in her own eyes. Dark storm clouds had eclipsed the sun, and a second later, she heard a terrible roar as waves battered her home island. She blinked back tears and continued to race to the castle, wondering seriously now if someone had drugged her the previous night. Her memories of the celebrations were even more blurred than her vision. She couldn't remember the castle ever feeling so far away, or her body ever seeming so helpless.

But there would be no hope for Atlantis if she couldn't save her baby. As she climbed the final steps to her castle, she could see the shelter through the open doors leading to the Keep, but she knew she would never reach it. Her weakness was overpowering her. She collapsed paces away from the shelter doors. Fading out of consciousness, she felt a tiny palm caress her face, and she embraced her fate with the last of her strength. She closed her eyes, kissed her baby one last time, and whispered three words. As the infant's crying silenced and the wave loomed overhead, she had never felt more alone.

Someone, she prayed, *please save Atlantis.*

Chapter One
BURNED

Save Atlantis.

Victoria felt her heart race as she read the text message from an unknown sender. It was the omen she'd been waiting for all morning. Her nightmare had unsettled her so badly that she'd checked news for natural disasters every hour since waking up, despite her best effort to stay offline. She just couldn't forget those final moments of fear as the catastrophic storm destroyed the most beautiful place she'd ever seen.

Stop worrying, she scolded herself, shoving her phone onto a box of wine glasses on her kitchen counter. *Someone sent the message to the wrong number, and the place from your dream isn't even real.*

The reality was that she had a serious amount of

work to do. Today was the day that her aunt and uncle had agreed to let her move into their guest house. She'd already moved boxes of clothes and books over from her childhood bedroom in the main house, but she knew it would take hours to unpack and arrange everything how she wanted. She'd be having a housewarming tomorrow, and her aunt, Andrea, had already taken the liberty of stocking the kitchen with food and wine.

Bracing to see some natural disaster in the news, she turned on her sitting room TV at noon. Nothing in the headlines caught her attention, but she left it on, hoping she wasn't tempting fate. While she arranged her kitchen, the BBC channel changed over to a program about some city scientists had recently found underwater.

You've got to be kidding me, she thought.

Despite her apprehension, she watched the documentary out of the corner of her eye while she worked through the boxes. She relaxed as she realized the city on TV wasn't the place she'd seen in her dream. While the program discussed new technology for mapping the seafloor, a knock sounded from the front door. Victoria turned off the TV and ran to answer it, guessing her aunt or uncle was visiting to see her progress.

But behind the door was a tall, handsome boy who made her heart race. Tom. A halo of blonde hair framed his tanned, smiling face, and Victoria was sure his beautiful silver eyes were sparkling behind his sunglasses. *My modern angel,* she thought. Even after three years together, she still couldn't believe such a perfect boy could exist. She threw herself into his arms, and his lips found hers before she could say how glad she was to see him. His cologne and the taste of his kiss far surpassed her memories, and the strength of his body made her feel complete.

"Hello, Stardust," he murmured into her neck. "I've got a charity meeting to go to in an hour, but I wanted to make sure you're settling in alright. You didn't answer your phone, but I hope you don't mind me stopping by."

"Not at all," Victoria said. "It's still a bit of a mess, but I'll show you around."

She gave a quick tour of her house, made a pot of tea, and snuggled onto one of the sofas in her sitting room with Tom. Aiden and Andrea had always trusted her to be alone with Tom, but she'd never had more privacy with him than now. She knew she had no reason to be nervous, but she glanced at Tom, wondering what he was thinking. He smiled, and a comfortable understanding fill the room.

"I can't believe your aunt and uncle have let you have your own house, Dusty," he said. He'd been in the guest house before, but Victoria could tell he was viewing it now with new appreciation. "You have such an amazing family. What would you like to do this summer, once you're settled in?"

Victoria sighed. "I should probably start researching universities," she admitted. "I've suspect Aiden and Andrea want me to start making plans for my future. Letting me have this house is probably only the first step in making me independent."

"We can go to university open days together," Tom suggested. "And why don't we order two copies of prospectuses so we can read together?"

"That would be brilliant," she said. The thought of spending so much of the summer with him, even if it was to research universities, made her heart soar. "The house should be ready in a few days. Just let me know if there's anywhere you want to book to see before then."

"Durham's got one next week. I can book us in," he said. Looking into her eyes, he seemed to stare into her soul, understanding her better than she did herself. "Is everything alright, Dusty? You seem a bit quiet today."

Victoria shook herself out of her daydreams. She took a deep breath, feeling like she was about to reveal a dark secret, which was ridiculous. *It was just a dream*, she reminded herself. "Was there ever an island that was destroyed by a wave?"

Tom laughed, catching her by surprise. "I'm have a feeling lots of places have been destroyed by waves, Dusty. You're probably thinking of Atlantis, though."

Victoria felt a shock hearing the word. *Atlantis*. The

message on her phone couldn't be a coincidence. The word lingered in the air, electric, and Victoria didn't know what to do it. She'd found her answer, along with so many more questions.

"Thanks," she said. "That must have been the name I couldn't remember."

"No problem," Tom said. "Just don't go looking for Atlantis. That's a dangerous errand."

It took Victoria half a second to realize he was joking. A second later, he looked at his watch. "Sorry for such a short visit, but I need to go to this meeting. Good luck with the rest of your move. Everything looks fantastic so far."

"Thank you," she said, giving him another kiss before they stood up. "See you tomorrow."

She watched Tom walk across the garden towards the main house, her happiness fading with every step he took. After everything he'd said, she wanted to prove that the message she'd received this morning wasn't related to her dream. She brought her iPad to her conservatory, took a deep breath, and fired off a search to see what she could learn about Atlantis.

Different versions of the myth attributed the destruction of Atlantis to various natural disasters, though most favored a cataclysmic flood or wave. Many of the Atlantis myths said gods had destroyed Atlantis as punishment for its vanity and corruption. Reading this over and over in different articles, Victoria began to feel sick as the truth became unavoidable.

Atlantis was the place from her dream.

She'd overlooked the dark undertones of Atlantis in her dream, but it made sense now. She'd been so amazed that such a powerful empire could fall that she hadn't even considered the obvious. Atlantis had been too arrogant, too corrupt, and probably too drunk to prevent its own destruction.

If it ever existed, she reminded herself. It reassured her slightly to read that modern historians believed Atlantis was nothing more than a morality tale. Explorers throughout history had claimed to have found the lost empire in every corner of the world, and scientists had scanned the seas, but the best technology throughout the ages had never found anything. To this day, nobody could say exactly where Atlantis might have been. It was the greatest ancient mystery Victoria could imagine, and she understood how easily the hunt could turn into an obsession for anyone.

You need to stop this, Victoria told herself after an hour of researching. She'd reached a dead end of unanswerable questions. She didn't know how she could dream of Atlantis so vividly when she'd never even heard of the place before today, but she was sure she could research Atlantis for the rest of her life and still never understand why the cryptic message about Atlantis had ended up on her phone the same day as her dream.

Feeling more confused than when she'd started her research, she returned to her bedroom and put her iPad away. She still had countless boxes to unpack, but her new furniture was already where she wanted in relation to the large windows. Her new bed was so much larger than her old bed, and it was the feature of her room that made her feel most like an adult.

Leaning against the wall was the enormous mirror her aunt and uncle had always kept in the guesthouse. Victoria had often admired it as a child, and she paused now to look at her reflection with a sense of how much she'd grown up. Her dark hair fell to her waist in gentle waves as ever, but her bright silver eyes, her favorite feature, were darker than usual with stress. She thought it was strange that even without a bit of makeup on, she looked older than she felt today. She smiled at her reflection, and then she noticed that a small, golden ball of light was floating behind her.

Victoria spun around, hoping the mirror was playing tricks on her. But the ball of light was there, and she sensed it was somehow alive. With her heart racing, Victoria took a few steps towards the door, ready to slam it shut. The orb soared to the mirror, and Victoria felt an unexpected force grab hold of her, trying to make her follow. She resisted, and the orb flared a shade of crimson that spoke of anger and frustration. After a second, Victoria relented and took a few steps forward.

And with a blinding burst of light, the orb disappeared. Victoria frowned. From where she stood, it looked like the orb had gone *into* the mirror. *Impossible*, she thought. She held her breath and waited, ready to dive for cover if the glass shattered, but the mirror stayed upright and still, and the room was silent.

"Where the hell have you gone?" Victoria whispered, edging towards the mirror. Even if the orb wasn't violent or dangerous, she expected it to burst back into the room any second. She ran her hand along the metal frame, wondering where the orb had gone, and with a few deep breaths, she summoned the courage to touch the glass. Her reflection seemed to ripple, making her doubt her sanity. Then, without any warning, she felt a sharp pain like fire consume her hand, binding her to the mirror. Before she could pull away, her body lurched forward, and her room began to slip out of focus.

She was falling through the mirror.

When she opened her eyes, she was standing in the middle of the strangest building she'd ever seen. She turned in a slow circle to take it all in. Thousands of massive square pillars surrounded her, each side of which supported a mirror larger than most doors. Each pillar was linked to its neighbors by towering arches and separated by large walkways, creating the impression of endless space. The layout of the building reminded Victoria of train stations in London, but this place was unnervingly empty. Everywhere she looked, it was only her own reflection that stared back at her, silver eyes bright and alert.

Where am I? she wondered, feeling uneasy. The orb wasn't here either. Noticing the glow around the nearest mirror, she held her hand to it, and her fingers slipped through her reflection into what she assumed was her bedroom. *I could turn back,* she thought, but her curiosity was impossible to ignore.

Spotting massive gates nearby, she ignored her reflections and began to walk, hoping she could exit that way. She expected the orb or another human appear any second from behind any of the hundreds of pillars, but she reached the gate uneventfully. Pushing it open, she found herself at the top of a set of stone steps leading down to a massive city square. The number of enormous, moonlit buildings around her suggested that she was in the middle of a capital city, and the beautiful mountain visible through the gentle mist of rain confirmed her suspicions that this wasn't just any city.

This was Atlantis.

But the place was nearly unrecognizable now. Even from a distance, Victoria could see that the buildings were deteriorating. Grass was growing through cracks in the stone cobbles that had once paved a busy city. The square was undeniably beautiful, but it radiated the same emptiness and silence that haunted the surrounding buildings. Looking into the dark windows of all the buildings, Victoria realized what was wrong.

"Atlantis is deserted," she breathed. She couldn't see any sign that humans had been in the city for centuries. *Was it the wave?* she wondered, feeling more uneasy every second. Not knowing where else to go, she walked down the steps, following a sign to the *Plaza*, which she assumed was the enormous courtyard before her. A beautiful, domed building was across the grassy square, but the ancient castle that overlooked the Plaza seemed the most important.

Within its walls, the grassy courtyard of the castle Keep had grown wild, though Victoria noticed a stone structure in the middle. Approaching it, she realized it was a modest throne, surrounded by paving in the shape of a sundial. As she approached it, she wondered how long it had been since someone had sat on it, let alone seen it.

And then a fire burst to light in the middle of the Keep, on the grass in front of the throne.

Victoria stared at the fire for a few seconds, deciding whether to run. The flames weren't spreading, and as she edged closer, Victoria couldn't help but feel that some deep magic was involved. She knelt, feeling an irresistible urge to touch the flames. They weren't radiating heat, confirming that this was no normal fire, and she dipped her fingers into the flames. At first, she felt a pleasant tingle in her wrist, and then, the fire seemed to explode in a burst of light. She pulled her hand away with a gasp, feeling like her arm had been scorched. The pain stopped instantly, but her wrist was covered in ash. She dusted it off with shaking fingers and stared in horror at the skin underneath.

Mene mene tekel upharsin.

Four black words were imprinted onto her wrist. The script was small and elegant, nearly identical to her own handwriting. Victoria had studied a few languages, but these words didn't mean anything to her. *Nick would know,* she thought. He was Tom's oldest friend and the smartest person she knew. The longer she stared at the words, she more she struggled to believe they weren't a curse. She didn't want them on her body. She tried to wipe off the words with the back of her other hand, and then on the damp grass, but they refused to smear or fade.

And then, the fire vanished as quickly as it had ignited. There was no smoke, not even a glowing ember, to indicate a fire had been burning there only seconds ago, only two words burnt into the grass.

Help us.

Chapter Two
MENE MENE TEKEL UPHARSIN

Victoria looked over her shoulder, suddenly feeling like she was in a nightmare. Somebody had written the words, and that person was invisible and powerful. The castle was empty, and the nearest walls were too far away for anybody to have hidden so quickly. Victoria shuddered, trying not to entertain the image of the castle keep filled with ghosts, and retreated to the Plaza. She had to get out of Atlantis. Arriving at the building with all the mirrors, she found the mirror that had brought her here still had the same glow around it. Praying that the portal still worked, she touched her hand to where glass should have been, and her fingers passed to the other side. Closing her eyes in relief, she stepped through.

For a horrible moment, she thought the mirror had made a mistake. She didn't recognize the guesthouse with its new furniture, until she remembered that this was her bedroom now. Glorious sunshine that contradicted her panic filled the room, and everything looked ordinary.

What the hell happened? Victoria thought, sinking onto her bed. Her visit to Atlantis felt like a nightmare, and she wondered for a moment whether she'd really been there. Holding her breath, she looked at her wrist. The words *mene mene tekel upharsin* stared back at her in beautiful black letters. *This can't be happening*, she thought. She grabbed the corner of her new bedsheets with shaking fingers and began to rub her wrist. Her skin stung with the friction, but the words stayed as dark as ever. She took a breath while reality crumbled.

There was no way the words on her skin could be permanent.

She fired off a text to Nick asking what the words meant. While she waited for a reply, she washed her wrist in her new bathroom. Three times, she watched the soapy water run into the sink without any trace of ink. She cursed under her breath and rummage through the toiletries and accessories she'd moved to the guesthouse, her desperation growing. Finding a pink silk ribbon, she prayed she had found a temporary solution. After a few fumbled attempts, she managed to tie a bow around her wrist. It didn't change the words underneath, but it was better than nothing.

How long was I in Atlantis? she wondered. She

glanced at the watch on her unmarked wrist. She'd spent nearly an hour in Atlantis, which was what she would have guessed. *At least I didn't travel though time,* she thought. *But how is it possible?*

She jumped when her phone buzzed in her hands. *The phrase from the Bible?* Nick said. *It was a warning from God saying they'd been judged, found guilty, and would be divided. You know the expression, the writing's on the wall? x*

Feeling nauseous, Victoria read his message a few times. She could only think of Atlantis, but she was sure Atlantis wasn't in the Bible. She composed a reply, hoping she was just being paranoid. *I think I've heard of it. But who is it about? x*

Nick's reply came less than a minute later. *Babylon, I'm sure. See Daniel 5. x*

Victoria thanked Nick and pulled up the Bible app on her iPad. She found the story about a disembodied hand writing the words *mene mene tekel upharsin* on a wall, confirming what Nick had said. It was a promise of doom, the punishment for immorality. A curse.

And it was now on her wrist.

Victoria buried her face in her hands. Whether this story was about Babylon or Atlantis, the meaning was unmistakable. The guilty would be punished. *But I'm innocent,* Victoria thought. Every second, she hated the words more and wanted them off her body. She tried to think of a better solution than the ribbon while she unpacked and organized her house. Eventually, she gave up and called her best friend, Sarah, to say she was ready to meet up. She locked her house for the first time and walked to town, relieved to return to reality.

"Smile, Vic," a voice said when Victoria had been waiting outside her favorite coffee shop in town for a minute. Victoria looked up in time to see a young woman with ruby red hair point a camera in her direction, standing a few paces away. "It's summer! Don't look so sad."

Victoria flashed a smiled and waited for the shutter to click before Sarah ran up and pulled her in for a hug. Flecks of paint covered her jeans and shirt, which didn't surprise Victoria. She was an artist.

"I been working on a project all day," Sarah explained. "I need a drink badly."

They ordered drinks and returned outside to a sunny table. "We should go somewhere this summer," Victoria said. If she didn't keep Sarah distracted, Sarah would notice the ribbon on her wrist in no time. "We can tell Andrea we're looking at universities and go to Europe or something. I've got nothing better to do, and I'm sure she'd love to take us on holiday."

"Sounds amazing," Sarah said. "Oh, my god, Vic," she whispered. "Turn around slowly and look at the guy at the table behind you. He's bloody gorgeous."

Reaching for her bag in what she hoped seemed a casual manner, Victoria glanced at the neighboring table, where a young man who looked her age was reading his newspaper. He had brunette hair tied back with a ribbon and a face Victoria was sure she recognized from somewhere, maybe a magazine. His cheekbones and chin were angular and defined, giving him an exotic look that any photographer would love, and his black shirt revealed the toned, tanned arms of someone who worked outside. *He is gorgeous*, Victoria thought, feeling a twinge of disloyalty to Tom, but something else about this stranger gave her an uneasy feeling.

As if he had heard her thoughts, the boy set his paper down. His piercing silver eyes met hers for a second, closing the distance between them, and the he looked away. Victoria didn't think he was Sarah's usual type, but from the way Sarah was still staring, it didn't seem to matter.

"Go on," Victoria whispered. "Ask his name."

Sarah shook her head, looking horrified. "I don't know him," she hissed.

"That's the point," Victoria pressed, rolling her eyes. It was a rare occasion for Sarah to find somebody she really liked, but she never made the first move. "If you don't ask, I will for you. That's a promise."

"Forget it, Vic," Sarah muttered. "He still has half

his drink left. I can see he's not going anywhere yet."

Victoria sighed.

"I see your point. I can't get a boyfriend unless I actually talk to guys," Sarah grumbled. "There's just nobody right for me."

"You should date Nick," Victoria said. "If you gave him a chance, you'd see how much he fancies you."

He's in love with you, she wanted to add, but now wasn't the time.

"He's too nice, and too smart," Sarah complained, though Victoria didn't think those were negative traits. "I can see myself getting bored after a day."

"I still think you'd be good for each other."

Sarah ignored the comment, which was exactly what Victoria expected. She glanced at the other table again as the boy lifted his drink. His sleeve suddenly slipped up his arm, and Victoria glimpsed a linear tattoo on his wrist.

The words *mene mene tekel upharsin.*

He and Victoria locked eyes for another moment, sending a shock wave through her body, before he stood up, leaving his drink on the table. He was even taller than Victoria had guessed, and he was already disappearing into the crowd by the time Victoria pushed her chair back, her heart racing. She had to follow him.

"Sorry," she said to Sarah. "I'll be right back."

Without waiting for a reply, she raced away from the

coffee shop. The boy was already some distance ahead on the street, nearing a corner that would take him out of sight. Victoria knew her time was running out.

"Excuse me," she shouted. "Wait!"

The boy continued without looking back. Victoria felt a flare of irritation. *He's ignoring me,* she realized. He turned down a little alley, but when Victoria reached it, he had disappeared. Victoria took a few deep breaths, staring at her frenzied reflection in the nearby window. The alley was a dead end, and there was nowhere he could have gone. She knew she'd seen the words on the boy's wrist, and she was convinced she'd seen him somewhere before, but she wouldn't have believed he was real if Sarah hadn't seen him, too.

The tattoo has got to be a coincidence, she reminded herself. *It's a Biblical phrase.*

She returned to the table, still unable to explain the tattoo or the boy's familiar face. Sarah looked up, nervousness apparent in her green eyes.

"I didn't talk to him," Victoria sighed. "He disappeared before I could get a word in."

"Good." Sarah lifted a pen over Victoria's left forearm. "May I?"

Victoria nodded and watched in fascination as Sarah began to draw. A beautiful, monochrome rose slowly took shape, sprawling across most of her forearm. Sarah began to hum and put her pen down after a minute, looking satisfied with her work.

"You've got a tattoo," Sarah said.

Victoria felt her eyes widen, thinking Sarah had seen the words under the ribbon, but Sarah was still looking at her artwork. "Very pretty," Victoria said, moving her other hand under the table. "It looks like a real tattoo."

"You'll smear it if you touch it," Sarah warned. "How's your move going, by the way? Seen any ghosts in the guest house yet?"

Victoria laughed, though Sarah's joke was far too close to the truth to be funny. She prayed she would never see the orb again. "I'll introduce everyone tomorrow."

To her disappointment, she returned home an hour later without seeing the mysterious boy, either. She was in the main house when family returned from work. Andrea was slightly shorter than Victoria and had the same silver eyes, but her hair was midnight black and barely brushed her shoulders. Everyone said she looked like an older version of Victoria, and today, her summer dress made her look particularly youthful. Behind her, Aiden looked astonishingly like a male version of his wife, but he kept his hair slicked back and preferred more formal outfits for work as a solicitor.

"Evening, darling," Andrea said, setting her shopping onto the kitchen counter to give Victoria a hug.

"How has your day been?"

"I'm nearly done moving into the guest house," Victoria said. She dropped her left arm behind her back to hide the ribbon and decided against mentioning the mirror, though she doubted Andrea had any answers. "I went to town for coffee with Sarah, and Tom stopped by earlier this afternoon. We looked talked about Atlantis and university."

The envelope Andrea had been holding fell to the floor with a loud smack, making Victoria jump. Andrea picked it up and handed it to Victoria. "That's lovely, darling," she said. Her lips formed a tight smile that contradicted her words, but Victoria wasn't about to ask what was wrong. "Speaking of universities, that booklet came in the post today. From Durham, I suspect."

Victoria tore the envelope open and found a palatinate Durham prospectus inside. She stared at it for a second, feeling another genuine surge of excitement about going to university. "It is," she said. The booklet was heavy, but she would enjoy perusing it with Tom. She was sure he'd gotten his copy today, too.

"Oxford, Cambridge, and Durham have a tradition of producing some of the finest scholars in the world," Aiden said, emerging from reading a letter to pour himself a drink. "I wouldn't dismiss their prestige lightly for any other university."

"I know," Victoria agreed, understanding that he was

speaking from experience. "Tom and I feel the same way, too. There's just something so amazing about those universities." She dreaded to think what Aiden would say if she decided to study elsewhere, but she hoped he'd support whatever decision she made.

"I want you to go wherever you'll be happiest, darling," Andrea said as she opened a bottle of wine. She poured a reasonable glass for herself and a smaller one for Victoria. "Your time at university is precious, and only you can truly decide what's best for yourself. I can take you and Sarah to look at universities in Europe this summer, if you would like to explore all your options."

Victoria gaped at her. "That would be amazing. We were actually talking about that earlier."

Their discussion about university continued throughout the evening. Victoria felt her evening was a vast improvement on her morning. Neither Aiden nor Andrea seemed to notice the ribbon on her wrist, and the only text messages she received were from Tom. Even after a few small glasses of wine, she wasn't inclined to ask him or her family about Atlantis.

At midnight, she returned to the guest house to get ready for bed. She could see the glow around the mirror, and when she touched the glass, her reflection rippled. But she had no interest in going back to Atlantis tonight, or ever. Like the words on her wrist, it was easier to pretend Atlantis didn't exist.

She shifted a few more boxes out of the way and collapsed onto her bed. Before she fell asleep, she vented about her day in her journal. It felt like days had passed since she'd received the mysterious text to save Atlantis, and yet the words on her wrist were proof that something in her life had changed profoundly since the morning.

Chapter Three
TRUE ALLEGIANCE

The next morning, Victoria ignored the mirror, though she could see it glowing in the corner of her bedroom. The words were still under the ribbon on her wrist, and she didn't feel any better about having them there. Even more than yesterday, she felt angry that Atlantis had imposed this burden upon her, and she still had no idea what to do about it. In the end, she distracted herself by finishing preparations for her housewarming party that evening.

At noon, her phone buzzed with a message from an unknown sender.

Victoria, you must decide tonight whether you will keep the Sentence of Atlantis. If you put your hand into the fire, you will lose the Sentence and sever all ties with Atlantis forever. If you do not touch the fire, you will remain marked, and the Sentence will be your key to Atlantis.

Victoria read the message a few times, making sure she understood. The Sentence, as the note called it, wasn't permanent. *There's no way I'm keeping it,* she decided. She slid the ribbon down her wrist for the hundredth time, just to check the words hadn't already disappeared. Though the rose Sarah had drawn on the other arm had faded slightly, the four words in black ink were still as dark as ever. The writing was pretty in a way, she thought, but remembering the ruined island she'd visited yesterday, the decision was obvious. She went to her bedroom, locked the door, and stepped through the mirror.

On the other side, the Atlantean building full of mirrors was still empty. Victoria walked through the Plaza and to the castle, feeling more confident than she had yesterday. But when she arrived, there was no fire burning in the middle of the ancient Keep, or anywhere she could see. She felt her heart fall.

The message said to decide tonight, she reminded herself. *You'll have to try again in the evening.* For half a second, she wondered if the text message was telling the truth, but she had to have faith. She'd regain control of her future tonight.

She was just about to leave the castle when she noticed a golden feather resting on the throne. She walked towards it, but when she leaned forward to pick it up, an electric shock passed through her fingers from the cool stone. Closing her eyes, the impulse to try the throne became easier to resist. Victoria took a breath and stepped back, and when she opened her eyes, the orb was in front of her.

"You knew I would be here early," she breathed, enchanted. She was sure it was glowing more brightly than before. She lifted her hand and leaned forward, but the orb flared a warning shade of red before she could get too close. Victoria stepped back, understanding perfectly. As much as she wanted to, she could never touch it.

"What are you?" she whispered.

The orb shot towards the sky and flew around in a large circle, pulsating with light like a heartbeat. Victoria had a feeling this was meant to answer her question, but she didn't understand the riddle. It floated up to the ramparts of the castle, and Victoria left the feather where it was and followed the orb on a walk on the castle walls. From this height, she could see that many of the main streets in the city had canals. The water was pristine, but they looked empty without boats.

"I could tell somebody about Atlantis," Victoria mused to the orb. She was sure fame and fortune awaited whoever discovered the lost empire, but when she imagined the media of the world infiltrating this beautiful island, she knew that revealing the secret would be a mistake. "Or I could just forget it all."

But she didn't want to forget Atlantis. She usually left photography to Sarah, but she took her phone out of her pocket now, tempted to document the place for herself while she could. The screen was blank, and the phone simply wouldn't power up. *Maybe something in Atlantis affects the signal,* Victoria thought. She returned it to her pocket with a sigh, thankful she had a watch that said she had an hour to spare before Tom was meant to visit.

The orb floated from the Plaza into the ancient city streets. Venturing further away from the part of Atlantis she was familiar with, Victoria began to worry whether she would get lost, but the streets and canals of Atlantis seemed to form such a perfect grid that she was confident she could find her way back if the orb abandoned her. It wasn't long before she realized it was giving her a tour of Atlantis. It led her around the streets of what was must have been the capital city, never stopping for more than a few seconds in one place. All around her, quiet canals reflected faded silver buildings. The city felt smaller than European capitals, but it had a majesty and elegance in its uniformity that Victoria couldn't explain.

Further from the Plaza, she passed through a few streets lined with balconied buildings that reminded her of apartments. Through the empty doorways and dark windows, she could see they were all abandoned. For a fleeting moment, she caught the scent of fresh bread in the

31

air, but she was sure it was just her imagination. The orb never gave her time to go into any of the buildings, and she had a feeling that she wasn't supposed to. She could only wonder what had happened behind each door, while one truth becoming painfully evident. The city was dead.

Atlantis really isn't dangerous, Victoria thought against her better judgment.

Passing an ancient storefront that she thought smelled of perfume, she brushed her hand against the wall. A thick layer of dirt transferred onto her finger, and a chunk of stone fell to the ground. Victoria picked it up. Beneath centuries of decay was the most beautiful silver stone she'd ever seen. She held it to building, her hand shaking. Atlantis was defenseless and damaged beyond repair.

"I wish I had a way to fix this," she whispered to the orb.

She felt a pulse of heat in her hand, and when she looked at the wall, the fragment of stone had reattached itself. Victoria gasped, looking at the orb and then back at her hand for answers, though she already knew.

It was magic.

Victoria searched the ground for another fragment of stone and found one at the bottom of the doorway. After a few seconds, she found where it had come from, and she held it up. The heat flared in her hand again, seeming ready to escape this time. When she let go of the fragment, it stayed on the doorframe, either defying gravity or genuinely repaired.

Victoria's pulse raced as she found a third fragment. But on this attempt, when she held it to its original location, nothing happened. She glanced at the orb for answers, suspecting it understood the significance of what she had done. Seeming to read her thoughts, it slowly approached her. She held out her hand, and the orb hovered inches away from her Sentence on her writ, never touching her skin. Victoria understood what it meant. The power was in the Sentence.

She returned to the Plaza, crossing over one of the largest canals in the city in the process, and sat down on the grass while the orb circled overhead. "I would never want to forget about Atlantis. Being marked without warning bothered me most," she admitted. Only a day had passed since then, but she understood better what it meant than she had yesterday. "But the words are a reminder that justice will always prevail, aren't they? Not doom."

The orb drifted away.

Victoria sighed. Atlantis had changed her.

With a glance at her watch, she discovered it was already late in the afternoon. Tom would be at her house any minute to discuss universities, and he would notice if she was missing. Deciding she would have to come back to Atlantis again later, she returned home. She'd barely put an extra bottle of wine into the fridge when a knock sounded on the front door. Victoria closed her bedroom door and ran to answer it.

"Afternoon, Dusty," Tom said, surveying her with a knowing look. "How have you been?"

"You wouldn't believe me if I told you," she said, managing a laugh. Her heart soared at the sight of him, and she felt pure relief coursing through her veins. As much as she wanted to share her adventures in Atlantis with him, she needed time to process her most recent visit. While Tom prepared drinks, she brought her pile of prospectuses to the conservatory and opened the doors to let the summer inside, determined to focus on her boyfriend. Tom laid his books next to hers, and they exchanged glances as they sat down. She would have hated researching universities on her own, but together, it seemed like an achievable task.

"Where do we begin?" Victoria sighed.

"You still want to study law like Aiden, don't you?" Tom asked.

Victoria nodded. "It must run in the family," she said. Her uncle was a lawyer in London, and for as long as Victoria could remember, she'd wanted to follow his example. Nothing bothered her more than injustice and inequality, and Aiden believed she had the discipline to fight for those causes. After a second, Tom removed a few booklets from the pile and set them on the floor. "Those universities haven't got the strongest law programs," he explained. "I wouldn't bother looking at them further. Agreed?"

Victoria nodded, flattered that he thought she was better than all those institutions. "Aim for the stars, right?"

"Indeed. Old or new university?"

"Old, for the history and tradition of it. I got a Durham prospectus last night, actually, though I don't remember ordering one."

Tom winked and pulled another few books from the pile. "Me too. Near to home or further away?"

"I want an adventure," she said. *That could be anywhere in the world*, she realized, wondering what subjects the university in Atlantis would have taught. "What do you think about Oxford?" she asked.

Doubt flashed in Tom's eyes for a second, and Victoria felt her spirits fall. She'd never considered that Oxford wouldn't be what he had expected or wanted. "All their programs are great," he said diplomatically. "There are just so many ways I could get into charity work, some of which are probably much easier and faster than a university degree. I want to make a difference in the world as soon as I can."

Victoria was torn. She admired his ambition, but the thought of his path diverging from hers terrified her. She busied herself with looking through a new prospectus to hide the surge of panic she felt. "We still have time to decide," she said. "I'm not worried yet."

"I have been thinking a lot about uni recently, Dusty," he said. The intensity in his eyes took her by surprise, commanding her attention. She put her prospectus down. "And it scares the hell out of me when I imagine going anywhere without you. You really are the most important person in my life, and the best thing that's ever happened to me. I really don't think I could survive without you." He leaned forward and kissed the back of her hand, his eyes fixed on her. "So, I have a question for you. Would you like to go to take a gap year together?"

Victoria felt her pulse race. Tom's proposal was a big, sudden step to deciding her future, but it felt right.

"Breathe, Dusty," he said, laughing. She hadn't realized she'd been holding her breath. She exhaled, still composing a response. "I'm not asking you to marry me or anything yet. I would just like us to spend the next year together on the biggest adventure of our lives."

"Where?" she asked.

"Anywhere in the world, as long as we're together. I could volunteer with some amazing charities, and you could get experience in law or do whatever you wanted. And if we're ready for university after that, we could go somewhere like Durham together. You could study law, and I could study business."

Victoria sensed this was the moment he'd been working towards all morning, if not the past few days. "That would be amazing," she agreed, "but Durham's not an easy university to get into."

"Shoot for the stars." He smiled. "As long as we're together, I'm happy."

Victoria took a deep breath. Tom was so persuasive. "It's not too early to start thinking about uni, is it?"

Tom shook his head. "The first deadlines at Oxford and Cambridge are still a few months away. But a few days ago, I had a feeling that if I didn't ask you soon, you'd make your own plans and disappear from my life forever. And I never want to lose you. I love you too much."

Victoria leaned over the table and kissed him. "I love you, too, and I'm not going anywhere. I think a gap year together would be brilliant."

They spent the next hour making a schedule of what universities to visit. It would be a busy and exciting summer, and Victoria couldn't wait to tell Aiden and Andrea. She could imagine how proud they would be of her plans for the future. By late afternoon, she and Tom had worked their way through all their university guidebooks and planned a busy summer, and she was ready for a glass of wine, even if Tom didn't drink.

"What on earth is that?" Tom asked, reaching for her left wrist as she picked up the pile of booklets to bring inside. Victoria detected an edge in his voice. Following his narrowed gaze, she realized he was looking at the rose Sarah had drawn on her left arm yesterday.

"Sarah was inspired when we went out for coffee yesterday," she said with a shrug.

His eyes lit up in comprehension. "She could be a tattoo artist, it looks so real. But you're perfect the way you are. Don't change."

Victoria hoped her blush was answer enough for him. The books were hiding the ribbon on her other wrist, and a knock sounded at the door a second later, saving her from worrying what Tom would say if he knew about the Sentence. "It's Nick," she said, recognizing his punctuality. "I'll put these books away if you let him in."

She ran to her bedroom, dropped the books onto her desk, and took a final look around. Everything was still in order, but the mirror was still glowing. *The others will want to see the house*, Victoria thought. Scowling at her reflection, she threw a blanket over the mirror and closed the door. She would have to wait to give her tour of the house after the alcohol started flowing and hope nobody noticed.

She returned to the kitchen to find Tom talking to a young man wearing glasses, a smart shirt, and unseasonably long trousers. His brown eyes surveyed the room for a moment, and Victoria knew who he was looking for. "Your place is amazing, Victoria," he said, holding out a crate of cider. "Congratulations. Is Sarah here yet?"

Victoria shook her head. "She's running late today. You really should ask her out if she means that much to you, before it's too late," she said. "Seriously. You two would be so good for each other."

Nick rolled his eyes. "She already knows I fancy her. There's no point."

"There is always a point if you like her that much, but never mind," Victoria said lightly. "Let's get drinks."

Sarah arrived a few minutes later, dressed in a skirt and a summery shirt. Victoria could tell she'd put extra effort into her appearance today. *Not for Nick*, Victoria thought with a sigh, deciding to ask Sarah about it later. She led the way to the sitting room, hoping there wouldn't be any drama tonight. Sarah greeted Tom with a hug and gave Nick a brief wave, which he returned. Victoria sighed and opened a bottle of wine while the others settled in the conservatory. When she joined them, Sarah and Nick were sitting on opposite ends of one of the sofas.

"I love your house," Sarah said to Victoria eventually. She'd paid more interest to her second glass of wine than she had to Nick. The group had ordered pizza and were waiting for delivery. "Everything looks so sophisticated. The three of us should just move in with you."

Victoria laughed. "You're more than welcome to, but

there's not enough beds. And I don't know whether my family would agree to it permanently."

"They could adopt us, too. You know they love us," Sarah said. "You do have the best family."

A second later, Victoria felt her phone vibrate in her hand. Assuming it was an update about the pizza delivery, she almost ignored the message. But seeing that it was from an anonymous sender, she couldn't help herself. She felt her heart sink further as she read the words.

STAY AWAY FROM ATLANTIS.

Who the hell is sending these messages? Victoria wondered. She could feel frustration coursing through her veins. For a fleeing moment, she worried that this new message was some sort of practical joke, but nobody knew about the mirror, her visit to Atlantis, or the words on her wrist.

"You okay, Stardust?" he whispered.

Victoria nodded, hoping he didn't see her hands shaking. The display on her phone had dimmed, so he wouldn't have seen the text. "Probably just the cider making me sleepy," she said, flashing the most reassuring smile she could manage. She hated lying to Tom, but he would only worry if he knew the truth. "I'll be better with food."

He kissed her forehead. Whether he believed her was difficult to gauge. Her phone buzzed again a few seconds later, but he didn't seem to notice her flinch. This time, it genuinely was an update about the pizza, but Victoria felt her composure crumble. She excused herself to get another drink, and as soon as she was alone in the kitchen, she sank to the floor, shaking.

Atlantis was meant to be giving her a choice about the Sentence, but now that she was seriously considering keeping it, Atlantis wanted her to stay away. The contradictory messages were cruel, and she refused to believe that Atlantis didn't need her.

Maybe these newest messages aren't from Atlantis, she mused while she prepared another round of drinks. The possibility reassured her slightly. She locked her phone in her bedroom, checked that the mirror was still glowing and the Sentence was still on her wrist, and tried to enjoy the rest of her evening. *Only a few more hours until you can decide,* she reminded herself.

An hour passed as the group worked through another bottle of wine. A chorus of Sarah's genuine laughter filled the conservatory. Victoria glanced from her watch to Tom, recognizing the sound of flirting, though she never would have expected Sarah to entertain Nick's attention.

"Sarah," Nick said. Something in his tone made everyone in the room look at him. He sounded much less sober than he had only minutes ago, but there was determination in his expression. Victoria glanced at Tom, but he didn't seem worried. "I dare you to kiss me."

Victoria nearly spilled her drink. When she'd suggested that Nick should ask Sarah out, she hadn't expected him to take her advice. And this was far from what she'd meant. *Please don't,* she prayed, wishing Sarah could hear her thoughts. A dare couldn't possibly end the years of tension and unrequited love between those two. Someone would get hurt, and that person would undoubtedly be Nick.

"Fine," Sarah said, and the room fell silent. Victoria groaned inwardly. "But just so everyone is clear, this doesn't mean anything. I'm only accepting a dare."

"The same goes for you," Nick said, before Victoria could advise anyone to reconsider. "This doesn't change anything."

Victoria knew he would leave the next move to Sarah, and the air filled with expectant tension. Sarah leaned in after a second, placed her lips on his, and pulled away, blushing fiercely.

"There," she said, swaying slightly on the spot. "That was easy."

Nobody said anything for a few seconds, and Victoria couldn't decipher either of their reactions. She sipped her wine, trying not to imagine what her social life would be like if two of her best friends never spoke to each other, and then Tom started to laugh. The sound filled the conservatory with a sense of relief, and everyone seemed to relax. Victoria glanced at the ribbon on her wrist. Whatever happened tonight, whether at home or in Atlantis, she knew everything would be alright.

She had only hours to decide what she wanted.

Chapter Four
THE DECISION

If you put your hand into the fire, you will lose the Sentence and sever all ties with Atlantis forever. If you do not touch the fire, you will remain marked, and the Sentence will be your key to Atlantis.

Victoria pondered these words from the morning's text message as she stared into the flames of the fire without a source. It was another warm, quiet night in Atlantis, a light rain was falling, and the unusual fire was burning in the front of the throne in the castle, presenting Victoria with a choice. For once, it seemed Atlantis was giving her what it had promised.

With a smile, she turned her back on it and the fire and ventured to the Plaza. She wanted to explore the city even more than she wanted to sit on the throne. She stopped in the Plaza only to check that the Sentence was still under the ribbon, and then continued towards the beautiful domed building she'd admired during her previous visits. An inscription above the building named it as the Grand Library. As she proceeded up the steps, the orb appeared out of nowhere between her and the enormous wooden door.

"I shouldn't be surprised," she said with a smile. The orb disappeared through the door, and Victoria hesitated until she heard the lock click. Pushing the door open, she could only see the orb in front of her. She took a step forward, trusting she wasn't in any danger. A strange sensation washed over her as her clothes became dry, and then, the building burst into light.

Choking back a scream, Victoria could only marvel at the view in front of her.

Countless torches around the building had ignited, providing a warm glow by which she could see that she was inside the largest and most beautiful library she'd ever seen. Hundreds of thousands of books lined the circumference of the building in shelves that reached from the floor to the base of the dome. The building was divided into stepped levels which were connected at regular intervals by straight staircases, reminding Victoria of an ancient theater or arena. The floor was a silver stone that looked expensive, though it wasn't a stone Victoria recognized.

She followed the orb on a tour of the ground floor,

resisting the temptation to touch any of the beautiful, old books. The orb then brought her up the grand staircase. Victoria stopped on the landing, noticing the most beautiful portrait she'd ever seen. Within the massive, gold frame, a handsome young man stood in front of an aquamarine sea. He had intelligent silver eyes, long brown hair with honey hues, and golden skin to match. His expression radiated kindness and wisdom. His clothes were what Victoria imagined of antiquity and were princely yet modest, and a metallic red bird perched regally on his bare shoulder.

Her gaze finally wandered to the inscription at the bottom at the frame. *Atlas, Beloved King.* Pleased with her discovery, she followed the orb upstairs. Thousands of thin booklets in identical black binding filled this floor. Victoria felt the compulsion to read them growing, but she resisted. The orb finally stopped over one of the tables in the aisle. On it were a few blank sheets of paper, a quill with a gold feather, and an atlas. Sensing the orb intended this for her, Victoria opened the book and discovered a map with a small cluster of islands labeled *Atlantis* near the middle. She began to look for England, curious about where the islands were in relation to each other. Failing to recognize anywhere, she sat down, suddenly feeling dizzy.

"Atlantis is so far from home," she whispered to the orb. "Getting here through a mirror shouldn't be possible." She looked at the beautiful sphere of light, wishing it could give her the answers she needed. It hovered in the air, expressionless. Victoria sighed and pulled out her phone from her pocket to take a picture, before she remembered that her phone didn't work in Atlantis. She caught sight of the ribbon on her wrist and sighed. "I really don't understand this place."

She returned her attention to the atlas and began to trace her own copy of the first map she'd seen, sorry that she lacked Sarah's artistic ability. When she finished drawing the outlines of the islands, she ran her finger along the edge of the main island, imagining its beautiful beaches with sapphire water. A second later, the parchment turned a faint shade of blue where she'd touched it. Wondering if she was imagining it, Victoria touched location of the mountain she'd seen from the Plaza, which she now knew was named Theus. She could visualize its beautiful, grassy hills, and a second later, the parchment surrounding her fingertip turned the same shade of emerald. She pulled away with a gasp.

Her touch was coloring the paper.

This must be magic, she thought. She labeled her map, created two more maps, and placed them all into the pocket of her jeans. Although she still had no idea where Atlantis was, she was amazed with her reproductions of the maps, and she resolved to look at them at home in the morning, when she had more resources around. She expected the orb to continue their tour of the library, but looking around, she realized it had disappeared while she'd been working.

Through the glass dome overhead, she could see that the rainy, midnight sky would not be light for hours. She had little inclination to explore Atlantis on her own, especially in the dark, and her brush with magic had left her exhausted. *I should go home*, she thought, stifling a yawn. She ran across the Plaza, wishing she could lock the library behind her to protect all the beautiful books, but she had a feeling she would return sooner than she thought.

Atlantis was taking over her life, but she wasn't worried.

Chapter Five
CONFLICTED

The Sentence was still on Victoria's wrist, bold as ever under the ribbon, when she woke in the morning. She was surprised to find that the uneasiness she'd felt over the past few days no longer fluttered in her stomach, now replaced by a stronger sense of relief and satisfaction. She had what she wanted. She looked up at the mirror, debating whether to go to Atlantis before breakfast, and her heart seemed to stop for a second at what she saw.

The mirror had shattered.

The glass was still in the frame, but she could see straightaway that the connection between the mirror and Atlantis was broken. She closed her eyes, fighting a wave of devastation. She couldn't help but think that the boy she'd seen with the Sentence was responsible, though she knew she was being paranoid. She was sure she would have heard someone walking through her house, and she could see the windows were still locked. *He doesn't even know where you live,* she reminded herself. *This was just a horrible accident.*

But the thought wasn't any consolation. She could feel her body growing numb with shock, her mind less willing to comprehend. The way to Atlantis was broken, and the orb wasn't here to help. After all the sacrifices she'd made in accepting the Sentence, she would never be able to go back to Atlantis.

It wasn't until she looked at the globe on her desk that she felt a small wave of hope. *I have maps of Atlantis,* she remembered. If she knew where Atlantis was, she could get there without the mirror. She rummaged through the jeans she'd worn yesterday, but the pockets were empty. Victoria frowned. *Maybe the maps couldn't go through the mirror*, she thought, sorry she hadn't checked as soon as she'd come home. She looked through her bed and desk, her desperation growing.

The maps were the key to her future with Atlantis, but they were nowhere to be found.

Victoria found a pen and paper and spent the next fifteen minutes trying to recall the details of the maps. But when she looked at the final attempt, she knew the exercise had been a worthless. Needing inspiration, she scanned her globe for familiar islands, but nothing caught her attention.

"It would take a miracle," she sighed. She tore the papers out of the notebook, stuffed them into a folder on her desk, and vented in her journal.

Receiving a text message from Tom, she remembered that she needed to have an important conversation with her family. In the afternoon, she heard voices in the garden. She wandered outside with a few prospectuses, reminding herself that she had no reason to be nervous. She found Aiden and Andrea reading in the sun with a bottle of wine between them, which seemed to be a good omen. She sat down on one of the spare chairs and took the liberty of refilling their wine before their glasses went empty.

"Hello, darling," Andrea said, setting her book down. "How was your weekend? Did you enjoy your housewarming?"

"I've had a busy few days," Victoria said, unable to find a better word to explain what the strangest weekend of her life. "I really love the house. Thank you again for the wine. I think it encouraged Sarah and Nick to kiss."

"You're welcome," Andrea said with a smile. "I'm glad you had a good weekend, and I hope it works out for them."

She's got no idea. Victoria took a deep breath, sensing her chance. "I've decided what I want to do for university."

"Oh?" Aiden said. He lowered his book, and Victoria knew she had his undivided attention. "What's that?"

"I definitely want to study law," she said. Saying these words filled her with conviction that this was the right decision, and Aiden and Andrea smiled at each other, though Victoria still couldn't bring herself to break her other news. "I've always been interested with the work you do, Aiden, and I can see myself studying it and making a career out of it."

"You would certainly excel at it, Victoria," Aiden agreed. "You're a very intelligent young lady, and the law is in your blood. What universities are you considering?"

Victoria couldn't fight her smile now. "Tom and I actually are hoping to get into Durham together and take a gap year beforehand."

Aiden stood up, all traces of his smile disappearing. "Absolutely not!" he barked.

Victoria saw the sternness in his eyes. He was deadly serious. "What?" she demanded, glancing at Andrea for support. But Andrea simply looked away. Victoria's indignation swelled. "Any parent would love for their child to study at Durham! You both studied there!"

"Durham is an excellent university, yes," Aiden said. His expression softened slightly. "Any parent would be blessed indeed for their child to receive an education there. However, I will not have you and Tom attend the same university together, no matter how prestigious it may be."

"Durham's not a small university," she protested. "We probably won't even be in the same college."

"I forbid it."

Victoria sank into her seat. "You can't," she whispered, trying hard not to whine. "I'll be eighteen. I can do whatever I want, with whomever I want."

"As long as you live under our roof, you live by our rules."

"Maybe I'll leave, then." The words were out before she could stop herself, but she meant them. "Sarah's family will let me live with them. They love me."

"Victoria," Andrea interrupted. Her face was lined with worry and hurt at Victoria's threat. Nothing else, Victoria knew, would have forced her to break her silence. "Tom is a lovely boy, but I agree with Aiden. University is not the right time or place to make such serious commitments. You're still young, and your education should still be your first priority. We don't want you to ruin your future with hasty decisions."

Victoria glared at her family across the garden table. *Andrea can't mean that,* she told herself. "Tom and I have been together for three years. We are not a hasty decision. I don't want anything or anyone else, and I'm old enough to decide that for myself," she said. The fact that Aiden and Andrea thought otherwise made her feel sick. "We're not asking you for permission to get married. I just want to take a gap year and go to uni with him. Is that really so unacceptable?"

"If Tom goes to Durham, you must go to Oxford or Cambridge or any other university, or we will not fund you," Aiden said. "And you certainly will not take a gap year together. That is my final word."

Victoria stood up, tears stinging her eyes. Aiden and Andrea were being so unreasonable. "Tom is the love of my life," she declared. Having nothing else to add, she stormed into her new house, slammed her bedroom door behind herself, and threw herself onto her bed, ignoring the broken mirror.

No, no, no.

A day ago, she'd been so happy with her plans for her future that she hadn't imagined how easily everything could unravel. The thought had never occurred to her that her family wouldn't support such an important decision. She had no idea how she would tell Tom or, even worse, what would happen next. She refused to believe this was the end of their relationship, but if it was, she would never forgive Aiden and Andrea. She could never choose between Tom or her family.

Someone I love is going to get hurt, Victoria realized. A second later, her phone rang. She glanced at the display with a sinking heart. She didn't want to have this conversation, but she knew Tom would spend the rest of the day worrying if she didn't answer. She took a deep breath and accepted the call.

"Hi, Dusty. How are you?" he asked. The warmth of his voice broke her heart. She desperately wanted to say that she wasn't alright and that she needed him in her life, but she couldn't find the words. The line fell silent for a few seconds that stretched for an eternity. Another moment passed before Victoria realized she'd pushed the button to end the call herself.

What have I done? she wondered, staring at her phone in horror. In all the time she and Tom had been dating, neither of them had ever hung up on each other or walked away in the middle of a conversation. A wave of guilt crashed over her with this realization. She desperately wanted to tell Tom about her horrible day, to hear him say that everything would be okay, and as she contemplated calling him back, her phone buzzed the with the arrival of a message.

What's wrong? You can talk to me. I love you, Dusty, his text said.

You shouldn't be apologizing, Victoria thought, fighting a fresh wave of tears. *It's not your fault.* It was no reassurance that he wasn't even angry with her, and she hated herself for hurting him. He was so loving and supportive and caring and exactly right for her. Right now, more than ever, she didn't believe that Aiden and Andrea were truly considering her best interests. Regardless of what anyone thought, she knew with every part of her being that she belonged with Tom, and she refused to let this be the end.

Tom was her everything, but she couldn't bring herself to respond to his message.

Fifteen minutes later, she still hadn't composed a response, and a knock sounded on her door. She sighed into her pillow, wishing Andrea would leave her alone. Unless Aiden had changed his mind, Victoria didn't want to talk to anybody yet. "Go away," she said, closing her eyes. When the door opened, she felt her temper flare. "Honestly, I need to be alone."

"If you really mean that, I'll leave," a gentle voice replied. *Tom.* Victoria gasped as her heart skipped a beat. "But I'd rather stay with you for a while if you're upset, Dusty, if that's okay."

Victoria nodded slowly, her misery slowly dissipating in his presence. He took his place at her side and wrapped his arms around her, enveloping her in a hug filled with love and understanding. His skin burned softly against hers, and she burrowed deeper into the contours of his body. Even if it didn't resolve the situation, she was thankful he'd decided to visit her.

"Tom," she whispered after a minute, lifting her face

from his chest to look at him. "Aiden and Andrea said I can't go to university or take a gap year with you. He said he won't pay my tuition if we do. It's so unfair."

She could feel the tears welling in her eyes as Tom hugged her tighter. He was silent for what seemed an eternity, and she wished she knew what he was thinking. "It is unfair, Dusty," he said at last. "Aiden and Andrea were having a serious conversation in the garden when I walked past. You're making decisions that will set your entire future, and they just want the best for you."

"Really doesn't feel like it," she grumbled. Aiden and Andrea could spend the whole summer talking about her future, but they'd already done the damage. "I want to make these decisions for myself. It's my life."

Tom brushed his fingers through her hair. "I know, and I promise we will work through it. Lots of people do."

"How?"

The question filled the room with silence. Tom spoke after a minute. "I feel like everyone should take time to reflect over the summer. Applications for university don't close for a while, and we're not in any real hurry to make a decision," he said. "Maybe we'll think of a better plan for our futures in that time or your family might change their mind."

Victoria nearly laughed. "You are such a bloody optimist." A thought occurred to her. "What are you doing here, anyway?"

Tom's expression became serious. His beautiful silver eyes met hers, seeming to search for an answer. "I don't know, to be honest. As soon as you hung up, I sensed something was wrong. I had the worst feeling that you'd be gone if I waited much longer, so I had to see you."

Victoria gaped at him. "What do you mean?"

"You're not going to do anything drastic, are you, Dusty?"

Victoria frowned, not understanding what he was implying. "Like what?"

"Leaving, running away, anything. I know you're upset with your family, and I have a feeling you'll want to put space between yourself and them."

Leaving, running away, anything. Victoria ran her hands through his soft hair as she marveled at that plan. It was certainly a drastic solution, but she had no reason to stay at home if she wasn't happy. Even a week away would be enough to get distance and clarity and give Aiden and Andrea time to reconsider. Tom's fears had unknowingly given her the perfect plan, though his expression begged her to deny it.

"I might go away for a while," she said, deliberately keeping her answer noncommittal. "But I really need you to understand that it's not your fault. This is all between Aiden and Andrea and myself."

Having given him the confession he wanted, she closed her eyes, bracing for his reaction. A second later, she felt his warm fingers brush against her face. He traced a path from chin up to her forehead and back down the other cheek, like he was trying to memorize her body. Victoria sensed he was debating whether to fight for her, or if her plans were already set.

"It's a bit drastic, but I understand," he said. He was speaking very carefully now. "You don't have to say where you're going, if you know yet, but at least let me know when you're leaving, please. I want to say goodbye before you go."

"I don't want to stay here too much longer," she said, leaving that to his interpretation.

"Tomorrow?" he translated. He sighed into her pillow, a sound of despair that broke Victoria's heart even further, and began to run his fingers gently along her arm. Victoria sensed he was forming reasons for her to stay, that he wasn't going to give up easily. "You'll miss the Open Day. There's no way I can talk you out of this, is there? Or any way you'll take me with you?"

Victoria shook her head, avoiding his gaze. Those silver eyes could persuade her to do anything. She briefly imagined running away with him, leaving everything behind, but this was her battle, and she refused to get anybody else involved. *Even if it kills me,* she thought "I am sorry I'm missing the Open Days. I would have loved to go with you."

Tom reached over, gently wrapped his hand around her waist, and flipped her onto her back. Victoria gasped. She could see the desperation in his eyes, eyes that she could lose herself in, as he leaned in and brought his lips to hers. His kisses were gentle, the way most of his kisses started, but after a few seconds, something changed. Victoria felt a growing intensity as he pulled her closer. He was asking her to stay in the most persuasive way imaginable. She knew leaving Tom would be difficult, but she couldn't stay.

With all the gentleness she could manage, she slowed her kisses and pulled away. Tom's eyelids fluttered shut. Victoria could feel his heart racing through his shirt, matching her own pulse. She had no idea what he was thinking, and she wasn't sure she wanted to know. She only wanted to stay with him on her bed forever and pretend that none of her problems existed.

"I should go now, Dusty," Tom said after a minute. "Would you promise me something? Stay safe, and please come back soon. I'll miss you."

Victoria knew he deserved that much. "I promise. I'll come back soon."

"I love you."

"I love you, too," she said. Her breath caught in her

throat. They'd never said such a serious goodbye before, but she knew now that it wouldn't be permanent. "I love you so much. See you soon."

He stood up and disappeared into the hallway, closing the door behind him.

I'm so sorry, Tom, Victoria thought. She stared helplessly after him, wanting nothing more than to follow. The warmth and safety of his arms around her meant everything, and it took every measure of her restraint to stay away. *Don't you dare follow him*, she told herself. She could feel her sense of being incomplete grow with each step he took, and she hoped he would pass Aiden and Andrea in the garden without incident.

Thinking of her family, Victoria buried her face into her pillow and started to cry. She cried because the portal to Atlantis was broken. She cried because Aiden and Andrea had said she couldn't go to university with the person who made her complete, and she'd never felt so misunderstood by her family. They'd gotten into petty arguments before, the way any family would, but this betrayal felt like war. Whatever she decided to do for university, she knew that spending the whole summer with her family would be unbearable. She had to leave, and she knew where. Nothing about Atlantis could hurt her as badly as Aiden and Andrea had today.

She needed to fix her mirror, or she needed to find

the maps, wherever they were.

Chapter Six
THE MISSING PIECE

Victoria spent an hour looking for the maps, then turned her attention to the mirror. The puzzle of broken glass seemed impossible to solve, but she persisted until her phone rang. She could see through her blurry vision that Sarah was calling. Wiping her tears away, Victoria answered it.

"Hey, Vic, are you okay?" Sarah asked. "I've just seen a text off Tom saying I should talk to you."

Victoria shook her head, trusting that Sarah would understand her silence.

"I can't believe Aiden and Andrea said no," Sarah said. She sounded genuinely worried. "They always seemed so liberal. I mean, they give you bottles of wine without you even asking and let you have your own place. Keeping you from going to uni or on a gap with Tom doesn't make any sense."

"I can't stay here any longer," Victoria said. Sarah's sympathy wasn't helping. "I need to go away for a bit."

The conversation fell silent. Victoria guessed that Sarah, like Tom, had anticipated this situation. *Everyone but m*e, Victoria thought, holding back a sigh.

"Want me to come over tonight?" Sarah asked. "We can have a girly evening. That would be fun."

Or I could run away, Victoria thought. She knew Sarah wanted to provide a distraction, but neither of them would say it. The more important thing was that she'd soon have some distance between herself and her family. "That would be great."

"I'll get ready now and let you know when I'm on my way this evening. Everything will be fine."

Slightly cheered, Victoria hung up and returned her attention to the mirror. During dinner, Aiden and Andrea acted like their argument had never happened, which was fine with Victoria. She had to wait for the right moment to mention her plans, and she could feel it approaching. Andrea brought out cake and sparkling wine for dessert, which Victoria sensed was her way of apologizing, and as they finished eating in the garden, Victoria felt her conviction and confidence return.

"Sarah and I would like to tour universities this

week," she said when Aiden and Andrea had opened another wine. It wasn't exactly the truth, but it didn't matter. "I'm not really asking for your permission, since I'd probably go anyway, but I thought I should let you know."

Aiden and Andrea exchanged a glance. "Thank you for your honesty, darling," Andrea said, sounding genuinely relieved. "I suppose you'd like a way to get there?"

"Yes, please," Victoria admitted, surprised and suspicious she was making progress so quickly. "We'll probably stay with Sarah's brother, so I just need some money for a train ticket there."

Aiden surveyed her thoughtfully. "Would a thousand pounds be enough to last you a few weeks?"

Victoria gaped at him. It was an incredibly generous offer. *Almost too kind*, she thought, her suspicions flaring. "Isn't that too much?" she asked.

Aiden shook his head. "Keep it for the summer. Spend time with Sarah, and look around a few universities. Maybe you'll find one that you like. If not, you and Sarah can go to Europe with Andrea later in the summer to view universities there."

There it is, Victoria thought, holding back a sigh. *Anything to get me looking at universities far away from Tom.* "I'll see how it goes. Thank you."

"You're welcome," he said, seeming relieved that she'd warmed to the idea. "I'll send you a text when I've transferred the money. Andrea and I will be setting off for the airport in an hour."

Victoria managed a smile, conscious that this was all an apology for their argument, though money couldn't buy her forgiveness. She finished her wine with a few sips. "Thank you. I'll be packing in my room if you want to talk about anything else," she said.

After Victoria had organized her room and retrieved her suitcase from the main house, her iPhone chimed with the arrival of an email from Aiden confirming the money transfer. Victoria felt a surge of gratitude despite her annoyance. Finances was one less thing to worry about now. A minute later, her phone chimed again. Sarah was on her way.

Victoria found Aiden in his study, thanked him for his generosity, and said goodbye. Andrea was packing in her bedroom with a glass of wine in her hand. Victoria sensed that the events of the day had upset everybody, but Andrea seemed determined to pretend nothing had happened.

"We love you, darling," Andrea said, wrapping her in a final hug. She glanced at the ribbon on Victoria's wrist as they separated, and for a second, Victoria had the impression that Andrea knew what was underneath. "Stay safe, and keep us updated. We'll be back in a few days."

"I love you, too," Victoria replied. She meant it as much as always, but she could sense the damage to their relationship. "See you soon."

Crossing the garden between the two houses, Victoria felt relief wash over her. For at least the next week, she was free from Aiden and Andrea's rules. She knew she could contact Tom and agree to go to the Open Day with him, but even more than that, she needed to go back to Atlantis.

Sarah arrived a few minutes later with a bag of essentials. Something about her looked different, Victoria thought, though it might have been the wine.

"Hey, lovely," Sarah said, pulling her into a hug. "Everything'll be okay. Do you want tea or anything?"

Victoria laughed. After such an emotional day, it seemed impossible that something so normal still existed. It was exactly what she needed. "That would be amazing. Thank you."

With the kettle boiling, Victoria retrieved her phone from the kitchen and managed a glance for new messages before Sarah gently pulled it out of her grasp. "Leave it for a day or two," she said. "I promise Tom will be fine. If there's an emergency, he can get in touch with me."

Victoria sighed as Sarah powered off the phone and put it on the far end of the counter. They moved to the sitting room and settled onto the sofa with their drinks.

"Can I talk to you about something?" Victoria asked

"Anything."

Victoria took a deep breath. "I know what I'm going to say sounds mad, but I really need you to listen to me, even if you don't believe me," she said. Sarah nodded in agreement and put her sketchbook down. "I've found Atlantis."

She told Sarah about the mirror and the messages she'd received, explaining everything except for the Sentence. She wanted Sarah to believe her out of faith, rather than because she'd seen the proof. She would show the words only if there was no other option.

"What does this mean?" Sarah asked when Victoria had said everything she wanted. She poured another cup of tea for herself and Victoria.

"Even if I can't fix the mirror, I need to try to find Atlantis again. Anything to get away from Aiden and Andrea for a while," Victoria said.

"And you're going alone?" Sarah asked.

Victoria nodded, feeling a small sense of relief. If this was the biggest objection Sarah could produce, nothing could stop her from leaving.

"You won't be safe," Sarah sighed, "especially not from yourself. I can imagine you spending weeks moping about Tom and university and the future. You'll be sad and probably make bad decisions. I'm coming with you."

"No," Victoria said. "Absolutely not."

"Why not?" Sarah countered. "If you give me three

good reasons, I'll let you go on your own."

"It'll be too dangerous for you."

"It'll be more dangerous for you if you're alone, Vic. Honestly."

Victoria could feel her argument failing. Sarah was right, and they both knew it. Slowly, Victoria nodded.

"Brilliant. I just have one more suggestion," Sarah said. "Hear me out, okay?"

Victoria hesitated, knowing she shouldn't give Sarah any more time to negotiate. She could guess what Sarah was going to say, and it wasn't what she wanted to hear, but she nodded in resignation.

"You probably want to leave straightaway, but we should take a few days first to look at universities," Sarah began, holding up a hand to silence Victoria's sigh. "Even if it's just two days, I'll be happy. We can look at local universities to make Aiden happy while we prepare. Then, if you seriously want to look for Atlantis, you've had a bit more time to think about it."

Victoria had to admit it wasn't the worst suggestion she'd heard that day. She did need more time to prepare, and as long as she was away from Aiden and Andrea, waiting a few extra days to find Atlantis wouldn't hurt. With a nod, she conceded. "Two days looking at universities," she said, "and if I want to look for Atlantis after that, we'll try. Promise?"

"I swear," Sarah said, pulling Victoria in for a hug. She glanced at her own phone again, blushing.

For a moment, Victoria wondered if Sarah was messaging Tom, but then she understood. "What's the deal with you and Nick?" she asked, hoping she sounded casual. "I haven't really had time to ask you about what happened at the housewarming."

"What do you mean?" Sarah asked, locking the display on her phone. Victoria met her gaze steadily, refusing to let Sarah evade an answer. Sarah knew exactly what she meant. "We had lunch in town today, but nothing is going on," Sarah amended, a defensive edge in her voice. "We're just friends."

"You wouldn't have told me if it hadn't been a halfway decent afternoon," Victoria said. Maybe she and Tom had been wrong hoping that one kiss could change everything, but the fact that Sarah and Nick had spent the afternoon together was a good start, even if Sarah didn't call it a date.

For the rest of the evening, Victoria sensed Sarah was paying more attention to her phone than the film or her artwork. "Should I message Tom?" Victoria asked when the film finished. She felt agitated that she hadn't spoken to him in hours and frustrated that she couldn't go longer without contacting him. She wanted to know how his evening had been and whether he'd thought of another plan for their future together, and at the same time, she didn't.

Sarah glanced up from her drawing, biting her lip. "Doesn't seem like a brilliant idea to me," she said gently. "Wouldn't a little space be better for now?"

Victoria sighed. "I miss him already."

Sarah closed her sketchbook. "I'm not here to stop you. It's your decision."

Victoria had her answer, even if it wasn't the one she had wanted. She retrieved her phone from the kitchen, showed Sarah to the guest bedroom, and said goodnight. She sat on her bed in her own room and stared at her phone for a minute before deciding against contacting Tom. She would have to survive a few days without contacting him. She was drifting asleep when she heard a knock on the front door.

Tom, Victoria thought, instantly wide awake. Wondering if Sarah had arranged a surprise visit, she raced to the door and found herself staring straight into the intensely silver eyes of a familiar face.

But he wasn't Tom. Victoria could only gape at the tall boy with long brown hair whose tattoo she had seen in the coffee shop. His lips formed the most annoying, arrogant smirk she had ever seen. Before he could say a word, she slammed the door in his face, secured the locked, and leaned against it for extra security, breathless.

Bloody hell.

She looked towards the guest bedroom and heaved a

sigh of relief. The door was closed and the light was off. This situation would have been impossible to explain, even to Sarah. Victoria could hear that the boy hadn't moved, and she doubted he would leave until she'd called the police or listened to what he wanted to say. *His tattoo of the Sentence isn't a coincidence*, she decided. *He knows about Atlantis.* "Who the hell are you?" she hissed at the door, trusting he could hear her.

"My name is Gryffin," he said. His voice was low and commanding and sounded even older than she had imagined. Victoria was glad he couldn't see her surprise through the door. "I need to talk to you. Open the damn door so we can talk properly."

Victoria seethed at the idea of someone telling her what to do in her own house. She raced for a response. "You're talking right now, aren't you?"

His sigh was audible through the door. "Are you looking for Atlantis?"

Victoria felt her breath pass through her lips. Against her better judgment, she found herself unlocking and opening the door to face Gryffin. "How do you know?" she demanded.

He smirked in a way Victoria found incredibly annoying. "To begin with, you have the Sentence on the wrist of your dominant hand. You might not have told anybody about it, but it's as obvious as a tattoo." Victoria reflexively reached for the ribbon on her right wrist but stopped when Gryffin raised an eyebrow. "You seriously need to forget about Atlantis. Forget it exists, forget you ever thought about it, and don't go looking for it. It's fucking dangerous. *Trust me.* Your life depends upon it."

Victoria could only stare at him.

"I won't warn you again," he said. And without another word, he turned his back to her and took off running. Victoria stared after him, too stunned to follow, though she now had a million questions. He knew about Atlantis and the Sentence, and she need answers.

"Wait," she called, breaking out of her trance, but he didn't stop. Whether he was ignoring her or too far away to hear, she knew she'd missed her chance to get information from the beautiful, mysterious, irritating boy. But his visit had still answered some of her questions. Atlantis had always wanted her to find it, and she had a sudden suspicion that Gryffin had sent the message telling her to stay away. *Did he break the mirror, too?* she wondered. She shivered at the thought of him being in her house without her consent or knowledge, but that was in the past.

For the first time since she'd chosen to keep the Sentence, she was absolutely convinced that giving her loyalty to Atlantis had been the right decision. She would see the words on her wrist every day and remember Atlantis, no matter who asked her to forget. If Gryffin wouldn't give her any more information, she would learn herself, even if it took the rest of her life. *He can't stop me.*

For a final moment, she wondered if she should follow him to ask about the mirror, and then she noticed that he had dropped a small bundle of papers on the doorstep. *He wouldn't have done that on purpose,* she thought, her interest flaring. She picked them up and retreated inside before he realized they were missing. Seeing the top page containing familiar shapes overlaying a grid, she couldn't quite believe her luck, or what his secret was.

It was a bundle of maps. And they were in her own handwriting.

Abandoning the idea of pursuing Gryffin, Victoria locked her front door and laid out all the papers across her kitchen table. From their delicate texture, she could tell that these were the exact maps she had made in Atlantis. *How the hell did Gryffin get these?* she wondered. He obviously knew more about Atlantis than she did, but that didn't matter terribly at the moment. She had the maps now. She pulled out her phone and got to work locating Atlantis on a real map.

She started her search in the Mediterranean, since most historians place Atlantis there. Feeling lucky, she held her breath and zoomed in on a random place in the sea. But there were no islands there. She tried a few more locations, feeling foolish for trusting blind luck, and stopped when she spotted a stretch of coastline that she was sure she recognized from the largest paper map. She compared the two maps for a moment, hardly believing her eyes. *They're a perfect match.*

When she zoomed out more on her phone, she found that Atlantis simply didn't exist on modern maps. Where the islands were supposed to be was nothing but empty sea, but Victoria wasn't surprise, and didn't care what modern technology said. She had found Atlantis.

The problem now was that it wasn't anywhere near England.

Victoria had to admit that she had no idea how she was supposed to get there, without her mirror. The distance was too great to swim, and trains, cars, or airplanes were out of the question. A boat really was the only possible mode of transportation, but it was too dangerous and would take too long. *And I don't have a boat, anyway,* Victoria thought. She put the maps under her pillow and forced herself to go to bed. She would find a solution in the morning, without Gryffin's help.

She slept restlessly, dreaming of a sandy beach where a wooden boat awaited to take her to Atlantis. When she woke, her bedroom was light with sunrise. She checked that her maps were still under her pillow, and she fell asleep again. In her next dream, she walked around the same beach from her earlier dream, but no matter how hard she pushed the boat, she couldn't get it into the water.

It was a rainy day when Victoria finally woke, but the weather couldn't ruin her satisfaction. She had the maps. The frustration from her dreams overshadowed her hurt about the situation, but she resolved to overcome the obstacles between herself and Atlantis. *At least I have control over that*, she thought. As Sarah made breakfast, Victoria stole a moment in the conservatory to research how she could get to Atlantis. She was so lost in her thoughts that she didn't notice Sarah standing behind her until it was too late.

"What are you looking at?" Sarah asked, sneaking up behind Victoria. She placed a steaming mug of tea on the table in front of Victoria and took a sip from her own drink. "You're looking very thoughtful."

Victoria switched off the screen on her iPad, but Sarah had seen. "It's a map," she admitted.

"Where'd you find it?" Sarah pressed, sitting down on the other conservatory sofa. "It looked really old."

Victoria wanted to tell Sarah that these were the missing maps, but she would then have to reveal that Gryffin had been here. She took a sip of tea, stalling for time. "I'll explain soon," she promised. "I don't quite understand it yet."

Sarah shrugged. "Let me know if you need help."

Victoria smiled. *If only you knew*, she thought. She

still wanted to talk to Tom, and she missed him immensely, but she had bigger preoccupations today. She didn't want to spend much more time at home, and she needed to plan the next part of her journey.

"I'm going to see to a few errands in town soon," Sarah said a few minute later. "Are you alright staying here, or do you want to join?"

"Errands or a date?" Victoria teased.

Sarah rolled her eyes. "I'll stay here," Victoria decided. She needed another opportunity the look at the maps in privacy. "Take the spare keys and have fun."

"You sure?" Sarah asked, though she looked grateful when Victoria nodded. "Call if you change your mind. I won't be gone too long."

"I won't crash your date. Say hi to Nick."

Sarah scoffed, but she couldn't hide her blush.

Fifteen minutes later, she had the house to herself. She reviewed that the location of Atlantis she'd saved on her phone matched the paper maps, and then turned her attention to the problem she hadn't solved last night. She still had no idea how she was supposed to get to Atlantis. Even after sleeping on it and considering the dangers, she desperately wanted to go, but she couldn't see how the journey was physically possible. She couldn't simply take a boat the rest of the way, like she'd wanted to in her dream.

Without a miracle, it looked like she would be stuck

in England.

Not knowing what else to do, she found herself debating whether she should message Tom. She started composing a text, and when she looked up, debating whether to send it, the orb was hovering a few feet in front of her.

"You're back," she gasped. "I need your help. The mirror is broken."

The orb floated towards to mirror as if it understood her, and Victoria followed, abandoning her message to Tom.

The room was still for a moment, and then a blinding light burst from the orb. Victoria buried her face into her hands, and when she opened her eyes, she understood exactly what had happened. The mirror had no cracks and provided a perfect reflection of her room, as if it had never been broken. The orb disappeared through the glass.

Even in the broad daylight, Victoria could see the mirror glowing, and she understood what she was supposed to do next. She raced around her house, throwing clothes and toiletries together into a bag. When she had enough to survive a week away, she surveyed her room. She didn't feel the nervousness she'd expected at leaving, only regret that Sarah wasn't here. Victoria hoped she would be able to return to her room for Sarah, but she refused to waste another chance of finding Atlantis because she'd promised to wait. She raced to her desk and scrawled a quick note.

I'll be back later. I'll be okay. Hope you had a great

date.

She left the note on the kitchen table and returned to her bedroom. The mirror was still glowing. She pushed her hand through her reflection, making it ripple, and gasped as her fingers brushed against soft sand through the bottom of the frame. She dusted it off and stepped through the mirror, knowing what she would find on the other side.

It was the beach from her dream.

"Thank you," she whispered to the orb, her heart racing. A wooden boat was on the sand not far ahead, exactly like in her dream. She felt a peace and conviction wash over her. This was exactly where she was meant to be. The orb was her guardian angel, and it was impossible to be afraid of what was next. She was going to Atlantis, whether anyone liked it or not.

Sitting on the warm sand, she pulled the map out of her pocket and tried to figure out exactly where she was. She couldn't see any distinguishing features on the island to help her locate herself on the map, but her gaze found one of the small islands at the far edge of the map, just beyond the Atlantean border. If her intuition was correct, the main island of Atlantis was only days away in the boat.

Seeing that the mirror was still glowing, Victoria examined the boat. The words *mene mene tekel upharsin* were etched into the top of the boat in small letters. The boat was in perfect condition, and there was plenty of space to fit two people and supplies. Despite her excitement, Victoria realized with a sinking feeling that she hadn't considered the essential provisions like food, water, and shelter, though they would be critical to surviving the journey.

"I can't go yet," she told the orb. Looking inland, she was relieved to see the large mirror through which she'd come to the island was still glowing. "Besides, I made a promise to Sarah. I can't just disappear."

The orb didn't seem to protest, but Victoria knew it communicated in ways she didn't understand. Hoping she wasn't wasting her only chance of going to Atlantis, she walked to the mirror and stepped through it into her bedroom.

Chapter Seven
DEPARTURE

"Where the hell have you been?" Sarah demanded, bursting through the bedroom door only a second later. "I saw your note, but I looked for you everywhere. I was getting so worried you'd gone without me." Victoria faltered, sensing that Sarah was genuinely upset, but something in her expression must have told Sarah everything she couldn't. "Can you please explain what's going on?" Sarah asked more calmly.

"Let me show you," Victoria said. "It's about Atlantis. You might want to grab your bag. I'll stay watch by the mirror."

Sarah rolled her eyes but grabbed everything Victoria had asked, adding her notebook and a few pens from the kitchen. "No food?" she grumbled.

"Of course," Victoria breathed. Sarah had only been joking, but it was a valid point. In her excitement, she'd almost forgotten the essentials again. She glanced at the orb, which hadn't moved. "I'll get those now. Can you stay here and watch? I'll be back soon."

Praying that the mirror would still work and the orb wouldn't go anywhere, Victoria returned to the main house. She found a tent, bedding, a medical kit, and more food and water than what she considered to be emergency rations. Though she wouldn't dream of telling Sarah, she had a feeling Atlantis would provide for them until the end, since it had taken them this far.

The orb and Sarah were still waiting when Victoria returned to her bedroom. Along with her relief, Victoria felt she would never be more prepared than she was now. "We might not be able to get back," she warned Sarah.

Sarah sighed. Victoria suspected Sarah thought she'd lost the plot completely, though her artist's eye had probably seen that the mirror was glowing. "I've already told you I'm not letting you go alone."

Feeling less guilty now that she'd warned Sarah, Victoria grabbed her bags and followed the orb through the mirror again. She heard a gasp behind her as Sarah followed onto a bright, beautiful beach.

"Where the hell are we?" Sarah asked. The expression on her face was a wonderful mixture of disbelief and amazement, and Victoria realized she had made the right decision going back for Sarah. "Is this Atlantis?"

Victoria bit her lip. "I'm not quite sure," she admitted, deciding not to mention the maps until she had looked at them more thoroughly, "but I think we're at the edge of Atlantis."

"You've been here before."

"I dreamt about this beach last night, and I was here when you were looking for me," Victoria said. "I was able to fix the mirror, but this isn't the place it used to go. We're supposed to take the boat to Atlantis."

Sarah swayed on the spot, and for a second, Victoria worried she would faint. "This is so strange, Vic. I really don't understand what's happening, and I'm not sure I like it, but I can see it makes you happy, so why not? I did make a promise."

They looked at each other for a moment, and Victoria felt a rush of gratitude. "I pray to the stars we'll be able to find Atlantis without any problem, and I'm sure we will," Victoria said, choosing her words especially carefully, "but if there's ever *any* emergency, you have to get yourself back to land straightaway. I don't want you to put yourself in danger."

Sarah looked at her with wide eyes, and Victoria realized she'd made her point. "Everything should be fine if we stay together," she concluded on a lighter note. Refusing to focus on the potential danger ahead, she marched to the boat. The orb followed close behind. As she loaded her bags into the space under the seats, Sarah suddenly seemed to realize what was happening.

"A boat?" Sarah asked over her shoulder. "Really? Isn't Atlantis supposed to be underwater?"

It was a fair question, Victoria had to admit. "That's what the myths say, but it isn't. I don't know why everyone has it wrong." She began to pull the boat into the sea. The wood moved through the sand effortlessly, and the boat was soon floating on the water. Victoria sighed in relief. The journey was progressing better than in her nightmare. "We could swim the entire way, but I doubt that would be much fun."

"Fair enough. Hope you're good at rowing," Sarah said. She brought her bags aboard and took a seat at the bow. Victoria pushed the boat until it was gliding through the water and jumped in, feeling enormous relief that they were moving. The orb floated to the front of the boat, as if it was leading the way, and then disappeared without a sound.

Victoria exchanged a glance with Sarah. "Looks like we're on our own now," she said, reaching for the oars. The mirror on the beach was glowing, but she wasn't going to turn back. "To Atlantis."

"Wait," Sarah said, "is the boat moving by itself?"

Victoria looked up, expecting Sarah to be joking, but

the boat was moving away from the island and picking up speed. Within a minute, she had no doubt. The boat was cruising along at a safe and comfortable speed, without Victoria having touched the oars.

It's magic.

"That makes everything so much easier," she said, laughing at her luck. "I thought I'd have to row the whole way."

"How's it doing it?" Sarah asked. She didn't seem as surprised or suspicious as when she had gone through the portal, now only amazed and curious.

Victoria shook her head, wishing she had the answer. "Your guess is as good as mine, but I would say magic." The only other possibility she could imagine was that the orb was somehow involved. She ran her fingers over the words etched into the boat, unable to decide which theory was more likely. "See this? I'm pretty sure it means this boat is Atlantean. If we're lucky, the boat will take us straight there."

"If Atlantis exists," Sarah added gently.

Victoria laughed. "You sound like Nick." She would have been offended if she wasn't so confident. Sarah had seen all the proof Victoria could offer and had no excuse to doubt anymore. "I know it does. You'll see soon enough."

When Victoria next glanced over her shoulder, the beach was disappearing into the distance. After a few more minutes, the island was nothing more than a thin stretch of white and emerald against a sapphire horizon. She took a few deep breaths, trying not to worry if she'd forgotten anything, because it was too late now for regret. She and Sarah were leaving the mirror behind and heading into open waters.

Even further out from land, the sea was perfectly calm. Victoria watched Sarah pull out her sketchbook and a pencil and begin to draw. *Going to Atlantis isn't supposed to be this easy*, Victoria thought. She kept her eyes on the horizon for a while and occasionally referenced her maps. According to her calculations, the boat was going straight to Atlantis.

"What are you working on?" she asked Sarah. "You don't seem worried with the journey."

"I'm just finishing a sketch of Tom," Sarah said with a shrug. Victoria's heart skipped a beat. "Nothing new." She held out her sketchbook, and Victoria couldn't help but marvel at it. Even though the art was still a work in progress, and couldn't deny that Sarah had talent.

"It's brilliant, Sarah," she said. "What will you do when it's done?"

"I might put it in my portfolio, if Tom says I can. I like it, but I can see now that I could use more practice drawing scenery than people."

"I think it's amazing," Victoria said. Sarah shrugged

the compliment away, and the boat fell into silence as she began to work again.

"Where do you think we are now?" she asked after an hour. Although she wanted to trust the boat with her life, she couldn't believe it was taking them straight to Atlantis without any problem. She retrieved the map from her pocket for what felt like the hundredth time. Looking at the map now, she could imagine a line showing the route to Atlantis. With the incredible progress they were making, she guessed they could be on the main island in a day or two.

"You can read that?" Sarah asked.

Victoria nodded. "You can't?"

"The writing looks like scribbles to me."

"You're looking at it the wrong way," Victoria said, handing the papers over.

Sarah shook her head after a second. "This isn't English, Vic."

Victoria frowned. "I drew the map myself. Of course the labels are in English." She couldn't think of any explanation that hadn't come from a fairy tale. She wondered if the papers had an Atlantean enchantment so others couldn't read them, and then whether Gryffin had understood the maps. She smiled, hoping they'd frustrated him fiercely.

"Is that a tattoo?" Sarah asked, breaking Victoria out of her thoughts. "What does it say?"

Victoria looked down. She'd been playing with the ribbon on her wrist without realizing it, exposing her Sentence. She pushed the ribbon up her arm, deciding it was time to reveal another secret. She told Sarah everything about the Sentence, including what Nick had told her about its Biblical history, and everything else she'd guessed since then. "I might be wrong," she concluded, "but the expression is important to the Atlanteans. It's probably some sort of motto."

"It's so dark," Sarah said. Victoria wasn't sure she was referring to the ink. "But it's not a tattoo?"

Victoria shrugged. "I have no idea how permanent it is. It hasn't faded yet, and it's been a few days."

The boat fell into silence, and Victoria evaluated Sarah's reaction. "If you could have one yourself, would you want one?" Victoria asked.

"Why not?"

Victoria hesitated, debating whether to tell Sarah about Gryffin. "It's felt like a curse when I got it. I wouldn't wish that on anyone, no matter how important it is to Atlantis."

Sarah shook her head. "Looks more like a sign of strength to me, but you know best. Did Tom know?"

Victoria laughed as adjusted the ribbon back into place. "If he noticed the ribbon, I don't think he saw what was underneath. He wouldn't have been happy about it.

Nick gave me a lot of information about the phrase, but he never saw the Sentence."

Sarah slammed her sketchbook shut with a sigh.

They definitely went on a second date, Victoria thought, but she didn't dare ask now.

"What do you think will happen if Atlantis is real?" Sarah asked, interrupting her thoughts.

Victoria took a deep breath. Sarah was changing the subject, but she was nearly admitting that Atlantis could exist. "People would go mad if they found out," she admitted. "It's been a mystery for so long that its discovery would make world news. And even if it's ruined, the place will be amazing. Everyone would try to see it, and tourism would only ruin it more."

"We probably shouldn't tell anyone," Sarah said.

"I think that would be a good idea."

"I just wonder why modern technology hasn't found it."

"I was thinking about that, too," Victoria said. "Either nobody has found Atlantis before, or they never told a soul if they had. If the truth was too amazing or dangerous, anyone with common sense would have kept Atlantis a secret to the grave."

"Seems promising."

Why me, though? Victoria wondered. She had the maps and this boat, which nobody who had looked for

Atlantis before would have had, but that wasn't enough to guarantee success. She mulled over the question until she realized that the sun was approaching the horizon quickly. Sleeping on the boat after sunset would be incredibly unsafe. Even if the sky was clear now and the boat had done well so far, the possibility of waking up in the middle of a storm would be a nightmare. *What else are we supposed to do?* she thought.

"Look," Sarah said, pointing to the distance, "an island. Is it Atlantis?"

Victoria looked to the horizon, her heart racing. She could barely make out a speck of land in the distance. It was impossible to gauge the distance, but she guessed it was less than hour away at the rate the boat was traveling.

"I don't know," Victoria said. "It's still too far away."

Half an hour later, the sky was beginning to get dark and cloudy, but the boat was close enough to the island that Victoria could see it was too small to be the main Atlantean island. She was surprised that the boat was going so close to land, but she wasn't going to get her hopes up that this was their destination for the night. The boat cruised to what Victoria could tell was the sheltered side of the island, where the sea became calmer. She was surprised to find a sheltered bay with a stone dock in it.

"Do we jump?" Sarah asked, voicing what Victoria

had been wondering. "The water is shallow here."

The beach was seconds away, but Victoria hesitated. This was their once chance to get to safety, but the boat could continue without them, leaving them stranded forever. "Not unless the boat stops. I'm not going to abandon our only mode of transportation."

The boat slowed, as if it had heard her, and a few seconds later, it bumped onto the sandy beach and came to a stop. Victoria stood up, testing whether her numb legs still supported her. Stepping onto land, she swayed, but she and Sarah reached for each other and held each other tight.

"I'm shattered," Sarah groaned. "It feels like we've been swimming all day, not sitting in a bloody boat."

"I know. I can't remember ever feeling so tired." The boat seemed to have taken them to a quiet beach. Beyond the sand was a little meadow that would make a good campsite, surrounded by a forest. "We're running out of daylight," Victoria said, a wave of exhaustion washing over her. "We should probably put the boat away for the night and stay here, if that's okay. The boat must have brought us here for a reason."

"Here looks fine with me," Sarah agreed. "Nobody is going stumble across us while we sleep."

"I hope you're right." Victoria unloaded their bags onto the grass, and she and Sarah secured the boat to the dock for the night before setting up shelter in the meadow.

Victoria brought their bags inside and unfolded their blankets onto makeshift beds. Using a lighter she'd found in Sarah's bag, she lit a candle and put it on a lantern in the middle of the tent.

Sarah crawled inside a moment later and surveyed the interior with an expression of appreciation. "This looks brilliant," she said. "I'm bloody impressed we've pulled this off."

That was the best compliment Victoria could have asked for. "I'd rather have a magic fire for light and warmth, but this should be safe enough. Atlantis must really want us to find it, if it's helping us so much," she said. Sarah made a sound of agreement as she curled up in her bed. "The orb helped me fix the mirror, and we've found a boat programed to take us the rest of the way to Atlantis. We haven't had to row, and all the sea within viewing distance of the boat was perfectly calm. If that's the case, I don't believe we have much to worry about tomorrow."

"Hopefully," Sarah agreed. "Anyway, I need to sleep, Vic. That boat ride stole all my energy."

Victoria felt her jaw drop. Sarah had obviously been joking, but the theory seemed strangely possible. Nothing else explained how the boat moved on its own, or why Victoria felt like she'd spent the entire day exercising when in reality she'd been sitting in the sun. *The journey today could have killed us,* she realized with a sense of horror, *even if the boat is there to help.* Wishing Sarah goodnight, she blew out the lantern and vowed she'd be much more careful tomorrow.

Chapter Eight
GHOSTS

Victoria slept dreamlessly until morning light filled the tent. She ate breakfast on the beach and checked that the boat was still secure before she decided to explore a path along the coast. It led her towards the cliffs she'd seen from the boat yesterday. Nearing the highest point of the island, she began to feel that she shouldn't venture further, but she caught sight of an ancient, pillared building and edged nearer.

What is this place? she wondered. Whoever had built the fortress here had obviously wanted it in an impregnable location, but it was too open to be residential or useful for defense. *There must be a reason it's protected so well.*

In the end, she ignored the feeling that she wasn't meant to be here and wandered closer. The stones in the building seemed to shimmer as she approached, like the stones in Atlantis. Victoria thought the ruins would have been incredibly beautiful if they didn't feel so intimidating. Standing in the middle of the structure, she had an amazing, panoramic view of the horizon. The ocean stretched in every direction as far as she could see, with no other land in sight. She could see her tent in the meadow and boat on the pier, and nestled within the forest was a lake she hadn't seen from the path. If the monument had been warning her to keep her distance, the lake was beckoning her to approach. Victoria set off, but halfway down the monument's steps, she noticed the sound of her footsteps change. She stopped, surprised.

The step is hollow, she realized. She sat down to investigate. Gripping the stone, she began to pull. It weighed less than she'd expected, and it only took her a few seconds to push the slab out of its spot completely. Seeing what was underneath, Victoria gasped.

The stone had been concealing a secret passage.

Through the gap, Victoria could see a set of steps leading deep underground. She couldn't tell what was at the end, but she began her descent. Her uneasiness grew more intense, but Victoria ignored it. When her foot touched ground after the last step, she could no longer see anything ahead of her. The air was cool but not damp or stale. Her intuition warned her to turn back, but she couldn't help but continue.

You could get lost, she reminded herself, looking over her shoulder after every few steps. As long as she could still see the light from where she'd come, she could make her way back. She wished she could see what was around her, and for a moment, she considered powering on her phone to use the flashlight, but preserving its charge was more important. A second later, she bumped into a solid object and fell forward.

The sound of crunching glass filled the room as Victoria landed on her hands and knees, and a searing pain shot through her right palm. She hissed, feeling a sticky mix of blood and dirt on her skin. *It could have been much worse*, she reassured herself, imagining herself plummeting into an invisible chasm. *It's probably just a scratch.*

She stood up and took her time retracing her way back outside. When she was in the sunlight, she sat down, shaking despite the warmth of the day. She knew she was lucky that she had only tripped. Holding her breath, she looked at her hand. The cut was shallower than she'd expected and barely bleeding, but it was still the worst pain she'd ever experienced. If there hadn't been sand in the wound, she would have gone back to the tent for the medical kit, but she knew she wanted to get to the lake first. Vowing to be much more careful with her future explorations, she managed to push the stone slab back into place with her foot and set off.

Up close, the lake was larger than Victoria had expected. A wooden bridge connected points the main shore to a small island in the middle of the lake. Victoria tested the structure with a few steps before she was convinced it would support her, then walked to the middle island and sat down on the grass. The pain in her hand had subsided into an unpleasant pulse, but she rinsed her cut in the water and bandaged it with part of her sleeve until she could get back to the medical kit in the tent.

Satisfied that the wound would heal, she pulled out the map and eventually found an unlabeled island that had a lake in the middle. By her calculations, she and Sarah were most of the way to Atlantis. *We could be there tomorrow if everything goes well in the morning,* she thought. Now that she'd been stuck on this island for the better part of a day, she was beginning to regret her promise to Sarah. *It's only one day,* she reminded herself. *The world won't end.*

After lying in the sun for a while, Victoria stripped out of her jeans and shirt, ready to swim. The water was so clear that she could see sand at the deepest part of the lake. She waded in and reveled in the feeling of blood, dirt, and sweat washing off her skin. Finding that her hand wasn't hurting, she dove in began to swim. Further away from shore, the water appeared to be sparkling, tinted with a hundred streams of colors that danced in the otherwise invisible current. *How strange,* Victoria thought. The streams began to move faster, then morphed from vague lines into more distinct, terrifying forms underwater.

Translucent ghosts.

Atlanteans.

Victoria screamed as a force pulled her underwater. The apparition nearest to her was a girl with pale hair. With a sad expression, she reached out and touched the Sentence on Victoria's wrist before Victoria could realize what was happening or recoil. The girl's hand seemed to pass through the skin as if she was not solid, though Victoria felt a stab of freezing cold where the specter had touched. She screamed, but the sound disappeared in a flurry of bubbles that nobody could hear.

And then an immense weight began to pull her down, dragging Victoria underwater. She kicked harder, but she couldn't propel herself to the surface or push the ghosts away. The Atlanteans blurred as her vision flickered, and Victoria knew she only had a few more seconds before she would need to breathe. She stopped struggling and let herself sink. As her fingertips brushed the soft sand at the bottom of the lake, a sense of serenity washed over her. Her fate belonged to Atlantis. Her vision darkened, and she began to fade out of consciousness.

And then, the weight lifted. Victoria sensed that the ghosts had disappeared. With a final burst of strength, she pushed herself off the sand. After what felt like an eternity, she broke through the water surface with a gasp that gave her new life. She splashed her way to shore and the instant she was on warm, dry land, she started to cry.

She had misread the signs about Atlantis. She'd fallen so hard for its call that she hadn't believed the danger behind it, even if Gryffin had warned her. And despite having convinced herself that she was safe from Atlantis if she had the Sentence, she'd never felt more afraid. Nothing in her life would be the same if she returned to England, but she had to try.

Sarah was sketching in the afternoon sun when Victoria returned to the meadow. She looked happy and peaceful and rested now, Victoria noticed with a surge of jealousy. Still shivering, she sat down on the blanket Sarah had laid out on the grass and sighed, wondering how much she wanted to reveal. Sarah looked up from her drawing.

"Everything okay?" she asked. "You don't look well."

Victoria shook her head, blinking away a new wave of tears. "I want to go home. Now."

"What?" Sarah surveyed Victoria carefully now. "We've only just left England."

Victoria shook her head again. Right now, in the middle of the meadow on this forsaken island, wasn't the time or place to tell the truth. "This is too dangerous. We really shouldn't have come here, and we should go home."

"I see you don't want to tell me," Sarah grumbled. "I don't know what's happened to stress you out so much, but it's okay to feel scared. It probably is a stupid idea to be out in the middle of the ocean with just a boat and a tent, but we've done so well in getting here. You should sleep on it, and if you still want to go home in the morning, I'll go. Sound good?"

Closing her eyes, Victoria could still see the ghosts, the young girl reaching out for her in the lake. She'd be lucky if she could ever sleep again, but if waiting a day was the only way to get Sarah to go home, Victoria had no alternative. She finally nodded.

"Great. What do you want to do now?" Sarah asked. Victoria knew she was deliberately changing the subject. "We've got the whole afternoon free, and it looks like a nice day."

"I'll get changed into dry clothes and fix my hand first, but I've got something to show you," Victoria said. "Bring your sketch pad if you want. I have no idea what it is, but you'll probably like it."

Sarah nodded. Victoria dipped into the tent for a few minutes, and when she returned outside in dry clothes, a small fire was burning on the blanket. Sarah had stopped drawing and was staring deep into its flames, looking too enchanted to comprehend what she was seeing.

"What are you doing?" Victoria asked.

"It just appeared a second ago," Sarah said. "It's not hot."

Victoria instantly understood. "Don't touch it!" she hissed.

But it was too late. Sarah had put her hand in the fire. She jumped back, like the heatless flames had burnt her, and the fire disappeared. Victoria closed her eyes, knowing what would happen next.

"Victoria?" Sarah whispered a moment later. "There's something on my wrist."

Victoria looked up, hearing the panic in Sarah's voice. She could distinguish the words *mene mene tekel upharsin* in faint letters against the pale skin of Sarah's wrist. "Look at the maps again," Victoria said. She dove into the tent again and found the maps at the bottom of her bag, and held them out to Sarah with a shaking hand.

Sighing, Sarah took the papers. "Oh, my god," she whispered, her eyes widening. "I can read it."

"I thought you might be able to. It must be the Sentence."

Sarah spent a few minutes examining the maps, talking through some calculations with Victoria until they both agreed on where they were. *Maybe Gryffin could read the maps*, Victoria thought, her heart falling. Her only consolation was a suspicion that Gryffin hadn't made copies of her maps. She knew he hadn't intended to lose them, and she could only hope that he hadn't had the time or foresight to make contingency plans.

"What happens next?" Sarah whispered.

"I need to bandage my hand," Victoria admitted, "and then I want to show you something."

Sarah helped Victoria, and they went to the monument together Victoria still had a feeling she was supposed to stay away, but it was easier to ignore now that the whole island made her nervous. Looking at the structure a second time, Victoria had no better idea of what purpose it had served. "What do you think this place is meant to be?" she asked Sarah.

"I don't know," Sarah said. She was pulling paper and a pen out of her bag. "A temple, maybe? It doesn't look fortified for defense, and it doesn't seem to be protecting anything. There's nothing on this island."

It seemed too obvious. With its beautiful details, open structure, and pillars that reached for the sun by day and stars at night, this edifice looked and felt like a temple from the ancient world. "It's got to be something more. There's a secret room hidden underneath the steps," Victoria said, deciding it wouldn't be unsafe to explore the area if she and Sarah stayed together. "I think the entire building was built around whatever was down there."

She led Sarah to the stone concealing the secret passageway and sat on the step nearby. After trying for a few seconds to push the stone aside, she could tell that something was different. It didn't sound hollow, and it didn't budge when she tried to slide it with her uninjured hand. The thought of using the other hand made her feel sick.

"Could you help me, please?" she asked Sarah. "My hand can't take the pressure."

Together, they pushed and pulled, but the stone still didn't move. Victoria would have doubted her sanity, but she could see the bloody spot where she'd touched the stone hours before. "It must be stuck," Victoria sighed. "It moved so easily before. I'm sorry."

"I can see you were here. I believe you," Sarah said. "Now, why don't you tell me about this room? What did you see?"

"Nothing," Victoria admitted. "It was too dark, and I didn't want to waste my phone battery."

Sarah looked down at the steps and back at Victoria. "Do you think this building is protecting that room?"

"I don't know what else it would be here for."

"It looks like a temple," Sarah suggested, looking uneasy. "You could have found the crypt."

"Of course," Victoria groaned. She shuddered, thankful she hadn't seen what had been around her. Sarah sketched the temple before they returned to the tent for the evening. They spent the evening on the beach and returned to the tent at sunset.

"Do you miss Tom?" Sarah asked as they crawled into bed.

Victoria flinched as sorrow shot through her body. "I do. I don't feel right when I'm not with him, but I'm not even worried about myself. The situation isn't fair on him, and I hope everything will be okay when we get back."

"We won't be gone forever," Sarah said. "They say absence makes the heart grow fonder."

Victoria pondered those words for a few minutes. She couldn't imagine a future without Tom, but she couldn't see how one with him was possible. Their relationship would have to survive years apart at university, if she didn't get her family's support, and they would face even more adventures taking a gap year together.

"I found this earlier. It was in the bottom of the tent bag by the way," Sarah said, holing a folded sheet of paper. "Is it yours?"

Unfolding it, Victoria found a symbol she'd never seen before. Beneath was a short message. *Draw this symbol above your navel and you won't have to eat or drink for a week.*

Victoria frowned, reading it a few times to make sure she understood. She refused to believe that a simple drawing on the body could end hunger. If it was that easy, someone would have discovered the secret centuries ago, and the world would have been a much better place since then. But she hadn't forgotten all the myths that emphasized how corrupt the Atlanteans had been.

Instead of sharing such knowledge with the world, they would have used it to their own advantage, Victoria thought. *Without the need for food, they would have had unlimited resources to trade and been invincible in war.* She hated the injustice of it, but given that she and Sarah were currently in the middle of nowhere with limited resources, she had to try. *Atlantis put it here for a reason,* she thought, though looking at the cloth around her hand, she wished Atlantis had provided a charm to heal injuries. *We're not going to start a war.*

"Can I borrow a pen?" she asked Sarah.

Sarah obliged. Victoria copied the symbol onto the skin above her navel and explained what it was.

"Can I draw it, too?" Sarah asked.

"Why not?" Victoria replied. "You already have the Sentence."

She handed the pen back, and Sarah drew the symbol on herself. Victoria had seen enough in Atlantis to believe in magic, but she still doubted whether the symbol would work. She drifted off to sleep, wondering whether the Atlanteans could have been so selfish. It was nearly midnight when she heard a branch crack in the forest, not far from the tent. She sat up, trying to ignore the images of the

Atlantean ghosts. Someone was in the forest.

Victoria listened carefully, praying it was Gryffin. Talking to him would be easy after everything she'd endured this week. A gentle breeze rustled the tent, and Victoria relaxed. *You're being ridiculous,* she scolded herself. She wanted to believe she and Sarah were safe, but she couldn't ignore the horrible feeling of someone approaching the tent. She crawled to the tent door, unzipped it without a sound, and peeked outside.

There were no ghosts. But since sunset, the island had undergone a transformation that made Victoria feel like she was suddenly in a nightmare. Fog had crept into the meadow, so thick that she couldn't see the nearest trees. Victoria shuddered. She was essentially blind, but her intuition was screaming at her now that someone was out there, that something terrible was about to happen. With a feeling that time was running out, she shook Sarah awake.

"Hide in the forest," she hissed, trusting Sarah would hear her urgency. "No matter how long I'm gone, *don't go looking for me.* I'll find you. Go!"

Sarah followed Victoria out of the tent without question. As soon as her ruby hair had disappeared into the fog, Victoria raced to the opposite side of the meadow. Nearing the edge of the forest, she felt the presence of something real and even more dangerous than the Atlantean ghosts grow stronger. Someone was watching her.

She ran faster, knowing she had no time to hide. In the forest, she threw herself against the nearest tree, trying to catch her breath without making a sound. Through the fog, she could sense the presence approaching quickly, and it wasn't Gryffin. *He never felt dangerous like this*, she thought. She took a final breath, not knowing how else to prepare for whatever was coming. The fog in front of her began to glow with firelight.

And then, Victoria felt her entire body immobilize against her will, as if by magic, as a hand touched her shoulder.

"Hello, Victoria," a deep, male voice murmured. "How wonderful to meet you, at last."

Chapter Nine
CAELAN

It was the strangest sensation Victoria had ever felt. Her lips refused to scream, and she had the feeling that her mind was disconnecting from reality, like a force was hypnotizing her. She tried to escape the stranger's grasp, but her body refused to obey her thoughts. Beneath her panic, she couldn't guess who this man was. She knew from his voice that he wasn't Gryffin, and he was too strong to be a ghost.

"Please don't struggle, Victoria," he said. His voice was pleasant and had an accent she couldn't place. "I'm being careful not to hurt you. We will talk in a few minutes."

Victoria felt her body relax, until she was standing limply. Only the stranger's hold on her back kept her on her feet, while his other hand held a burning torch.

"Let's walk," he said. He gently took a hold of her arm and began to lead her across the meadow. They climbed up the hill, following the same path Victoria had taken in the afternoon. *We're going towards the monument,* she realized. She had no idea what they would be doing there, but she had a horrible vision of him locking her in the crypt. She felt herself swoon. *Sarah will never find me. I'll die there.*

She forced herself to stay calm. Until she knew who he was or what he wanted with her, there was no point in wasting valuable energy. *Maybe it's all a misunderstanding*, she thought. *Maybe he knows about Gryffin.* Reaching the point where the path split, the man turned towards the forest instead of continuing up the mountain steps. Victoria felt her heart race faster. *He's taking me to the lake,* she realized with horror. The prospect of seeing the ghosts again was even worse than being locked underground. And still, she had no choice but to go where the stranger led, her own body betraying her with every step.

After what felt like an eternity, the procession stopped in the middle of the bridge. The man muttered a few foreign words, and glittering, crystal bars sprung up around the bridge, making a prison. Victoria felt herself regain control of her body. Her instinct was to run, but she knew the fog would slow her down if she got past the bars. Glancing into the lake, she couldn't see past the reflection of the firelight. Victoria swooned, realizing she had no way to escape, but the man supported her. Either he didn't know about the ghosts, or he wasn't afraid.

"Who are you?" Victoria gasped.

The man rotated her to face him. For a second, she was struck with a strange impression that Gryffin had aged twenty years in a matter of days. The man before her had had the same angular face, brunette hair that brushed his shoulders, and piercing silver eyes that were both captivating and dangerous. He was even taller than Tom, but his arrogant air forced her thoughts back to Gryffin. He was wearing a cloak Victoria knew hadn't come from modern day.

"I am Caelan," he said. He flashed an unreadable smile. "I've been waiting a long time to meet you."

"What do you want with me?"

Caelan said nothing for a moment. Victoria wondered if she'd discovered the crux of who he was. "It's very simple," he began. His eyes, silver and unfathomable, met hers steadily. "I exist to ensure you stay out of Atlantis. I know you're meant to restore the empire, but doing so would endanger the entire world. Atlantis is an ungodly, reprehensible place, with power that must stay broken and forgotten. If you do not believe me now, you will discover so at your own peril."

Victoria stared at him, trying to determine whether

he was serious. He seemed to believe that Atlantis was real, but his faith that she was supposed to restore the empire was laughable. "How do you expect me to help Atlantis? I'm only seventeen. I can barely drive, let alone save an empire."

"Are you denying your intent to restore Atlantis?"

He likes a debate, Victoria realized. It was her only way to buy time to make a plan. "I wouldn't even know how."

"Not yet," he agreed. "But you're not like most people. You're not even like most Atlanteans. In time, you will find ways of restoring Atlantis that nobody else could imagine, and the repercussions will be severe. I'm sorry, but I simply cannot risk letting you reach Atlantis."

"The whole world thinks Atlantis is a myth."

"It's in your blood, Victoria," he retorted. Victoria heard a sudden sternness in his voice and sensed he had lost interest in her debate. "I know you can feel the truth. You know Atlantis is real, and you never doubted it for a moment."

Victoria decided it was best not to say anything.

"You are an intelligent young woman, Victoria, and I do not intend to trick you or cause you any harm. You should believe me when I say that the only way you can save yourself is by swearing to stay away from Atlantis," he said. Victoria felt a shiver run through her body as he met her gaze directly. Something in his eyes lacked the generosity in his words, though she believed him, for some reason. "If you cannot give me your promise by tomorrow morning, I have other ways to make you forget about Atlantis."

"I promise now," Victoria said, crossing her fingers behind her back. Some promises were meant to be broken.

An amused smile crossed Caelan's lips. "I should explain myself," he said. In a flash, he unsheathed a dagger from his cloak. Its sharp, silver blade glittered in his torchlight, and Victoria instinctively recoiled. "Spoken promises are too fragile. I require a blood oath, sworn on your own life and enforced by the magical contract of your words. Any violation of your promise will kill you instantly."

Victoria stared into his eyes, hoping he couldn't see her fear. Magic like that didn't exist in the real world. *But he's serious,* she realized. She'd seen enough this week to know she should believe in these blood oaths, even if she didn't want to. She stood there, too stunned to stay anything.

"You have until midday to decide, Victoria," Caelan said. "It is a simple decision. You must swear on your life to stay away from Atlantis, or face great consequences."

With a bow, he walked through the bars at the edge of the bridge and disappeared into the fog.

As soon as the light of his torch disappeared, Victoria collapsed to the ground, shaking. She suspected that

Sarah would start looking for her late tomorrow afternoon, when Victoria had been missing for most of the day. By then, it would be too late. The only glimmer of hope Victoria could find was that Caelan didn't seem to know about Sarah yet, but even that would change once Sarah stepped out of hiding.

I've got to get out now, Victoria realized. She wasn't sure if Caelan would return before morning, but now was her chance to escape. Taking a deep breath, she glanced into the lake. Without the light of Caelan's torch, the water was black, and it was still impossible to tell whether the ghosts were still lurking there. She ventured to the small island in the middle of the lake and saw that Caelan had barricaded this, too. *He must not know about the ghosts,* she thought. If the only way off the bridge had been through the water, she would have faced them again. But even that wasn't an option now.

Victoria returned to the bridge and sat down. Her next plan was to kick through the bridge's wood railings, which she guessed were the weakest part of her prison, but the bridge was sturdier than it looked, and it refused to budge. After a few minutes, she turned her effort to the diamond bars, feeling helpless. She pushed and pulled until she was in tears, suspecting that Gryffin could have escaped from prison within minutes. *How the hell would he do it?* she wondered.

And then, she had a revelation.

Gryffin was the baby from her first dream of Atlantis.

She stopped pacing the bridge, stunned. Gryffin and the woman from her dream had the same hair and the same silver eyes, and she was amazed she hadn't realized it the second she'd seen him. He had lost his mother and grown up into a young man with some sort of Atlantean magic. Though she had no idea how any of it was possible, it was the only answer she had. *That's why he's got the Sentence and knows so much about Atlantis,* she mused. *There is still at least one Atlantean around.*

Thinking about his mother again, she felt a wave of sadness and surprising empathy for him, though it didn't excuse his behavior. She deeply regretted not talking to him properly when she'd had the chance, to glean any information he had about Atlantis. She felt helpless as she resumed pacing along the bridge, and then slapped the wood in frustration. She was locked in, and she had no power to escape.

A second later, a warm feeling spread through her hand, intensifying until a few bursts of sparks burst from her fingertips like miniature fireworks. *I'm going mad,* she thought, sinking to the wood planks beneath her. Despite Gryffin's warnings, she'd never expected this danger when she'd set off for Atlantis, and now she would never return home. She'd left so much behind in England that she'd taken for granted until now. Aiden and Andrea had only wanted to protect her, and Tom wouldn't forgive himself for letting her run away if she never came back. Her disappearance would hurt everyone.

Shaky and exhausted, Victoria closed her eyes. After what felt like an hour, she had no tears left to cry, and even if she did, she wasn't going to waste them on herself. Sarah might never return home. Victoria was sure there was hope for Sarah, though she couldn't see it yet. After what could have been a minute or an hour, it began to rain. Victoria moved to the little island in the middle of the lake for shelter under the trees, and after what felt like hours of laying in the dark on the soft grass, exhaustion overwhelmed her fears. Drifting off, she wished she could see Tom and her family one last time and tell them what she most wanted to say. *I love you, and I'm so sorry.*

Chapter Ten
ESCAPE

Victoria woke on the island an hour later. She was sure she had heard someone in the distance through the mist, but after a moment, she realized it was the bridge creaking in the wind. The night was still dark but surprisingly warm, and a light rain had begun to fall. Wiping rain off her face, Victoria stretched and stood up. She had to break out of her prison while Caelan was still gone. *Gryffin has the Sentence, and he could probably do it,* she thought. *He and I aren't that different.*

A moment later, a shattering crash filled the air. Running to the bridge, Victoria saw that one of the wooden bars had shattered, leaving enough space for her to escape. With her heart racing, she slipped through the gap and dove into the lake. She reached the shore before she remembered the ghosts, but the water had remained calm and, for the moment, undisturbed apart from her own movement. Victoria ran down the mountain without a glance back or a second thought about her soaked clothing. Reaching the meadow, she came to a halt and surveyed her surroundings.

Sarah was nowhere in sight, and the tent was gone.

Fighting a wave of nausea, Victoria she ran to the edge of the forest. The island wasn't massive, but the search for Sarah would take time they couldn't afford. Victoria prayed for a miracle, realizing she had no idea how or where to begin. Sunrise wouldn't be for at least another hour, by which time Caelan would probably be looking for her.

And then, a twig crackled overhead. Victoria froze, sensing this sound hadn't been from the wind. There was only a handful of people who could possibly be on this island. Holding her breath, she looked up. After a second, she noticed a figure sitting on a branch halfway up the tree, silently watching her. Despite the darkness, she recognized the flash of red hair instantly.

"Sarah?" she whispered.

"Vic?" Sarah replied, sounding relieved. "Bloody hell. You scared me. I thought I saw someone coming, so I hid. What the hell is going on?"

"I was hoping you could tell me," Victoria admitted. "Have you seen anyone else here?"

"Nobody but you, until now."

"Right," Victoria sighed. "Could you come down? We need to leave this island. Now."

"What's going on?" Sarah repeated. For the first time this week, she sounded genuinely afraid. "You just disappeared overnight without any warning. Where did you go?"

Victoria shook her head. She felt horrendous for putting Sarah in danger, but she couldn't explain now. "Later. We need to go."

Sarah sighed and climbed down the tree. "You will tell me as soon as we're on that boat," Sarah hissed. She reached around the tree and pulled into sight an enormous bag containing their tent and supplies. Victoria felt her spirits soar. The stars had answered her prayers. "I was worried sick about you."

Victoria knew she'd lost the debate, though she could only feel relief that Sarah was ready to leave. "I will," she promised. Scanning the meadow, she could see that their path to the beach was clear, and it would only take a few more seconds to get to the pier. "I'm going to run to the boat now. Follow me and don't stop."

Holding their bags of supplies, they ran.

The boat was still on the dock at the beach. *Caelan must not have known about Sarah or our resources*, Victoria thought with relief. She untied the boat, Sarah jumped in with her bag, and Victoria pushed off before jumping in herself. This time, she didn't have to instruct the boat to move. It glided through the water without a sound, picking up speed by magic, and five minutes later, the island had disappeared into the darkness. Victoria could swear her clothes were getting dry.

"Vic, please tell me what's going on now," Sarah said. "You've really scared me. I've been up all night worrying about you."

Victoria took a deep breath. Sarah deserved the truth. "When we were on that island, a man named Caelan found me and imprisoned me on the bridge on the lake," Victoria said. "He said he would kill me if I didn't promise to stay away from Atlantis."

Sarah's eyes widened in horror. "He threatened to kill you? Who the hell does that?"

"I don't know," Victoria admitted. "I didn't know so many people thought Atlantis was real."

"How did you get out? Did you promise to stay away?"

Victoria shook her head, and Sarah rolled her eyes. Victoria could see her perspective, though she knew Sarah would never fully understand "He probably would have killed me anyway. But I do want to go home," she said. "Right now. England might not be perfect, but at least nobody wants to kill me there."

Sarah nodded, not seeming surprised with her

decision. "If that's what you want, I'm happy to go back. You mentioned it yesterday, and I see I should've listened earlier."

They looked at each other for a moment, and Victoria knew she and Sarah had realized the same problem.

"How do we change the course of the boat?"

Victoria wished Sarah wouldn't have asked. She didn't have the heart to admit that she still had no idea how to control the boat or, even worse, that it was probably still going to take them to Atlantis.

"Turn back to England," Victoria begged the boat, feeling agitated and helpless. The boat continued through the water in what seemed to be a straight line. They had already reached open waters, and the island was quickly disappearing into the distance. Victoria repeated every command she could think of while touching the Sentence on the boat until she'd she felt exhausted. The horizon was getting lighter with dawn, and she sensed they were getting closer to Atlantis every second.

"I give up," Victoria sighed. She buried her face in her hand, on the verge of tears.

"Don't worry, Vic," Sarah said. She yawned and pulled Victoria in to a hug. "If you can't control the boat, there's nothing we can do. Let's just try to go to sleep and see what the situation is in the morning."

Victoria grumbled. Sarah didn't sound upset or

worried, but that didn't make her feel any better. Her only consolation now was that they were safe here. Seeing that her clothes were dry, she let herself drift to sleep, trusting the boat would protect them, even if she had no idea where she would wake up in the morning.

Chapter Eleven
WISHES

Atlantis was spectacular.

This wasn't the deteriorating Atlantis that Victoria had visited, or even the beautiful Atlantis she'd seen in her first dream before the wave had destroyed it. This was New Atlantis.

The most skilled masons had rebuilt the city, working the beautiful silver stones so that they glowed. The buildings were even stronger than before, but somehow more modest and elegant. People filled the streets with life and business from sunrise to sunset. Society thrived, people respected the new laws, and the country prospered again righteously.

Out of the city, the Eternal Forest was once again home to the most beautiful trees, the leaves of which reflected sunlight everywhere. They seemed to sing in the sun, whisper at night, and dance in even the gentlest of breezes. The air carried the fragrance of fruit and spices and baking, and a sense of peace.

Atlantis had not fought in a war for thousands of years.

Victoria and Tom stood together on the highest steps in the Plaza, holding hands as they admired the harbor. Tom looked to be in his thirties and was dressed in Atlantean couture with a simple gold wreath on his head, matching hers. A giggle sounded as a beautiful young girl peeked out from behind Victoria's long, white dress. She had her mother's silver eyes but her father's fair hair. Laughing, she pulled at her mother's free hand, asking to play on the beach. Victoria and Tom exchanged smiles and let their daughter sweep them away.

Everything was perfect.

This was New Atlantis.

Chapter Twelve
RESOLUTION

"We're going to Atlantis," Victoria announced with a smile when Sarah woke up the next morning. She missed Tom desperately after her dream, but she knew what she had to do. They were still on the boat and had been journeying for hours. She was convinced she would see land any minute, but she couldn't help but worry that the boat had listened to her desperate pleas last night. Without any way to determine where they were, Victoria could only pray that the boat had seen her soul and knew what she really wanted.

Sarah responded with a blank expression. "I thought you wanted to go back to England?"

"I've changed my mind."

Sarah sat up straighter, looking interested at this news. "Why?"

Victoria had spent the past hour watching the sunrise, and she could only think about the beautiful little girl and the amazing life she'd seen herself living in Atlantis with Tom. Even if she could find the words to explain this vision to Sarah, it was so personal that she wasn't sure she would want to. All she knew was that everything had changed. None of the threats or fear of the past week mattered anymore. "Atlantis is important to me," she said finally. *Very important.* "I didn't realize until now how badly I want to see this through. We're so close anyway that we should at least try."

Sarah stared at her like she'd spoken in a foreign language, then held out her hand. "Could I see the map?" she asked, catching Victoria by surprise. Victoria handed the papers over, and Sarah spent a minute looking at them before she pointed to an island around the middle of one of the more detailed maps.

"This looks the same shape as the island we were one yesterday. We must be getting close to where Atlantis is supposed to be," she said. "I have no idea how fast we're going, but if we're going the same speed as the other day, we should be there soon."

The next hour was one of the slowest Victoria had ever endured. Eventually, she stopped looking at her watch and set her sights on the horizon. When she felt that she couldn't stand another minute of suspense, a dark outline appeared in the distance. *It could be a cloud*, she thought, her heart racing. But after a few minutes, she could distinguish the shape of a mountain, and she would have recognized the island anywhere.

She had found Atlantis.

"Oh, my god," Sarah breathed, looking at Victoria with astonishment and apology in her eyes. She must have seen the truth in Victoria's expression. "I'm so sorry I didn't believe you sooner."

"I told you Atlantis isn't underwater," Victoria said, smiling. She was exactly where fate intended, and doubt belonged in the past. The next hour seemed to be even longer than the previous as they neared the island. Both time and the boat seemed to slow, and Victoria was sure it would have been faster to jump off and swim to shore. After what felt like an eternity, they approached the biggest beach Victoria had ever seen. In the middle of the bay was an enormous shipwreck, the bow of the ship pointing to the sky. After what felt like an eternity, the boat finally bumped onto the white sand of a beautiful beach and came to a stop. Victoria took off her shoes and jumped onto shore.

"The sand is as soft as it looks," Sarah said as they dragged the boat out of the water. "This is amazing." She sounded nothing like the skeptic who hadn't believed in Atlantis over the weekend, and Victoria smiled halfheartedly, feeling disappointment consume her. This wasn't the paradise from her dream, lush with trees and flowers and beautiful scents. This was the desolate, lifeless Atlantis she hated.

"Let's explore," Sarah suggested, pulling Victoria inland. "We might find people."

Victoria wished she had the same optimism. She followed, confident she would find their boat again by the shipwreck. Sarah took the path that Victoria was sure went all the way around the island, and it wasn't long before Victoria recognized her surroundings. Wizened, grey buildings at the edge of the city towered above lifeless streets and drained canals. The expression on Sarah's face conveyed awe that words couldn't.

"I could make so much great art here," Sarah said, reaching unconsciously to where her camera usually hung. Victoria smiled. Sarah had no idea what potential existed in the treasures around them. She braced herself when they arrived at the Plaza a few minutes later, and Sarah started to run, pulling Victoria's arm in excitement. "This place is beautiful. I wonder if the buildings are locked."

"I've only tried the Grand Library," Victoria admitted, looking at the domed building. "It wasn't locked then, but I don't know about the others."

Sarah took off for the steps at the north end of the Plaza, and Victoria followed. Passing through the main gate of the castle, she was sure Sarah could imagine the Keep filled with people and beautiful flowers and plants, but, it had now regressed to a simple but beautiful structure. Even for Atlantis, it seemed particularly old and weathered. Victoria found herself wandering towards the throne again, once again tempted to sit on it, but before she could, Sarah gasped behind her.

"Did you hear that?" Sarah asked. "I swear I heard whispers."

Victoria jumped away from the throne, listening carefully. She was sure that whispering wasn't a good sign. She couldn't hear anything, but Sarah had sounded convinced.

"It was coming from that direction," Sarah continued, pointing at the tower to their left. Victoria approached the open doorway cautiously and found a large, circular room. In the dim light, she could see that the walls were lined with hundreds of old books, but nobody was inside.

"It's another library," she said. A large table in matching mahogany wood stood in the middle of the room, with a pile of books strewn across it. Victoria felt like there was something important, right in front of her, that she should be seeing, but it was such an amazing room that it was impossible to tell what. She pulled a few identical black books out of the nearest bookshelf and brought them to table, careful to not damage them.

"We shouldn't be here, Vic," Sarah chimed over her shoulder. She sounded nervous. "Something doesn't seem right."

Victoria wasn't sure what Sarah was sensing that she couldn't, but she didn't see any problem. At the far end of the room, opposite the door through which they'd entered, was a dark passageway. She ruffled through a few more books before she walked closer to the other doorway, hoping she could see further in.

"We shouldn't go there," Sarah said. "It's bloody dark."

Victoria couldn't see anything down the hallway, either, but she felt like she was supposed to go there. As she stepped in, she could hear Sarah sigh. Victoria began to walk, knowing that was probably all the encouragement Sarah needed. A few seconds later, she heard footsteps following her as she led the way through the dark.

"It's not that bad," Victoria said lightly. "Our eyes will adjust soon."

Sarah huffed in response. After a few seconds, Victoria had to slow down. The passageway was growing darker, reminding her of the crypt on the other island. When she could no longer see anything in front of her, she finally stopped. "We could use our phones for light, or turn back," she suggested.

A second later, a blinding flash of light filled the

corridor. Sarah screamed and grabbed Victoria's hand. Hundreds of torches had burst into flame along the wall, lighting the way forward. Victoria stood motionless for a moment, her eyes adjusting, before Sarah laughed.

"Atlantis is mad," she said. "Absolutely mad."

Victoria laughed with her, relieved to see that there was nothing to be afraid of. Atlantis was full of magic, even if she had no idea how it worked. "We can't turn back now," she said. She grabbed a torch and resumed walking. As she neared the end of the passageway, Victoria could hear moving water. At the end of the hallway, she found a large wooden door with a key in the lock. Victoria hesitated, reluctant to go anywhere she wasn't explicitly allowed, though the key seemed a good indication that she could continue.

"Just open it," Sarah grumbled.

Victoria twisted the key and pushed the door open. The scene in front of her, only visible by the light of her torch, took her breath away. Directly in front of her was a bridge which crossed over a wide, dark river. A stone path ran along both sides of the river. She exchanged glances with Sarah, beginning wondering what exactly this place was, when the feeling hit her. It was a magnetic pull like she'd felt on the other island, which had made her stay away from the temple and go closer to the lake, but it was completely different. This time, it was telling her to cross the river, and she trusted her intuition completely. She began to walk, lighting a few of the torches hanging on the wall along the way. Sarah grabbed one and followed silently and unquestioningly, but when they reached the middle of the bridge, she stopped.

"I don't like this place, Vic," Sarah said. "It's spooky."

Victoria hesitated, torn between exploring whatever was on the other side and accommodating Sarah. While she waited for Sarah to follow, she looked into the river. In her lingering paranoia, she partly expected to see more translucent ghosts, but what she found was possibly worse.

The water level was rising.

A second later, a thunderous roar filled the cave. Victoria and Sarah exchanged glances, and when Victoria looked up the river, a massive wave was rushing towards her, filling the tunnel. "Sarah, run!" she shouted. She turned around and ran towards the hallway they'd come through. When she stopped to look over her shoulder, she saw that Sarah had run the opposite direction and was at the other side of the river.

Before she could say anything, the wave rushed past.

The ledge under her feet was dry and the torches were still on fire when Victoria found the courage to open her eyes. She looked across the river with a racing heart, wondering if she had imagined everything, but it was still too dark to see anything past the bridge. The water level of the river was dropping closer to normal every second.

But Sarah had disappeared.

"Sarah?" Victoria called.

She received no response but the echo of her own voice.

Victoria grabbed a torch and began to run. As she crossed the bridge, another group of torches lit in front of her to illuminate blocks of small, stone buildings that had been hiding in the shadows. An endless path stretched ahead of her, crossed at intervals by perpendicular aisles. Everything on this side of the river was laid out in a massive grid. Each building had an inscribed metal gate, which Victoria didn't have time to read as she ran and called for Sarah. *What kind of maze is this?* she wondered. Getting lost in here would be easier than breathing. Finding Sarah would be nearly impossible.

After a minute, Victoria noticed a trail of footprints on the main path. *Was Caelan here, too?* she wondered. She had no choice but to follow them, hoping they would lead her to Sarah. She stopped running after another minute to listen for Sarah, but she couldn't even hear the river anymore. *Maybe she didn't go this way*, Victoria thought, allowing herself a moment of hope before she set off again. Any other explanation for silence was too morbid to consider.

The path ended at the edge of a small lake. With her heart racing, Victoria finally stopped running. She could hear a river in the distance and realized she was in a series of caves, probably nearing the edge of the main Atlantean island. She wasn't sure if it was just her imagination, but there seemed to be a light glowing at the other side of the lake, leaving her two options. She could turn back or hope she'd find a way out ahead.

Swearing under her breath, she shoved her torch into the sand and waded into the water. For a moment, she thought of the Atlantean ghosts in the lake on the other island, but this lake felt different. She couldn't see anything in the inky water, and she began to swim when it was deep enough. Even if Sarah hadn't gone this way, she had a feeling she was supposed to cross the lake.

At the other end, she found a large hole in the rock through which mute sunlight was spilling into the cavern. She pushed herself out of the water onto a ledge in the stone. The howling wind was warm, and the view of the sea took her breath away. She'd reached the edge of the island, like she'd guessed, and massive waves were looming in the horizon, approaching Atlantis with incredible speed. With a sinking feeling, Victoria realized exactly what was happening.

History was repeating itself.

She was on a dirt path that wrapped along the

mountain. Sarah was still nowhere to be seen, and the wave would be here in fifteen minutes. *Sarah's probably safer in the caves than anywhere else in Atlantis,* she decided, and she took off running, praying that this path would lead her to the city.

She needed to reach shelter.

A bare forest appeared to her left, and she wondered if it was the same one she'd seen in her first dream. Like the woman in that dream, she was racing for her life, and the dream was the only reason she knew what to do next. The secret steps to the castle were somewhere on this path, if only she could find it.

As the path approached an empty beach, Victoria glanced at the horizon. The waves were only minutes away now. Feeling faint, she ran even faster, until she reached the steps up the mountain. She was relieved to find the ancient castle at the top. The doors of the antechamber to the right of the throne were open, promising shelter, but there was no sign of Sarah. The advancing shadow was swallowing Atlantis, and the hum of the waves was amplifying into a thunderous roar, but the sound of grinding stone was still unmistakable. The entrance to the shelter was closing.

Victoria closed the distance with only seconds to spare before the sliding wall sealed her inside the room. In the silence and darkness, she prayed that Sarah was safe, wherever she was. A second later, the bright light of the orb appeared in front of her, and Victoria crashed to the floor, unconscious, as the wave roared over Atlantis.

Chapter Thirteen
ATHELEA

Opening her eyes, Victoria wondered if she'd woken up in a parallel universe. She was lying on her back in the middle of a very dead forest. She could see bright blue sky between bare, white branches and tree trunks. It took her a second to remember that she was in Atlantis, and she sat up gingerly, her body aching. After another second, she realized this was the forest from her first dream about Atlantis, but all the beautiful leaves and flowers were gone.

How did I get here? Victoria wondered. Something was wrong. She had no recollection of anything after getting into the shelter from the wave. She looked around, expecting to find herself in a scene of destruction, but the forest was still standing and seemed unharmed.

And a beautiful woman in a black dress was sitting

silently against one of the nearby trees. She had brilliant silver eyes, proud cheekbones, and dark hair that fell in waves to her waist. But her most distinctive feature was her air of nobility. Victoria didn't recoil. She would have recognized the stranger anywhere, but in this forest, it was impossible not to know.

The woman was the princess from her first dream about Atlantis.

"Hello," the woman said, offering a warm smile. Her voice was soft and her accent strangely familiar. "I'm Athelea. Don't be afraid. I'm here to help you."

"What happened to Atlantis?" Victoria asked, looking around the forest. The ground looked dry, and the sky was perfectly blue. "It was flooding, and the waves were coming."

"I believe what we just saw was an echo of the storm that destroyed Atlantis long ago," Athelea said. "It wasn't real, and it didn't cause any damage."

Victoria breathed a sigh of relief. "Where's Sarah?" she croaked, asking the next question that had come to mind. She needed so many answers. "Please help me find her."

"I'm sorry," Athelea said, "but who is Sarah?"

"My friend, Sarah," Victoria repeated. Every syllable hurt. "Ruby hair, pale skin, almost my height, and my age. She was here with me earlier, but we got separated."

Athelea's silver eyes widened in alarm. "You

brought someone with you?"

That was exactly what Victoria had been trying to say. She told Athelea an edited version of her story, starting with her dream about the destruction of Atlantis and ending with the echo of the wave. She decided not to mention Gryffin until she'd determined what Athelea knew about him. Athelea listened without asking any questions, and Victoria slowly felt suspicion replace her frustration. Nobody else had believed her so readily this past week. There was no reason that a perfect stranger should be the exception.

"And now I can't find her," she concluded, her voice breaking.

Athelea frowned. "I haven't seen her yet, but I will find her. Atlantis has always been full of both mysteries and miracles. Don't lose faith."

"What about Caelan?" Victoria asked. "Can we do anything about him?"

"Possibly," Athelea said. Victoria could tell she was uncomfortable with being uncertain. "It doesn't all make sense to me yet. It would help if I knew exactly what he is."

What he is. Victoria shuddered, unsure if Athelea was implying that he wasn't human. A week ago, she would have dismissed the thought instantly, but it wouldn't surprise her now if more legends were real than she'd thought. "What do you mean?"

Athelea frowned at her hands, seeming reluctant to meet Victoria's eye. "In Atlantis, there were ancient prophecies about a woman who would destroy us. Nobody ever believed that one person could do what armies couldn't, but Atlantis has never been weaker than it is now."

Victoria knew without any doubt that the prophecy was referring to Caelan. She was about to say that the prophecy had been wrong, that the destroyer was a man, but Athelea held up a hand to silence her. "I do not believe for a second that you are that person."

Victoria snapped her mouth shut. Until she'd met Caelan, she hadn't considered that anyone would doubt her intentions in Atlantis. She'd been so convinced from her previous visits that Atlantis was deserted that she hadn't been prepared to meet people, and certainly hadn't considered she might be intruding.

"I'm sorry," Athelea continued, punctuating the prolonged silence. "This information must be terribly overwhelming."

Victoria shook her head. "It doesn't change anything, really. I'd rather know the truth than be unprepared."

Athelea raised an eyebrow, but Victoria maintained her stance. Ignorance wouldn't protect her the next time Caelan found her. "I'd genuinely rather know. Please tell me everything, Athelea."

139

"It could be many years before you see Caelan again, or it could be days. I will try my best to protect you for as long as you're in Atlantis," Athelea said.

"He's already gotten to everybody else, hasn't he?" Victoria whispered. Athelea's promise didn't make a difference. "That's why they're all gone. Except for you."

"I regained consciousness as the storm faded. The Atlanteans have been gone since the moment the real waves struck, long before Caelan ever thought of us," Athelea said. Victoria couldn't hear untruth in her words. "To my knowledge, he has not destroyed the Atlanteans or harmed Atlantis in any way."

She's got no idea Gryffin is alive, Victoria realized. "Has anybody ever found Atlantis?"

"Never. I suspect any protection around Atlantis fell when you arrived, which is why Sarah was able to enter with you."

Victoria felt a twinge of guilt. "Could anybody find Atlantis now if they make the journey?" Victoria asked, thinking of Gryffin again. *He's her son*, she reminded herself, but she still wasn't going to mention him until she knew Athelea better. *She deserves to know eventually, but a few more days won't make a difference after all these years.* "Couldn't you restore the protection around Atlantis?"

Athelea paused. Victoria guessed the process was complicated, and unless they knew exactly where Caelan was, there was a risk of sealing him inside. Athelea suddenly looked years older and more weary than she had moments before, and Victoria sensed she'd spent many years with preoccupations.

"How do I know you're not with Caelan?" Victoria asked, remembering suddenly. Her suspicion flared. "He said he wasn't alone. It seems terribly coincidental that you've shown up in Atlantis after I've escaped from him."

"You don't believe we are the same person?" Athelea said. The surprise and offense in her voice seemed genuine, but Victoria didn't respond. She hadn't suggested anything along those lines, but it was interesting that Athelea had offered it herself, without prompt. Victoria bit her lip, trying to figure out what to say next. Trusting Athelea seemed so instinctual, but she couldn't shake her suspicion that Athelea was hiding something from her.

"I've been here for what feels like centuries," Athelea said, seeming to sense her hesitation, "and I haven't seen a single soul since the Destruction. Caelan's interest in Atlantis is news to me, though I realize I have no way of proving this to you. You must simply believe me on my word that I knew nothing about him until today."

Victoria said nothing.

"Let's walk," Athelea suggested. She offered her hand, and Victoria caught a glimpse of the Sentence on her wrist. "I will show you what's left of Atlantis, teach you our history, and we can talk more. If I must earn your trust slowly, I will."

Victoria hesitated before letting Athelea help her up. The royal's palm was not rough from manual work but not perfectly smooth, either. Something bright flashed at Athelea's hip, and Victoria imagined for a second that it was a sword. *Why does she need that?* She wondered with another wave of suspicion. Despite Athelea seeming honest enough, reminded herself that this was Atlantis. Nothing was what it seemed.

"The Eternal Forest was always my favorite place in Atlantis," Athelea said as they left the meadow. If she sensed Victoria was nervous, she didn't show it. "The trees had leaves like diamonds, and the whole Forest would glow with the most amazing light. I would come here whenever I needed a quiet place to relax or think."

Victoria remembered this from her dream, but she didn't know how to reply. Until now, she'd only been reasonably confident that the events from that dream had happened how she'd seen them. Seeing this woman in the Eternal Forest confirmed it all. "That sounds beautiful," she said simply.

Athelea offered a smile. "I come here often to reflect on how Atlantis used to be." There was sadness in her words, and Victoria sensed Athelea would be the last person in the world to help Caelan destroy Atlantis. *This is her home,* Victoria realized. *She's trying to protect what's left of it.* She instantly felt guilty for distrusting Athelea, but there was just so much she didn't understand.

After a minute of walking in silence, they reached the edge of the forest, and Athelea cast a final glance at the trees before stepping on to the main path that Victoria now knew ran around the island. "Please don't take this the wrong way," Victoria said, "but why are you still here, when everybody else is gone?"

"I'm the exception, for a reason only the stars know. I've spent years seeking a way to bring the Atlanteans back," Athelea replied. The pressure of this task was apparent in her melodic voice. "But I believe the stars have kept me here because I was supposed to witness your return and guide you to success where I have failed."

Victoria sensed Athelea had been working up to this moment since the start of the conversation. "Please explain."

"I've researched every prophecy Atlanteans have ever made about the Destruction. The only one that was correct was never completed, but it did say that an Atlantean would return to restore the empire."

"You're wrong," Victoria said. "I'm not Atlantean."

They were in the heart of the city now. Athelea stopped at the top step leading down to the Plaza and gently took a hold of Victoria's wrists. She adjusted the dirty pink ribbon, revealing the black words beneath. "Only an

Atlantean can wear the Sentence," she said. She met Victoria's gaze steadily, then looked at the cloth Victoria had tied around her injured palm. "You're hurt."

Victoria hesitated, embarrassed to tell the story to a stranger. "On the other island, I found an underground room and fell on some glass in the dark. I cleaned it and made a bandage."

"It would only take me a second to heal it," Athelea offered. "You should sit down, so you don't faint. I'm not sure how your body will respond to this treatment."

Victoria still didn't trust Athelea entirely, but she knew it would be dangerous to leave her wound unattended any longer. The cuts didn't look infected when Athelea unwrapped the cloth, but Victoria sat down, accepting help. A second later, she felt a gentle heat radiate along her palm, and when she blinked, the cuts were disappearing. She looked at Athelea in surprise, and when she looked down again, the wound had healed completely.

"Stand up and test it. Is that any better?"

Victoria obeyed. Even though her hand hadn't been hurting before, it seemed perfectly fine now, and she couldn't help but think that magic was responsible. "It disappeared."

Athelea paused, then muttered an oath and produced two shimmering objects from within her dress. "Take this," she hissed, shoving a heavy object Victoria's hands. After a second, Victoria realized it was a diamond dagger, glittering in the afternoon sun. Athelea held the longer sword that Victoria had seen earlier, which now seemed perfectly capable of slaying. Victoria immediately thought of a medieval dragon.

"What's going on?" Victoria asked, her hands shaking. She tried to keep the panic out of her voice, but she knew she wasn't fooling Athelea. She'd been right about the sword. "Is this another echo?"

Athelea shook her head, scanning the horizon with her piercing silver eyes. "Something very dangerous is out there, but I don't yet know what."

"Since I'm a trained warrior," Victoria murmured.

Athelea laughed without breaking her stare. "I am. Use the sharp end of the dagger when you fight. If you trust me and do exactly as I say, we will be fine."

Victoria clenched the dagger, expecting to see a massive pair of wings on the horizon, but nothing happened. The ocean was visible from the Plaza, and it reassured her slightly that another wave, real or echo, wasn't approaching. Athelea remained tense and observant, radiating calmness and confidence that Victoria wished she could absorb.

And then, Victoria felt the stone beneath her feet begin to shake.

Athelea muttered something under her breath that Victoria could tell wasn't polite. "It seems Caelan has sent us an earthquake."

Victoria heard her dagger clatter onto the steps of the Plaza, safely missing her feet as she dropped it. She didn't see any point in retrieving it. "An earthquake? Honestly," she gasped, not sure how anybody could control the ground. "I'd rather face a dragon."

"Oh, Victoria." Amusement flashed across Athelea's face. "Dragons only exist in legends."

Victoria laughed, surprising herself. "So did Atlantis, until this week," she said. She had no idea how they could be joking at a time like this. "What are we supposed to do now?"

"We're going to fight it. Focus. Find your quintessence and bring it forward."

"My what?"

Athelea took a fast breath. "I don't know what you would call your essence, perhaps your energy? The Atlantean word for that is *quintessence*."

Victoria nodded.

"Perfect," Athelea continued calmly. The ground shook so violently that they both took a step back for balance. "Close your eyes and feel for that energy. When you find it, push it out of your body against the earthquake. You'll probably going to fall, but I'll catch you, and everything will be fine. Do you understand?"

"Yes." Victoria closed her eyes and began to search

for her mysterious quintessence. The earth groaned and rolled beneath her feet, and for a second, she couldn't even feel her own breathing. She could hear stones crashing in the distance as ancient buildings began to lose their integrity. *This is no way to fight an earthquake,* she thought. But when she finally found her pulse, everything outside her body suddenly became unimportant.

She understood exactly what Athelea meant. Deep within her, at a level she couldn't quite define, was a shimmering mass of sparkles. She tugged at it gently with her mind and found that it followed her command, flowing effortlessly to her fingers. She pushed it out so it collided with the earth. The energy met resistance, but the violent tremors softened every time Victoria pushed her quintessence against them.

When only one sparkle of energy remained within herself, Victoria stopped pushing. The earthquake had ended. She exhaled, losing consciousness, and gentle arms cushioned her fall towards the unmoving earth of the Plaza.

Chapter Fourteen
AFTERSHOCK

"Victoria, you won't believe the history this place has," a familiar voice enthused, gently breaking into Victoria's consciousness. "It's really incredible. I hope you feel better soon and can see everything."

Victoria just wanted to sleep. She felt exhausted, and it took her a few seconds to remember why. *Earthquake.* The memory of falling stones and shaking ground felt distant, like days had passed since then, and even now, it seemed to be slipping further away. And then, she realized who had spoken and opened her eyes.

Sarah.

A figure with familiar ruby hair was sitting next to her on the bed. Her bright emerald eyes were glittering, and a beaming smile lit her face. Victoria sat up, and Sarah threw her arms around her in a massive hug. Victoria felt her fill with tears. Blinking them away, she realized she and Sarah were in the Plaza. She was laying on the bedding that had been in their tent a few days before. Athelea was watching from a few paces away with a smile.

"Thank you," Victoria mouthed to Athelea over Sarah's shoulder. Nothing could express the gratitude she felt to see Sarah alive and well. Athelea smiled in acknowledgment.

"This place is amazing, Victoria," Sarah said when she pulled away from the hug, practically bouncing on the bed. "Athelea's already showed me a bit of the city and palace, but we were waiting for you to recover before we did the whole tour."

Atlantis doesn't have a palace, Victoria thought, looking to Athelea for answers, *unless Sarah means the castle.* Even if there had been a palace, it would be amazing if Atlantis was still intact after that earthquake. The Plaza didn't seem to have sustained any damage, but it was only a small part of the city. "How long have I been sleeping?" she asked as Athelea approached.

"Just for the afternoon," Athelea said. "You lost a lot of energy fighting the earthquake, but that's to be expected. How do you feel?"

Victoria stretched. Her entire body was sore, but she had a feeling Atlantis was in worse condition. "I'll be fine tomorrow," she said. "How bad is the damage?"

Athelea took a deep breath that seemed ominous to Victoria. "There's no significant damage," she said, keeping her voice steady. Victoria braced herself for bad news. "But it could take quite a while to repair everything."

"The whole island?"

"Fortunately not. The earthquake shook a few buildings in the city badly, but Mount Theus seems to have absorbed most of the shock. There is no damage to the Isle of the Gods."

"The Isle of the Gods?" Victoria asked.

"The royal island," Athelea said.

Victoria gave up pursuing an explanation. If Athelea wasn't worried, it couldn't be that bad. There was still so much she needed to know about Atlantis, and she had no idea where to start.

"Would you like a tour of Atlantis?" Athelea asked, seeming to read her thoughts. "Sarah and I thought you would want to explore, so we were waiting for you to wake up. Do you feel strong enough for that?"

Victoria nodded, thankful that the others had waited for her. "We could probably clean up the streets a bit along the way."

"That's a wonderful idea," Athelea said. She held out her hand, revealing the Sentence on her wrist again, and helped Victoria to her feet. Sarah flashed Victoria a reassuring smile. "To begin, this courtyard is the Plaza. Our first king, King Atlas, built it from the ancient castle grounds during his reign, along with the Grand Library, which I believe you've both seen, and the Reflector, which I'll show you later. Follow me."

Victoria and Sarah followed Athelea out of the Plaza. Although Victoria had expected to find heaps of debris on the streets after the earthquake, she was pleased to see that the buildings were still mostly intact. Only a few chunks of stone had fallen to the ground, leaving gaps and cracks where they'd once been. *My quintessence must have helped,* she thought with a sense of relief. Athelea stopped in a wide street of uniform buildings, four stories tall and made of the dark silver stone that was everywhere in Atlantis. Victoria guessed this area had once been part of the shopping district.

"Is it safe to be here?" Victoria asked Athelea. "Are the buildings unstable now?"

Athelea surveyed the nearest wall. To Victoria, the building appeared to be a basic building, but she suspected Athelea saw much more. "They should be perfectly safe," Athelea said after a second. She picked up a stone fragment from the ground and held it up. In the light, it seemed to have a pearlescent glow, though Victoria wasn't sure if she was just imagining it. "This is Atlan stone. It comes from mountains in the outer Atlantean islands, and since it is remarkably versatile, masons have used it in nearly every building in Atlantis. It is the strongest material in the world when cut correctly, but it also requires dexterity to be most effective."

Victoria blinked at her, not following entirely.

"The stone used in most Atlanteans buildings is remarkably strong," Athelea concluded. "I believe that the dexes fortifying them may have broken during the earthquake, causing more damage than the earthquake itself. The buildings, however, should be perfectly safe."

"What is a dex?" Victoria interrupted.

"Sorry!" Athelea exclaimed. "I forgot you aren't familiar with Atlantean words. Dexterity is simply the manipulation of energy. I suppose you could think of a dex as a sort of magic spell. Atlanteans have used them for thousands of years. I'm sure you've already seen me use a few."

Victoria thought back to when Athelea had healed her hand in the Forest. It had reminded her of magic, and she was sure she'd seen both Gryffin and Caelan do something similar. She had so many questions now. "Is that why the stones broke in places? The dexes have stopped working?"

Athelea nodded. "I believe so. Atlan stone is even stronger than diamond. Only something as powerful as a dex could break them, and only something as powerful as that earthquake could break a dex."

"Oh," Victoria said. "Can we fix the dexes somehow?"

Athelea looked at Victoria with an expression of intense curiosity. *What's that about?* Victoria wondered. "I suppose so," Athelea said. "The most difficult task will be determining exactly which dexes the original masons used, which could take significant time. Once we know, I'd imagine we could restore all the dexes on the island in a matter of weeks."

Weeks. Victoria sighed, glancing at Sarah to gauge her reaction. She didn't look anywhere near as lost as Victoria felt, and Victoria understood. The others had probably already discussed this in greater detail, and Sarah knew whatever truth Athelea was withholding.

"We should look for a temporary dex as soon as possible, but why don't we focus on moving this rubble away in the mean time?" Victoria suggested, trying not to sound too frustrated. "At least we can make the streets cleaner and safer."

"That is a strong plan," Athelea said, though Victoria sensed she would have much preferred to work another time. They spent a few minutes moving the lighter stones into a pile at the side of the street, and Athelea fell silent. Victoria could only imagine the hopelessness and despair she was feeling at seeing the city deteriorating more every day.

"Athelea's fighting a losing battle," Sarah whispered

after they'd been working ten minutes. They stopped for a moment to watch Athelea use dexterity to float an impossibly large stone to the side of the road with no apparent effort. Together, the women had cleared up nearly the entire block, but Victoria was conscious that the rest the rest of the city was still a mess. "Atlantis is too big for one person to manage, and it's not like the Atlanteans are just going to show up and help her."

Victoria suddenly understood what they were doing wrong. "We should be protecting these buildings before anything happens, instead of fixing them every time something breaks."

Sarah inclined her head in a gesture that looked like reluctant agreement.

Passing a block of abandoned houses, Victoria could feel emptiness and silence in the dark windows and doorways. She couldn't grasp how these streets had once been bursting with an entire civilization. "How did everyone disappear?" she wondered to Sarah. "Not even Athelea knows what had happened."

"Atlantean society is very different from the rest of the world," Athelea said. Victoria jumped, not having heard her approach. "To us, technology and science are a blessing that became a curse. They were the reason we existed and thrived and, I believe, the reason we fell. You ladies must learn some of our history while you are here. Understanding our past could provide great insight into not only the present, but the future."

"Our history?" Victoria asked, wondering if this was something else she'd missed while she was unconscious. "You're English?"

Athelea laughed. "Of course not. But I want to tell you about my past here so that you can better understand what happened to Atlantis. Hopefully you'll be able to make some sense of why you are here now and what we should do next."

"Go for it," Sarah panted, rolling a stone to the side of the street. Victoria didn't see any reason why she and Sarah shouldn't get to know Athelea better. She hoped her earlier suspicions had been unreasonable, especially since Athelea had found Sarah, but she sensed Athelea still wasn't being fully honest. That secrecy, coupled with the fact that Athelea was the only Atlantean left, made it difficult to trust her. But they were probably going to be in Atlantis a while, and Athelea was their only ally.

"I will start at the very beginning, as even the earliest details are incredibly important," Athelea began when they moved on to a new street. This bordered one of the larger canals, which was still empty. "Atlantean legend says that the gods became jealous of humanity while they watched over us thousands of years ago. They envied our freedom to love who we wanted, to go where we pleased, and to forge our own destinies. One day, they created Atlantis so they could live amongst us. It was a perfect, beautiful place, a paradise. The gods took human lovers and lived here for a thousand years, but they began to long for their home in the heavens.

"When the gods eventually left, our first king was a wise man named Atlas. He united the Atlanteans, expanded the city, and established the guilds that helped Atlantis thrive. His laws were fair, and the Atlanteans loved and respected him. Atlantis grew even more prosperous, but after generations, the Atlanteans became discontent. They wanted more land, wealth, and power than ever before. They fought, firstly amongst themselves, and later with other countries around the world, to secure this. Atlantis became so militant and so hungry for what it didn't deserve that any other civilization in the world could have sense we were doomed."

Victoria looked around the street with a new perspective of how much history Atlantis had. Athelea's story wasn't anything like the Atlantean mythology she'd read at home. It was so similar to mythology from other ancient cultures, but so incredibly different because she was here, and it was history.

"Nobody remembers exactly when the Great War began, since we had been at war for generations, but it was many centuries before I was born," Athelea continued when they finished clearing the section of the street, which contained more buildings that Victoria guessed had been stores. "Most Atlanteans in my generation believed victory would ensure our return to prosperity, and the Atlantean military was unrivaled under my father's command. Our technology and dexterity would have secured our victory in any battle we fought, but my father refused to use it. He was a strict and incredibly traditional man. As his only heir, my education was his foremost priority, and I attended nearly every diplomatic event with him. He hoped that one day I would be fit to rule Atlantis."

Victoria could only imagine the sheltered life Athelea had lived, burdened with responsibility and expectations. But the woman she saw now was the only survivor of a horrible disaster, and Athelea still seemed enslaved to her responsibility to Atlantis. Victoria couldn't imagine a more difficult fate.

"I met a man named Tristan a few years before the end of the war. We were both eighteen, and though he came from a civilian family, we quickly fell in love. When I wasn't fulfilling royal obligations and he wasn't busy with his education and the military, we met in secret. I led a normal life when I was with him, one where I didn't have to live up to my father's expectations or the demands of our citizens. For the first time in my life, I was free to be myself, I realized within one summer that I had found my Forever

Love."

Sarah coughed. Athelea looked at her with a quizzical expression, but Sarah didn't say anything. Victoria knew she didn't believe in true love but wouldn't ruin Athelea's story with this fact.

"Quite a few Atlanteans in every generation are lucky enough in their lives to find their true soulmate," Athelea continued. "The legends say that these Forever Loves are destined to be together and find each other in every life they live. Though many Atlanteans no longer believed in reincarnation by my generation, the idea of Forever Love, a profound bond between two Atlanteans, was still holy. To hinder Forever Love is the greatest crime in our society, after murder."

Victoria couldn't help but think of Tom now. The similarities between in their relationship and Athelea's story were unsettling, but Athelea didn't know any of that. Victoria had a vague sense of where the story was going now, though she wasn't sure how it related to what she knew about Athelea moments before the Destruction.

"At that time, Atlantean law prohibited the marriage of royal blood to common. These laws were the only exception to the rules of Forever Love. The commoners were modern people and couldn't care less about who the royals married, but these ancient laws were still scared to my father. Hell broke loose with his fury when I told him that

Tristan was my Love, and I didn't dare to ask if he could move into the palace. My father forbade me to ever see again."

Victoria heard the sadness in her voice and knew the story wouldn't end well. For the second time that night, she felt a connection with Athelea that she was certain Sarah wouldn't understand, and again, she felt another twinge of guilt for distrusting Athelea.

"There's one more place I need to visit before we go to the Isle of the Gods," Athelea said. "Follow me, ladies. It won't take long."

Victoria and Sarah followed Athelea down the street. After a minute, they stopped in front of a building that took up the whole block of the street, surrounded by low walls covered in some of the only flowers Victoria had seen in Atlantis. It reminded her of a cathedral, and she wondered how she'd missed it walking around with the orb. The Atlan stone gave it a medieval look, though the design seemed Mediterranean to Victoria the more she looked at it. They walked through a beautiful garden to the building's enormous front doors.

"This is the Hall of Divinity," Athelea said, unlocking the doors with a wave of her hand. Seeing inside the building, Victoria found herself speechless, and Sarah looked equally staggered. The interior resembled a cathedral as much as its exterior, but thousands of small candles were burning on the pews, in the aisles, and around the building, some even floating in the air like a starry sky. Real roses twirled up the pillars, and it took Victoria a second to realize that underneath it all, the ground was grass rather than Atlan stone, making the building seem at harmony with nature.

"I've lit a candle for the Atlanteans every night since the Destruction," Athelea said softly. Victoria felt her throat constrict. Athelea's sorrow was palpable, but all the prayers in the world hadn't helped bring the Atlanteans back. Athelea gently picked up a candle from the altar. The wick burst into flame a second later, though Athelea hadn't used any sort of match or lighter, and Athelea pushed the candle away. It began to float towards the others in midair, beautiful magic to behold.

"Isn't it dangerous to leave these burning?" Sarah whispered.

"They won't set anything on fire," Athelea said, not sounding offended by the comment. "It's a special type of flame monitored by a dex."

Sarah flashed a guilty look at Victoria while Athelea closed her eyes in what appeared to be a prayer. Victoria busied herself by walking around the building with Sarah. She guessed it must be Atlantean magic, probably dexes, that kept the candles floating and burning for so long. "Athelea had put so much energy into this place," Victoria whispered to Sarah when they were at the far end of the

Hall. "I don't think she's dangerous, do you? She misses the Atlanteans."

Sarah shook her head, seeming unusually somber. Victoria sensed she was pondering the meaning of Athelea's story. *It's still too soon to tell them about Gryffin*, Victoria thought, though still couldn't help but wonder where the Atlanteans had gone. With Sarah close behind, she slowly made her way back towards Athelea, wondering when the opportune moment would be.

"My father forbade me to ever see Tristan again and ensured I had no communication with anyone outside the palace," Athelea continued when she'd finished her prayers. She had a mischievous glint in her eyes now, and the gravity of the moment subsided. "At the end of the summer, despite being under constant watch, I received a final message from Tristan through one of my cousins. I managed to leave the palace unescorted that night, and Tristan found me in the city. He said he had accepted military duty and would leave Atlantis the next day, fearing what my father would do if he discovered we were still in love. In this very Hall, the High Priestess secretly married us. Maybe she didn't recognize me, or maybe she did and wanted to help. Tristan and I spent the entire evening together, and he was aboard a warship before the sun had risen."

Victoria looked around the building with a newfound appreciation for her surroundings. Atlantis had richer history than she'd realized, and she was sure that if the buildings could speak, they would have countless more amazing stories to tell. "This would be a beautiful setting for a wedding," she said.

"After Tristan left, everything in my life changed. Atlantis started to feel like a prison, and I resented my father for pushing Tristan from me. It was the darkest time of my life, and I believed I had nothing to live for. My mother could see how deeply separation from my Forever Love pained me, and she begged my father to bring Tristan back to Atlantis, but it was too late. Only weeks after he had left, I received a letter from the military saying that Tristan had died in battle. I would never see him again."

Even now, her eyes filled with tears. She took a few deep breaths before she seemed to regain her composure. Victoria could see that no matter how many years or generations had passed on the outside world, the loss of her Forever Love still pained Athelea. Sarah seemed to be fighting tears, too, but Victoria knew there was more to the story than the others realized.

Your son is alive, she wanted to tell Athelea, but she couldn't bring herself to say the words. The implications were too severe.

Finished with her vigil, Athelea led them out of the Hall and locked the doors. "But it's getting late now," Athelea said, "and we still have much to do. I'm sorry, ladies, but the rest of my story will have to wait for another time."

Chapter Fifteen
THE ISLE OF THE GODS

Athelea led them to the Plaza, taking a route Victoria didn't recognize. The massive building with all the mirrors seemed to be glowing in the evening sun, and it seemed to be perfectly intact after the earthquake. "That is the Reflector," Athelea said, catching Victoria looking at it. "From the reign of King Atlas, it has been the heart of travel in Atlantis. Every important room or building in Atlantis has an enormous mirror in it that is linked to its twin mirror in the Reflector. They are used as portals, going in both directions. Unfortunately, they haven't worked since the Atlanteans disappeared. I have not done extensive research on portals, but I would love to find a way to fix them. Traveling would be much simpler if they were functioning. I suspect the dexes supporting the system have grown weak."

Victoria stared around the Reflector in amazement. She'd always thought the building had a lot of mirrors when she'd visited on her own, but knowing their function made her see everything in a new light. "Can we go in quickly?" she asked.

Athelea diverted their course without question. Peering into the Reflector from its entrance, Victoria felt her breath catch in her throat. *There must be hundreds of mirrors*, she thought, amazed, *hundreds of portals to get around Atlantis.* She wanted to count, but she had a feeling it could take longer than the others would be willing to wait.

"There are exactly a thousand mirrors," Athelea whispered.

Victoria grinned in thanks and walked to the third mirror on her left. It looked darker than the others, like it was soaking up the evening sunlight instead of reflecting it. Even if the Reflector had been dark, she was sure she couldn't have missed it. *I really wasn't paying attention when I was here before,* she thought.

"What's the story about the mirror on the left?" she asked, walking up to it.

"That is the Broken Portal," Athelea said with a smile. "For as long as anybody can remember, it has just been a mirror. Many scholars have tried to explain why it hasn't worked or where it might lead if it did, but nobody knows. It is one of the biggest mysteries in Atlantis."

Victoria looked at the mirror more closely, intrigued. Her reflection stared back, like it knew a secret that Victoria never would, and she was disappointed that nobody had found out. It was strange to think that Atlantis had its own riddles, when the place was still such a mystery to the rest of the world. For a second, Victoria imagined the building bustling with people as they commuted to work or brought their children to school, and tears suddenly stung her eyes. Everything Athelea had said about the missing Atlanteans was insufficient. Victoria wanted to see them, to talk to them and hear about the lives they'd lived.

"Why aren't they here?" Victoria whispered, shivering despite the warm evening. She knew she'd asked before, but the question was still burning within her since she'd seen the Hall of Divinity.

Athelea lowered her gaze, and for a second, Victoria wondered if she would cry, too. But Athelea simply took a deep breath and shrugged. "I don't know why or where they have gone, or how to bring them back," she admitted. "After all the research I've done, I only have a few theories remaining."

Victoria felt her pulse speed up. The Broken Portal suddenly seemed unimportant. "Really? Like what?"

"I haven't been able to test many of them," Athelea disclaimed, "but I believe fate has sent you for that purpose. Together, we might finally be able to restore Atlantis and bring the Atlanteans back."

Victoria fought a sigh. Caelan had nearly the same words, and she had no idea where everyone was getting such a ridiculous notion. "Why do you think I could, if you couldn't? It's not like I can go back in time and change anything, right?"

"True. But you managed the journey here, which nobody else has ever done."

Victoria nodded. There was dark truth in those words, though she couldn't take full responsibility for her success. The conversation ended there, and Athelea led them out of the city on foot. Passing the Eternal Forest, they gained elevation the mountain that Athelea said was called Mount Theus, and they continued on the same path until it reached the edge of a cliff. Athelea incanted something under her breath, and a second later, an enormous bridge burst into light over the sea. Shimmering with an internal light Victoria couldn't explain, it looked like an endless plank of glass with elaborate rails. She exchanged a glance with Sarah. She'd always known Atlantis was special, but there was more magic here than she'd ever expected.

"Is that a dex?" Victoria asked.

Athelea nodded. "This bridge is made of Atlan stone, so it can be turned it any color. For the most part, generations of royals have kept it invisible for the added security of the Isle of the Gods. It does have railing on both sides, so you won't fall off between the islands."

Looking up, Victoria finally noticed the island at the other end of the bridge. All she could see was a massive wall and the turrets of four enormous towers, which she guessed were also made of Atlan stone. An intimidating metal gate swung open for the group as they approached the other end of the bridge, revealing an enormous, beautiful garden. Once they were all on land, Athelea made the bridge invisible again and closed the gates behind them.

Victoria understood why someone had name this place the Isle of the Gods. The palace was magnificent, the most beautiful building she'd ever seen. It reminded her of grand medieval castles in England, though she could see influences from many other palaces around the world in its design. The effect was unlike anything she'd ever seen. In the light of sunset, the palace was glowing magically. *Atlantis might be a myth,* Victoria thought, *but this is a fairytale.*

"The palace was essentially built around the Garden of the Gods," Athelea began. Calling it a garden, Victoria thought, was an understatement. It was more of a grand park, like those she loved in London. Through all the trees, she couldn't even see the other side of the palace. A main path cut through the middle of the garden, lined with torches glowing at various heights, and Victoria could see smaller footpaths radiating from an enormous pool in the center of the garden. On an evening like this, the grounds seemed perfect. Victoria couldn't imagine how the island had more beautiful better in its prime.

"The palace is divided into quadrants," Athelea said as they walked along the main path. "The royal family lived in the west tower, which is ahead. The south tower was for lesser nobility, and the north tower was for valued guests, especially visiting diplomats. The east tower was for staff and is now essentially where I have my various workshops. All the functional rooms, such as halls, libraries, and meeting rooms are on the ground floor around the palace."

After a walk through the Garden, Athelea stopped at the base of the Royal Tower. Victoria peered through an open door into what appeared to be an elegant ballroom or hall. The benches around its perimeter were made of a material that looked suspiciously like gold, but Victoria guessed it was Atlan stone. Going up the spiral staircase of the tower, she caught glimpses into a few other rooms. They were all larger than her bedroom in England, and each was decorated with a table, bed, and immense mirror. *Those would have led to the Reflector,* Victoria thought. She couldn't help but feel that the rooms were ghosts of their pasts, missing something that made them welcoming and habitable.

People.

Athelea led them to the top floor of the tower and

pushed the wooden door open, revealing a room similar to those Victoria had spied. There was a bed on each side of the balcony door and a large table in the middle of the room, covered in bottles and baskets of fruit. In the corner of the room were the bags with the tent and supplies she and Sarah had brought from England. Victoria ran to the balcony and gasped at the view. The city of Atlantis was only a silhouette on the horizon, but she imagined it would have glowed with lights and activity when the Atlanteans had lived there.

"This is the safest place for you ladies to stay," Athelea said, smiling warmly. "I hope you find it satisfactory. It was always one of my favorite rooms in the palace."

"It's perfect," Victoria said. She couldn't believe she would be spending the night in an Atlantean palace. "Thank you."

Athelea smiled. "You're very welcome. I've made you both dresses, by the way. I hope I've estimated your sizes correctly."

She picked up the two dresses that had been hanging on the back of the door. She handed the stream of mint green fabric to Sarah and the teal to Victoria. Like the dress Athelea wore, the ones she'd made looked classic and beautiful, like they'd been on a Grecian statue in a museum.

"They're so soft," Victoria breathed, running the fabric between her fingers. She glanced at Athelea, marveling at how she'd found the time to make them. The last of her distrust was fading quickly. "Thank you, Athelea. These are beautiful."

"Wow," Sarah breathed. "Can we try them on now?"

Victoria tore her gaze away from her own dress. Sarah had never cared much about fashion or clothes, usually preferring to dress in jeans and a shirt that she could get dirty working on her art. There was now a sparkle in her eye as she twirled the dress around her body, probably imagining what she would look like in it. Athelea nodded and gave a wink. "Of course."

Forgetting her modesty, Victoria pulled off her shirt. She was just about to step into the dress when Athelea gasped, looking in her direction. "Where did you get that mark?" she asked.

Victoria followed her gaze and realized she was talking about the symbol she'd drawn above her navel days earlier. It was still quite dark against her skin, but it had faded over the past few days. Victoria told Athelea about how she'd found the symbol on a note, and only then did she realize she hadn't eaten in over a day. "I wasn't sure whether it would really work," she admitted. "I've been so preoccupied since then that I haven't thought about it."

"It is a complicated dex, but fortunately, there's no way it could have harmed you or Sarah," Athelea said. "It simply slows your metabolism to a minimal level so you consistently have energy without needing to eat. The more often you use it, though, the less effective it becomes. It is really meant to be used in emergencies only, but the Atlantean army often used it in battle when they needed to travel long distances quickly and lightly."

Victoria bit her lip, processing this information. Her earlier suspicious about this dex hadn't been wrong, but she was reassured to know it had limits. She sensed Athelea had her own reservations about the dex, too. *Not all Atlanteans are selfish,* Victoria thought with a sense of relief that she wasn't alone in objecting to this dex.

"Nothing powers the body better than real food," Athelea continued. "This dex was never meant to be a permanent substitute, but I'm sure some Atlanteans abused its power. At any rate, I'd feel much better if you removed the dex markings now. They would go away on their own on after a week or so, but we shouldn't waste a dex when there's still enough food in Atlantis to feed an army. May I?"

Victoria nodded. Athelea examined the mark for a moment and then incanted something Victoria couldn't catch. The ink began to fade, and after a second, it had vanished. Victoria couldn't see any sign that it had ever been on her skin.

"And Sarah has one, too?" Athelea asked.

Sarah nodded.

"I wish you had told me about this earlier, ladies," Athelea sighed. Sarah flashed a guilty grimace at Victoria while Athelea worked her magic. "At least no harm was done. There you are."

"Thank you," Victoria said, securing her dress around her shoulders. "I'm so glad you're here to help us." It was the sincere truth, and she meant it more every minute. "I have no idea what we would do or how we would manage if you weren't here."

"I'm glad you're here, too," Athelea said. She flashed that mysterious smile again. "Look at your dress in the mirror. You and Sarah look like true Atlanteans."

Sarah fastened her dress and walked to the mirror. The pale green fabric complemented her ivory skin and ruby hair, and the style brought out a delicate, feminine beauty that she never seemed to embrace in her own clothing. She twirled on the spot, smiling.

"You look amazing, Sarah," Victoria said.

Sarah laughed. "Look at yourself." She pulled Victoria in front of the mirror. Next to Sarah, Victoria saw a young woman who she struggled to recognize. After a few days in the sun, her skin was tan, her hair shades lighter than it had ever been. She was nearly a stranger behind the beautiful dress. But the bright smile and silver eyes with a hint of uncertainty were still there, and they would never change. The length of the dress wasn't outrageously formal, as Victoria had expected, and a few seconds passed before she realized what made these dresses so perfect. Something about them was quintessentially Atlantean.

"I love them, Athelea. Thank you very much."

"You're very welcome. They look wonderful on you," Athelea said. She glanced at the fruit and bottles on the table. "You're probably hungry now that you no longer have that dex. Shall I make dinner?"

Victoria realized she was suddenly ravenous, after so long without a proper meal, and she was sure Sarah felt the same. "That would be amazing," she said. "I'm so hungry."

Sarah nodded in agreement, and Athelea excused herself. Victoria admired her dress for another moment before moving out to the balcony. There was so much she wanted to ask Sarah, but now wasn't the time. Athelea returned a few minutes later a with a large pot of soup and a fresh loaf of bread.

"This soup uses some of some of the vegetables I've grown in Atlantis," Athelea said, bringing three steaming bowls of soup to the balcony. It was some of the most delicious food Victoria had ever tasted, especially without a dex to prevent hunger.

"Would you ladies like a glass of wine?" Athelea asked. "We can still enjoy the weather outside for a while before the rain starts."

Victoria exchanged a glance with Sarah. Drinking at

home with her family's approval was safe enough, but this was a completely different environment.

"It's not strong alcohol," Athelea said, apparently sensing their apprehension. "I brewed it myself."

"Why not?" Sarah agreed after a second, and Victoria nodded.

Athelea poured three generous glasses of wine from the decanter. "Don't worry if you can't finish it all."

Following the others, Victoria took a sip. The wine was like nothing she'd ever tasted. It was fruity and incredibly sweet, nearly a juice. For a second, she wondered what she would do if the drink was poisoned, and she instantly felt terrible for doubting Athelea. The day had been a whirlwind, and she knew she wasn't rationalizing properly anymore. After a glass of wine, though she couldn't shake the feeling that Athelea was hiding something from her, she found herself warming to Athelea.

When the bottle of wine was finished, the evening dew to an end, and Athelea departed with a goodnight. Victoria realized she had no idea which room was Athelea's, or when and where or if they were supposed to meet in the morning. She still had so many questions, and her head was spinning with the combination of alcohol and everything she'd learned today.

"Oh, my god," Sarah said falling onto her bed, "Athelea is so cool. Who is she?"

Victoria felt a flash of annoyance and jealousy. She couldn't help but feel like the others were excluding her from their discussions, or that they were both withholding a secret from her. "You know her better than I do. You've spent so much time with her since the earthquake."

Sarah nodded. "Possibly. But she hadn't told me much about herself."

"She was in my first dream about Atlantis. It was all real," Victoria said, and then she hesitated. *Revealing Athelea's secret would be an invasion of privacy,* she thought, *but Sarah should know*. "She had a baby then. I don't know if it was even hers, and I'm honestly terrified to ask what happened to it. But since my dream of Atlantis, I've stumbled across one person too many times for it to be coincidence. His name is Gryffin, and he's about our age. He's got the same tattoo on his wrist as Athelea and I, and he had the maps of Atlantis. I have no idea why, but I'm sure he's her son, even though he looks our age."

"How is that possible?" Sarah asked, looking dumbfounded.

"Athelea is still around. Dexterity is real. Anything is possible here."

"You could ask her about him. Don't you trust her?"

"She carries around a sword. She was hiding it when I met her," Victoria said, more harshly than she intended. Voicing her concerns relieved some of the confusion she'd felt since meeting Athelea. "I don't think she's being entirely truthful."

"So?" Sarah asked. "She hasn't used weapons on us, and she's had plenty of chances. I see no reason to distrust her based on suspicions. But you tell her about this boy when you see best."

"You're probably right," Victoria sighed. Sarah was tipsy. "I'm just glad you're okay. I was so worried."

Sarah nodded. "You too. Maybe tomorrow we can figure out what we're supposed to be doing here. Athelea still seems convinced that you're here to do something special with Atlantis."

Victoria was still unsure why everyone thought that. From what she'd seen, Atlantis needed much more help than she could ever provide, even with Athelea's support. Deciding Sarah wouldn't have said that if she was sober, she ignored the comment, said goodnight and turned off the lights, letting the Atlantean sea breeze and rain lull her to sleep.

177

Chapter Sixteen
PURPOSE

The rain had disappeared and it was a fine morning when Victoria woke. Looking through the open balcony doors, she found that Sarah was already drawing in the sunlight, dressed in a silk robe that matched her dress from the night before. The ocean was glittering an amazing sapphire color, and Atlantis was glowing in the sun like an emerald. Smiling, Victoria pushed herself out of bed and slipped into a teal robe she'd found at the foot of her bed. *English summers have it all wrong.*

"How are we meant to find Athelea?" Victoria wondered when she joined Sarah outside. "She didn't say anything last night."

Sarah set her sketchbook onto her lap. "That's a good question. I have no idea. She didn't show me her room."

A second later, a knock sounded on the door. Victoria and Sarah both looked up, then exchanged glances with each other. While Sarah laughed, Victoria suddenly realized they had no way of knowing who was visiting until she opened the door. If Caelan had found them, they had no escape.

"It's Athelea," a familiar voice called.

Victoria ran to unlock the door, with Sarah following close behind. Athelea breezed into the room, wearing a different black dress and carrying a large basket on her arm. "Good morning, ladies," she said with a warm smile. "I hope you slept well?"

"Very well," Sarah said. Victoria nodded in agreement.

"I'm so glad," Athelea said. "I've brought breakfast, swimwear, and new dresses. I thought you might need it for a new day in Atlantis." She laid out an assortment of fruit, bread, and juice on the balcony table while Victoria and Sarah dressed into their new clothes. Victoria ate with a renewed appetite and felt a wave of energy and excitement fill her as Athelea brought them through the Garden of the Gods to one of her workshops in the east tower. She could smell beautiful fragrances from the tower before they entered it, but she wasn't prepared for what she found inside. Simple wooden tables filled the bottom room, and shelves of glass phials of various sizes lined the wall.

"I make perfumes here, using flowers and fruits from the Garden," Athelea said. Victoria could tell she took great pride in her work. "I make shampoos and soaps upstairs, and candles in the floor above that."

"It smells amazing," Victoria said. "It's a brilliant workshop."

"Thank you. You may have a look around and help yourselves to any scents you enjoy. I keep these rooms unlocked if you ever want to visit."

Victoria spent a while exploring the workshops with Sarah and found a sweet scent that reminded her of Tom. She sprayed a bit on her wrists and looked at the Sentence for the first time in days. Her skin was becoming more tanned with every day in Atlantis, but the ribbon had protected the words, which was still dark as ever. Seeing the words, she instantly remembered that her priority was to help Atlantis.

"Should we clean up more of the city?" she wondered.

Athelea gave her a long look which seemed to gaze into her soul. "We shall, if you'd like," she said. "I know it's not terribly exciting, but it is undeniably necessary."

After a few minutes in the perfumery, the women returned to the Garden of the Gods. Stepping into the sunlight, Athelea muttered a few words that Victoria could swear didn't sound like English. Victoria felt a strange sensation wash over her like a warm breeze, though it didn't touch her hair or the nearby trees.

"What was that?" Victoria asked, hoping she sounded more curious than suspicious.

"You ladies just felt a dex," Athelea said. "It should protect you from sunburn when we're outside today."

"Wow," Victoria breathed. She understood what Athelea meant when she said dexterity was a part of everyday life in Atlantis. There seemed to be a dex for everything. Sarah looked equally impressed, though Victoria was sure she was slightly skeptical, or at least curious, about how the dexes worked.

The women spent the morning cleaning up more rubble around the city. In the light of a new day, the damage from the earthquake didn't seem anywhere as bad as Victoria had remembered. She still didn't recognize most of the buildings around her, but she had a better grasp of her surroundings. The main difference today was that, now that Sarah had mentioned it, she noticed Athelea looking at her often with that expression of curiosity while they worked.

What is that about? Victoria wondered. She hoped Athelea wasn't putting too much faith into her ability to restore Atlantis. At the moment, the most she felt she could do was perhaps fill the empty canals with rowboats, but even that wasn't going to bring the Atlanteans back. Something needed to change in their approach to helping Atlantis, but she wasn't sure what or how.

"I feel we've cleared up as much as we reasonably can, ladies," Athelea said after they had eaten lunch in the Plaza. It was early afternoon, and from what Victoria could tell, they'd made their way through every main street in the city. "Thank you both so much for all your help. Shall we rest on the beach for a while?"

"Yes, please," Sarah answered, while Victoria looked at the sky. The morning had been warm, and even though the day was hot now, it felt humid, like it could rain later. Her body ached, even though Athelea had invoked various dexes to prevent sunburn and keep her and Sarah from tiring. She had never imagined she'd work so hard in Atlantis.

"Don't worry about the weather," Athelea said, following her gaze. "Every day since the Atlanteans disappeared, it's been sunny in the day and rainy at night. I don't know exactly why, but the weather never seems to change. I call it the Night Rain."

"That's probably the only predictable part of Atlantis," Victoria said, fighting a smile. She and Sarah followed Athelea out of the city and walked along the coastal path for a few minutes, until they reached the enormous beach with the shipwreck in the bay.

"What happened here?" Victoria asked. "I've always

wondered about the wreck."

"This is Shipwreck Beach," Athelea said. "Legend says that a drunk Atlantean sailor took his lover here on his ship on a summer night and accidentally crashed it when the tide went out the next morning. The wreck has been left here ever since."

"I'm so glad you're here to tell us these stories," Sarah said, voicing what Victoria had been thinking. Victoria realized they could easily spend all summer in this amazing place, though she wasn't sure how such a long stay would work logistically. Aiden and Andrea would worry, even if they thought she was safe somewhere in England. *Even if today was the only day I ever had here,* she thought, *it was worth it.*

"I will leave you here for an hour, if you wouldn't mind terribly," Athelea said, interrupting her thoughts. "There are a few more errands I must attend to before evening."

"Of course," Victoria said. She was used to Athelea disappearing and returning like breath. "I could spend the whole day here."

Athelea said goodbye and disappeared down the coastal path. For a moment, Victoria wondered where she was going, but before she could speculate, Sarah had stripped to her swimsuit under her dress and splashed into the water.

"This beach is amazing," Sarah said. "Atlantis is amazing."

Victoria followed, happy to be doing something so normal for summer. The water was a perfect temperature, and the fine sand felt like a cloud under her feet. She walked nearly halfway to the wreck before the water became too deep, and she followed Sarah in swimming the rest of the distance.

"Is the ship made of diamonds?" Sarah asked as they pushed themselves onto the deck. "It's glittering."

"Probably Atlan stone," Victoria said, touching the door leading to the cabin. It swung open to reveal a large room which the captain had probably occupied. "It looks and feels like the stone around the city. It's amazing that it could float."

"It's completely empty," Sarah observed from over her shoulder. "I wonder why?"

Victoria shrugged. "Someone probably emptied it after the accident. I bet it was carrying valuable cargo."

Victoria led the way out of the room to the bow of the ship and sat on the deck. There was enough breeze here to make the warmth of the afternoon comfortable, and the view out onto the rest of the bay was spectacular from this height.

"Wouldn't it be amazing if the boys were here?" Sarah asked.

Victoria's heart skipped a beat at the thought of Tom laying shirtless next to her on the beach. "It would be. Tom would adore the architecture and the dexes, and Nick would love all the history Atlantis has to offer," she said after a moment. For a second, she considered asking if Sarah had thought much about Nick these past few days, but decided against it. "But I couldn't imagine them ever being here. I'm still amazed we managed the journey ourselves."

"I know what you mean. I can see you miss him, though," Sarah said.

"I do miss him," Victoria said. She felt a stab of regret that the he and Nick would never know about Atlantis, but she understood now that it would have to stay a secret forever. "We've never been apart this long. I don't feel complete without him."

Running her fingers along the deck, Victoria noticed a frosted glass panel on the floor. She stared at it for a few seconds, debating whether it was safe to touch. "Steering system, maybe?" Sarah guessed over her shoulder, echoing Victoria's thoughts. It didn't look like a window into the lower decks.

Victoria ran her fingers along the panel, applying pressure in a few different directions. With even the slightest motion, she could swear that the ship shifted in response to her touch. Victoria looked around the deck of the ship again. There wasn't any sort of helm in sight.

"Definitely a steering system," Sarah said, watching with interest. A hissing sound recalled their attention to Victoria's hand. The stone underneath seemed to be dissolving. Victoria pulled her hand away, leaving a glowing blue imprint of her palm with a small, glittering key in the middle.

"Sarah, do you see any locks around here?" she asked.

Sarah looked around the boat for a few seconds, then shook her head.

Victoria hesitated, then picked up the key. The metal was smooth and perfectly preserved, and the head had a beautiful design that looked like a bird. "This could go anywhere," she mused. "Why do you think it was hidden?"

"No idea. Can we keep it?" Sarah asked, staring at the key with longing. Victoria hesitated before handing it over. Sarah looked at her impatiently. "It's a key, not a bomb. We can ask Athelea what she thinks."

Looking back at the island, Victoria realized what the problem was. She wanted to leave everything exactly where it was until the Atlanteans returned. *Moving any of their belongings around doesn't seem right,* she thought. She was disappointed that Sarah didn't feel the same way. But before she could say anything, Sarah dove into the water and began to swim away. Victoria followed with a sigh. They stayed in shallow water for another ten minutes and had nearly dried off when Athelea appeared on the beach, holding a few large bundles of fabric.

Sarah bounded up to her, holding out the key. "We found this on the ship when we were swimming. It was in the middle of the deck." Athelea set the fabric down and held out her hand, and Sarah gave her the key. "We were wondering if you knew what it's for."

Athelea laughed. "There are a million locks in Atlantis, and you would be lucky if you ever found the one meant for this key. Since you found it on the ship, I would assume it belonged to the sailor or his crew. This key was probably to his home or somewhere else on the boat."

"Can I keep it?" Sarah asked.

"Of course," Athelea said, taking Victoria by surprise. "I doubt the previous owner has any need for it anymore."

Sarah laughed, but Victoria didn't find their banter the least bit funny. The Atlanteans were missing, and she and Athelea weren't getting any closer to bringing them back. With growing agitation, she watched Sarah unclasp her necklace, feed the chain through the holes in the head of the key, and secure it around her neck.

Avoiding Athelea's inquiring gaze, she sulked off to her towel without waiting to hear what else Athelea had to say. *They're both as bad as each other,* she thought. After a few minutes on her own, she began to feel less annoyed. It was a beautiful day, and she could only imagine what the beach would have been like when Atlantis was at the height of its glory. Parents would have gone out with their children to play in the water, young couples would have fallen in love during romantic walks on the sand, and friends would share secrets with each other when nobody was listening.

Down the beach, Sarah began building a sandcastle, and Athelea contributed a few dexes to make it stronger. Victoria stopped paying attention to their conversation, but she could still hear their occasional bursts of laughter as their castle grew grander. *Sarah gets so much of Athelea's attention,* she thought. She could admit to herself that she was jealous, but she knew it was irrational and she didn't have any claim to special treatment just because she'd been to Atlantis first.

Sarah's my friend, though, she thought, torn between regret and happiness that she'd brought Sarah to Atlantis.

After a while, the others' laughter became easier to ignore, and Victoria began to wonder what Caelan was doing. The uncertainty of whether he was staying somewhere in Atlantis or planning his next attack from a distance made her nervous. She jumped when a hand gently touched her back, and she realized Sarah had snuck up on her while she'd been lost in her thoughts.

"Athelea and I are going to throw kites. Want to join us?"

Victoria had no idea what Sarah meant but nodded.

"Are you okay?" Sarah asked. "You look upset."

Victoria nodded again. It was easier to pretend than to bother everyone with the truth. "Just tired."

Sarah frowned, apparently seeing through the lie. "If you want to talk, I'm here for you. And so is Athelea."

Then why is Athelea ignoring me? Victoria thought. She stood up, ending the conversation, and followed Sarah past a magnificent sandcastle to Athelea. Three triangular objects were on the sand, looking nothing like the kind of kites Victoria had imagined. Athelea smiled at Victoria in greeting and picked up the kite with the yellow ribbon tail. Victoria could see that the kite was no thicker than a few sheets of paper, and she had no idea how it could fly. *Athelea probably made them herself out of the fabric,* Victoria reminded herself. *She probably used a dex that defies gravity.*

Athelea stepped back into what appeared to be a throwing stance, with her back to the ocean and her shoulders forming a line down the beach. "Throwing kites is one of the most popular competitive sports in Atlantis, but it is very simple," she said. "Hold the kite in one hand, aim slightly upwards, and throw it very gently."

With the slightest flick of her wrist, she sent her kite off. It flew parallel to the beach for a few seconds, picking up speed, before it began to rise, spiraling up towards the sun. After twenty seconds, Victoria could no longer see it against the bright sky.

"That's amazing," Sarah breathed.

"Thank you," Athelea said. "You should try."

Sarah glanced at Victoria, seeming to ask for permission to go first. Victoria shrugged, genuinely indifferent now. Sarah picked up the green kite, held it slightly higher than Athelea had, and used her whole arm to throw. Victoria could tell her form wasn't right for this sport. The kite flew a few feet before diving straight into the sand.

"That didn't look right," Sarah said, laughing as she ran to pick it up. "What did I do wrong?"

"You held it slightly too high and threw it too low," Athelea said, with a faint smile that only Victoria could see. "Hold it at your shoulder and aim just above the horizon."

Sarah nodded and got into position again. This time, she seemed to take a few seconds to aim, and the kite flew along the beach. It stayed parallel to the sand for ten seconds before it began to rise, slowly turning into an upwards spiral.

Sarah turned to Athelea, sporting an elated grin. "Not as fast as yours," she said, "but so cool."

"Still a respectable throw," Athelea enthused. "Would you like to try, Victoria?"

Victoria picked up the last kite and was surprised by how light it was, exactly like the paper she'd imagined.

Taking her stance to throw, she didn't bother to ask whether the kites could break. Brilliant Atlantean engineering was apparent in its firm frame and soft yet sturdy fabric. Feeling slightly absurd, Victoria aimed just above the horizon, took a breath, and flicked her wrist like Athelea had done. The kite rolled off her fingertips and began to fly parallel to the beach. After a second, it started to gain height and began the same spiral dance that the others had, but it was easily the fastest out of the three. Half a minute passed before it was out of sight, flying enormous circles over the island with the other two.

"Very impressive," Athelea said. "It's like you've been throwing for years."

Victoria smiled, secretly flattered. "Thank you. What happens now?"

"We should be able to see them again in an hour," Athelea said. "They'll descend slowly and hopefully land right where we threw them."

"Nice," Victoria said. "What will we do until then?"

"What would you like to do?"

The question caught Victoria by surprise. *Athelea doesn't just care about Sarah's opinion,* Victoria scolded herself. Although she'd only been in Atlantis for a little while, she knew her answer. "Could we look at the Broken Portal again?"

Athelea looked equally surprised by Victoria's

request, but they arrived at the Reflector fifteen minutes later. The Broken Portal looked no different than it had before, though Victoria didn't know what else she'd expected. She sensed that Sarah and Athelea were generally uninterested, that they believed the portal would never change. But Victoria couldn't shake her fascination. She was sure the Broken Portal would lead somewhere important if it was working, and she wanted to know more.

"Were there any portals outside of Atlantis?" she asked.

"I'm not sure," Athelea said. "They might have changed over time, but I believe all these portals functioned within Atlantis for many generations before the Destruction."

Victoria frowned. *Athelea really doesn't realize the implications of this,* she thought. "If the Broken Portal linked Atlantis to the outside world, somebody like Caelan could have access to cause destruction if he found a way to fix it," she said. "It's not a risk worth taking."

"The Broken Portal has never worked. There is no risk."

Victoria held her breath to keep from replying. She would have to research portals herself, sooner than later, especially since Athelea hadn't. Athelea lit another candle for the lost Atlanteans in the Hall of Divinity before bringing Sarah and Victoria back to Shipwreck Beach.

"Those are the kites," she said, pointing to three black spots barely visible above Mount Theus. As the kites approached, Victoria began to distinguish their shapes and strange yet captivating motion.

Athelea's kite was the first to hit the sand. She picked it up with a smile, and Victoria watched as the other two kites approached in wonderful spirals. Sarah ran a few paces to pick up hers more gracefully than she'd thrown it, and Victoria's landed directly at her feet. She bent down, glad that Athelea had introduced them to this sport, and her fingers had barely brushed the kite when her vision darkened and she collapsed to the ground.

Chapter Seventeen
DEXTERITY

"Are you okay?" a voice asked. Victoria wasn't sure if it belonged to Athelea or Sarah, or both speaking simultaneously. She tried to nod or to say that she wasn't in pain, but she couldn't move her body. Her head seemed foggy, and all she could process was the warmth of the sand beneath her body. Being out of control was strangely blissful, but Victoria knew it wasn't right. She could hear Sarah's constant stream of questions and Athelea's calm responses, but in her state, their words were meaningless sounds.

She took a few deep breaths, reminding herself that she was unharmed. After a what seemed like an hour, her body seemed to reconnect with her mind. Her vision slowly returned, and she could think rationally again. The spell had passed. Sarah and Athelea were both looking at her with expressions of concern. Victoria sat up with a sigh, sensing that Athelea would probably never stop worrying about her now, would always think she was fragile.

"What the hell happened?" Sarah asked. Under her newfound tan, she was whiter than Victoria had ever seen her. "That looked horrible."

"I don't know. It was like a fog took control of my body," Victoria said. "I wasn't in pain, but I couldn't do anything."

Athelea frowned. "Do you feel better now?"

"Just shaken," Victoria admitted. "What happened? Was it Caelan?"

"It was not," Athelea said. She sounded certain, though Victoria sensed she was racing for an explanation. "Whatever took control of you was a force of which I have very limited knowledge. If it is what I fear, we must take action immediately."

Exchanging glances with Sarah, Victoria realized neither of them wanted to ask what that was. *It must be bad if Athelea is worried,* Victoria thought. They packed the kites away and returned to the palace without any delay, and Athelea locked the gates to the Isle of the Gods behind them. She prepared dinner somewhere in the castle while Sarah sketched and Victoria drank tea on the balcony. Victoria suspected it was part of Athelea's scheme to make sure

Victoria wasn't alone.

"Don't take this the wrong way, but are you vegetarian?" Sarah asked Athelea after a glass of wine. The somber mood of the late afternoon had lifted slightly with food and the sunset, and this question made Victoria laugh for the first time in what felt like days.

"I haven't eaten meat since the Destruction," Athelea said. Victoria and Sarah exchanged glances. "There aren't many animals left in Atlantis, and I've never been skilled at fishing, so my options are scarce."

"We should teach you," Sarah said. "My dad used to take me fishing when I was younger. It was a bit slow sometimes, but I still enjoyed it."

"I would enjoy that very much."

Victoria couldn't believe she and Sarah were having this conversation with Atlantean royalty, but at least they could contribute something in return for everything Athelea was doing for them. When they finished eating, Athelea lit a lamp on the balcony for Sarah to sketch and gestured for Victoria to follow her inside.

"What happened to you this afternoon at Shipwreck Beach could have been terribly serious," Athelea said, closing the balcony door behind them. "Some power that even I don't comprehend has tried to possess you. I don't know where it has come from, or whether it will happen again, or what it is. I do believe, however, that we must ensure your protection immediately."

"How do we do that?" Victoria asked.

Ten minutes later, they excused themselves from Sarah and proceeded through a series of paths and hallways around the palace gardens. Athelea gestured to an open doorway off the Garden of the Gods inscribed with the words *Neutral Room*, and Victoria stepped through. Immediately, she sensed that this enormous, windowless room was different from anywhere else she'd been in Atlantis. It felt full of energy, like it was alive. A layer of water seemed to cover the floor, and Victoria had a fleeting impression that there wasn't anything solid beneath it. Only a bench and table in the middle of the room convinced her otherwise. Taking a step forward, her foot met solid ground, and the illusion shattered.

A white line of fire ran horizontally across the dark walls, halfway between the ceiling and floor. The flames reflected in the water, sending dancing prisms of light around the room. "That is Atlan fire," Athelea explained, sliding the stone door shut behind her. She took a seat on the bench and gestured for Victoria to follow. "It prevents any ambient dexterity from leaving or entering the room, making a perfect learning environment. Let's take a moment to walk around the room so you learn its energy."

Victoria followed Athelea in a slow stroll around the perimeter of the room, still bemused by the unusual floor.

The room made her feel uneasy. She could walk and see and talk and the way she did anywhere else, but a faint headache gave her the impression that the room was closing her in and somehow dulling her senses. After such a long day, she wasn't sure if she was imagining it or losing her mind.

"As I mentioned earlier, Atlan stone conducts dexterity better than any other material," Athelea said when they were halfway around the room. "When the Atlanteans were here, their dexterity made the stones incredibly strong. In return, the stones refined their dexterity. Together, the stone and fire should manage your dexterity so that nothing can go seriously wrong during your training. That is the purpose of a Neutral Room."

"Do you think anything could go wrong?" Victoria asked, hoping she didn't sound as nervous as she felt.

Athelea shook her head. "I doubt it. We'll begin by working with dexes that can protect you. I trust you're intelligent enough to never go searching for Caelan, so offensive dexes would be a waste of time. Defensive dexes, however, will help you whenever he goes looking for you or you find yourself in trouble."

"That makes sense," Victoria agreed darkly. She had no inclination to start a fight with Caelan. "Do you really think Caelan has dexterity?"

"I fear he has powerful dexterity that he has grown from experimentation. The earthquake was a perfect example of his skill," Athelea said. She scowled darkly around the room, as if it was somehow responsible for his behavior. "Unfortunately, he has probably planned countless ways to harm you by now. If you can name it, he can use it against you."

Victoria closed her eyes, suddenly feeling hopeless.

"You must learn how to block Caelan's dexterity. I honestly do not know what he is capable of, but if he could control your mind, or if he could put foreign thoughts in your head, you and Atlantis would be entirely at his mercy. You would rather be dead than ever find yourself in that situation where you lose your free will."

Victoria felt faint as the fire on the wall of the Neutral Room slipped out of focus. She understood exactly what Athelea was implying. "Could he really possess me?"

Athelea said, and Victoria felt the last of her hope of safety in Atlantis shatter. "While you seemed to resist the attack earlier today, you might not be so fortunate if it happens again. Caelan probably could possess you successfully, but I wonder what purpose that would serve. He couldn't kill you that way without destroying himself in the process. If he tries to harm you, I am quite confident that his methods will be either physical, if he can get close enough to you, or an attempt to manipulate psychologically."

"How do I defend myself against his dexterity,

then?" Victoria pressed.

Athelea beamed, and Victoria realized she'd finally asked the right question. "If you could learn to use your dexterity to put up a shield against outside dexterity, you will have an incredible defensive advantage over Caelan. With your consent, I will try to access your thoughts, and you will try to block my dexterity. There is no established method for your part, so we might have to experiment to find a system that works. Are you ready?"

Victoria hesitated. She had a horrible feeling that she knew what was next, and she wasn't sure she was ready to expose her innermost self to someone she'd only known a few days. *You trust Athelea,* she reminded herself. *She would never hurt you.*

"Everything will be fine," Athelea assured her. "We can finish whenever you've had enough."

Victoria nodded. *Better Athelea than Caelan*, she reminded herself. Not knowing what else to do, she closed her eyes and waited, trying to distract herself with insignificant thoughts. A second later, the middle of her forehead began to tingle, and then the pressure stopped. Victoria opened her eyes.

"That is what the dex feels like," Athelea said. "So you are aware, I am going to try to learn about the people you love. Even if our experiment fails, I hopefully will have gotten to know you a bit better."

Victoria knew this disclosure was part of Athelea's strategy. It was impossible not to think of Tom now. She tried desperately to keep Athelea from accessing those memories and thoughts, but as a sudden breeze rushed past her in this strange, enclosed room, she knew she stood no chance of hiding her personal life.

"Is he your boyfriend?" Athelea asked.

Victoria nodded and took a few deep breaths, wary about where this conversation was going. Athelea had succeeded so quickly. "His name is Tom. We've been together for about three years."

"Tom seems a very charming young man," Athelea said. "How did you meet?"

"We met through a mutual friend named Nick and have been together ever since," Victoria said. "Tom is the best person I know. He has never had a bad thought or word about anyone. He cares so much about other people that he wants to get into charity work. Sometimes, I feel he's too good to be real, but anyone who meets him can see he is the most genuine person."

"That's lovely," Athelea said.

Victoria couldn't find words to further express what she was feeling. All her love for Tom and the pain of separation came streaming to the forefront of her mind, impossible to ignore. She was going to have to fight harder if she wanted Athelea to stay out.

Athelea lifted her eyebrow in challenge.

It's part of the game, Victoria reminded herself. *Stay calm.*

After what felt like an hour, even though it was only minutes, Victoria simply couldn't fend off Athelea's intrusions. With every attempt to keep her memories concealed, she revealed more about her life within a matter of seconds. *If Caelan ever did this to me,* Victoria thought, *we would all be in trouble.*

The process repeated for what felt like an hour. Victoria tried to fend off the attacks, but every time, Athelea managed to break through her defense.

"You ran away from home?" Athelea asked after what felt like the hundredth attack.

Victoria nodded. "I needed some space from my family," she said. If Athelea didn't already know, she didn't want to get into details of their argument now, while she had a pounding head and aching heart. Athelea already knew more about Aiden and Andrea, Nick, Tom, and Sarah than Victoria had thought was possible, and Athelea didn't ask any questions but proceeded with another invasion.

"I can't do this anymore," Victoria panted, collapsing onto the bench. She wasn't any closer to shielding her mind. She was only getting more frustrated with her failure, and she knew she would lose her temper if they continued any longer. She suddenly realized why she was struggling so much. "Athelea, do you have to be Atlantean to have dexterity?"

Athelea hesitated. Victoria realized she'd probably never thought about that before. "I've never known anybody who didn't have Atlantean blood," Athelea admitted. "I have heard stories of foreigners who thought they could invoke dexes, but I don't believe any of them were ever proven. I would say that dexterity is purely an Atlantean power."

Victoria nodded. "So Caelan is probably of Atlantean descent. That's why he has dexterity."

"It would seem so."

The Neutral Room fell silent. The more Victoria knew about dexterity, the less she felt she understood it. But if Athelea was right, Gryffin had to be Atlantean, too. *He must be her son*, she thought. It seemed impossible, but the fact that Athelea was here proved otherwise. For a second, Victoria thought again of mentioning Gryffin, but she didn't know where to begin.

"The fact that one can bear the Sentence is a strong indication of an Atlantean bloodline," Athelea continued, when Victoria said nothing, and the moment passed. "In the years before the Destruction, Atlanteans spread out around Europe, which is probably why even Sarah can bear the Sentence."

"Do all Atlanteans have dexterity?"

Athelea shook her head. "There have been a few Atlanteans throughout history who either were not born with it or decided to give it up."

"Is that why I can't do it?" Victoria sighed. "Is something wrong with me?"

Athelea shook her head, looking torn between amusement and sympathy. "Many Atlanteans seriously struggle with once dex or another. You've probably heard of the warrior Achilles. He was a brave Atlantean soldier who knew very powerful defensive dexes, but his one heel was his weakness that he could never quite protect or heal. That's where the phrase originates, and it describes exactly what you are facing."

Victoria felt her frustration falter. Nick would absolutely love to hear that story. "Do all Atlanteans go to school?"

"Yes. Most Atlanteans attend school as children for training in math, literacy, and the sciences especially, to strengthen their knowledge for dexes. The process is effective yet predictable. They leave school with an arsenal of practical dexes for everyday life. Then, many attend university to learn how to use dexterity at a more complex or professional level."

Victoria nodded, making a mental note to ask later what those dexes were but stayed silent for now to let Athelea continue.

"Dexterity, however, does come most naturally to those with royal blood. Members of the royal family are often born with inherent dexterity. Royalty use dexterity for protecting themselves and Atlantis, and for managing situations when nothing else will work."

Victoria bit her lip. The hierarchy sounded deeply unfair, and Athelea didn't seem to understand how the system looked to anyone on the outside. Royalty could have abused their power so easily, and Victoria was sure that the commoners had thought similarly. "Is there any other way to learn?" she asked, though she wasn't sure she wanted the answer.

"The most dangerous education," Athelea admitted, "is when Atlanteans experiment with their strengths and discover their lack of limitations. Without supervision, they can learn dexes that destroy civilizations instead of build them."

"Caelan," Victoria muttered.

"Most likely. I believe Caelan must have some form of traditional training, perhaps through dexologs, before he decided to experiment. That combination makes his dexterity unpredictable and unstable."

Great, Victoria thought. She didn't like the sound of it, and even Athelea had a glint of worry in her eyes.

"What you must remember, Victoria, is that the way you learn is not nearly as important as what you learn,"

Athelea said. "I desperately wanted to study at university, but my father never let me. I had a tutor, and although I learned everything from her, I despised nearly every minute of the process."

Victoria managed a smile, feeling slightly reassured. Athelea was full of surprises, and it was impossible not to admire her confidence and faith.

"Ultimately, dexterity is a strange force," Athelea concluded. "I suspect yours is still not fully developed because you haven't been in Atlantis very long. It may take time for your body to become familiar with Atlantean energy and learn how to handle it. We can try again tomorrow. You've had a long day."

Victoria didn't hesitate to conclude their session. Following Athelea out of the Neutral Room, she felt her headache disappear as the weight of the room lifted. She said goodnight and goodbyes at the top of the Royal Tower, and Athelea returned down the tower to wherever she went at night. Sarah was still sketching on the balcony, so Victoria got ready for bed in silence, feeling her mood worsen as she processed the events of the day. Sarah joined her inside a few minutes later and put her sketchbook and necklace on the side of her bed.

"You shouldn't have kept the key," Victoria said, her irritation flaring before she could hold the words back.

Sarah looked up, seeming shocked for a moment,

before she reached for the necklace. "You can have it, Vic. I didn't know you wanted it."

"I don't want it," Victoria said. "That's the point. I want everything to be exactly how it was when the Atlanteans left, so that everything is the same if they ever come back."

Sarah paused, and Victoria knew she didn't have an argument for this. "I see what you mean," Sarah said gently, "but it's just a key. Is there any harm in me having it for now?"

Victoria sighed. "I suppose not."

"You should talk to Athelea about her plans going forward. I can see how much it means to her that you're helping."

Athelea would probably leave everything broken forever, Victoria thought, though she didn't dare say it to Sarah.

"What do you think of Atlantis now you've been here a bit longer?" Sarah pressed. "Has your time here been what you expected?"

Victoria smiled. "It's obviously beautiful, but I don't understand it. It's so *broken*, and I really don't like the fact that nobody else is here. It feels a bit like a ghost town, or a country that's been ruined by war."

"It is strange," Sarah agreed. "I'm glad you and Athelea are trying to help Atlantis, even if it's going to be a lot of work."

"I don't feel like we're doing much yet," Victoria admitted. She wanted to tell Sarah more about her training in dexterity, but she had no idea where to begin. "It's hard to explain."

"Does it have anything to do with her magic?" Sarah asked.

Victoria stayed silent, meeting Sarah's gaze significantly. "Dexterity. It's essentially manipulating energy to perform an action. I couldn't do it, and Athelea ended up finding out everything about Tom and Aiden and Andrea."

"I'm sorry," Sarah said, pulling her in for a hug. "Don't worry. I know you've been stressed recently, but you'll get it soon, you'll see."

"Thanks," Victoria said. Sarah's faith reassured more than would have expected. "How have you been? I noticed you've been drawing a lot this week. Could I see?"

Sarah handed her notepad to Victoria and sat back, ready for the appraisal. Her current sketch of the view of the Atlantis from the Royal Tower was still missing color but otherwise complete. Victoria flipped to the front of the book and found the sketch of Tom, which made her heart ache. Next were drawings of the meadow and temple on the other island, which she skipped over with a shiver. Sarah had drawn the exterior of the Grand Library while Victoria had been unconscious after the earthquake, capturing the graceful curves of the dome, the commanding pillars and scholars of the entryway, and the detail of the stones perfectly. They really were stunning sites, and Sarah's representations did them justice.

"They're beautiful," Victoria said, handing the book back to Sarah. "What will you do with them?"

"I'm going to ask Athelea if I can take them home," Sarah said. "I'd love to keep them, even if I can't use them for my portfolio."

"I'm sure she wouldn't mind," Victoria said. "You know what she's like."

They laughed together. Victoria felt better for having voiced her concerns about the dexes and the key and having explained to Sarah what it meant to her. And no matter what happened in the future, she was thankful that Sarah was experiencing Atlantis with her. They talked for a while longer about England before turning the lights out and saying goodnight. Victoria fell asleep, exhausted but ready to see what the next day in Atlantis would hold.

Chapter Eighteen
THE DARK DEX

"We should devise a plan of action, ladies," Athelea announced at breakfast the next morning before Victoria had remembered to suggest it. She surveyed the balcony table over her goblet of juice with a practiced air of importance. Victoria suddenly felt like she was at some sort of official meeting and took a long sip of her mango tea. It felt too early for such a serious discussion, even if she had slept incredibly well.

"Yesterday, we discussed how we could restore the dexes that once protected Atlantis," Athelea continued. "I went through my father's personal library last night, and I couldn't find any information about what dexes the masons used to fortify the buildings originally. I will continue my search until I find something helpful, but until then, we have many other preoccupations."

Victoria nodded automatically. She knew she should have been excited that Athelea had used her initiative to figure out how to restore Atlantis, but Athelea had missed years of making a genuine effort. Victoria felt like they were wasting time still, though she couldn't see what more they could do.

"What about the people?" Sarah asked, turning to look at Victoria with a hopeful expression. "Is there no way of getting them back? They could really help us."

Athelea looked at Victoria, too.

They're gone, Victoria thought. *You can't magic them back to life.* She knew better than to say any of this out loud, but she wasn't sure what else the others expected. They were putting too much faith in her for no reason. She gave a noncommittal shrug and retreated behind her tea, hoping somebody else would speak.

"Until recently, I thought I had tried everything possible to bring the Atlanteans back," Athelea said, seeming to take the hint. "But then, Victoria told me about her journey to Atlantis. She said that she had found some sort of monument or temple. There are many remote Atlantean islands with these features, so I didn't think much about the location at the time. But last night, I remembered you said you had fallen onto something in the dark. Could that object have been an hourglass?"

Victoria closed her eyes, thinking back to that moment. She *had* felt something gritty in her wound that could have been sand, even if she hadn't realized it then. "It might have been," she said, careful to not express too much confidence. Athelea and Sarah didn't need higher hopes than they already had. "But why would that be important?"

"One island in Atlantis, called the Isle of Time, was rumored to house special hourglasses under its temple, called the Domain," Athelea said. Victoria noticed triumph flicker in her smile, matching the sparkle in her eyes. "Atlantean legend says that the island was home to countless thousands of what we called Lifeglasses, each of which was linked to an Atlantean soul. A new Lifeglass formed with each birth and expired when its corresponding Atlantean died."

A long silence punctuated the conversation. Victoria waited, though she sensed where this conversion was going.

"Do you think the Lifeglasses are broken?" Sarah asked after a long pause.

"Perhaps. They may be broken or frozen, but I believe something catastrophic must have happened to disrupt them," Athelea said. "You can decide yourselves whether you believe the legend, but it's the only theory I have presently."

"I need to learn more Atlantean mythology soon," Victoria said, barely following what Athelea was saying.

Lifeglasses sounded impossible, but if they were real, they could be the key to getting the Atlanteans back. She felt a flutter of excitement. "Have you ever been to the island?"

Athelea shook her head. "The thought didn't occur to me until late last night. The Isle of Time was forbidden to everybody except the few Watchmen who protected the Lifeglasses. Until yesterday, I had not considered it could be relevant to our efforts."

"That must be what the strange building was," Victoria said to Sarah. The ghosts in the lake made sense now, if the home of Atlantean souls was so close. For a second, she considered telling Athelea about them, but the mere memory sent a shiver of terror through her body. There wasn't much point discussing the ghosts until they knew the Lifeglasses were even real, and there was only one way to find out. She turned to Athelea. "Could you take us there?"

Athelea hesitated for a second too long, and Victoria felt her hopes crash. "Eventually," Athelea said, "but not yet. Sarah and I should go to the Isle of Time first to make sure it's safe. If Caelan has been there again, we could be walking straight into a trap."

Victoria felt her heart sink further. "Without me?" she clarified.

Athelea nodded, barely meeting her eye.

Victoria found herself blinking back tears. She was tired of Sarah and Athelea leaving her out of everything they did, tired of laying around while the others explored interesting places and did important work. For a moment, she felt a flare of anger with both of them, even though she knew they weren't doing it to hurt her. She wanted to decide for herself what was best, though nobody in Atlantis or England seemed to understand.

"Until we know more about the Isle of Time, it would be wise for you to stay in Atlantis," Athelea said directly to Victoria, more gently now. "Sarah and I can scout first to confirm that it is safe and hopefully see whether the Lifeglasses are there. Your time will be much better spent studying dexterity than sitting in a boat."

Victoria shook her head, refusing to defeat. She didn't want to miss out on another adventure, but Athelea's logic didn't leave much choice. Victoria glanced to Sarah for support and received a neutral shrug. *At least I'll have a chance to research portals,* she reassured herself. She was sure she'd dreamt of the Broken Portal last night, though she couldn't remember exactly what had happened, and she wanted to learn more about the Reflector. "You two can go to the Isle of Time, as long as I can do something useful in the Grand Library," she conceded. "I don't want to stay in a Neutral Room all afternoon."

Athelea took her to the Library after breakfast without any question. The three enormous floors of books and the massive glass dome were simply breathtaking in the full light of day. The building still reminded Victoria of an ancient theater, and Sarah look enchanted as the group crossed the floor to the main staircase. Victoria was sure she was seeing how many drawings and paintings she could add to her portfolio.

"This is such a beautiful building," she whispered as they proceeded upstairs. "I could spend days here."

"That's probably what King Atlas intended," Athelea said with a smile as they passed the portrait of the monarch. "The most prominent scholars used the highest floor, which also contains indexes, and the ground floor was open to the public at all hours of the day. Access to the middle floor was granted mainly to University students, but I am confident we are now exempt from those rules." She stopped in front of one of the tables on this level and motioned for Victoria to sit, while Sarah fell behind to admire the painting of Atlas on the staircase landing.

"Would the Grand Library have any information about where the Atlanteans might have gone?" Victoria asked.

Athelea looked around the building, her expression thoughtful. "A copy of nearly every book ever written in Atlantis, or by Atlanteans, can be found here. I suspect that anything of such importance would probably be in the restricted section of the Grand Library, which obviously is not cataloged, or in my father's personal library on the Isle of the Gods," Athelea continued. "Any sort of prophecy would be archived in the Hall, though I've read nearly every document there already. At any rate, finding such information within any of these collections would require quite an extensive search."

Victoria sighed. At least there was plenty for her to do in the Grand Library while the others were away, and she wasn't going to ask for permission to look around. "We've got to start somewhere, I guess."

"Before we go, I'll find something for you to do, if you'll excuse me for a moment," Athelea said, seeming to read her thoughts. She disappeared among the bookshelves for a minute and returned with a pile of booklets, which she set onto the table gently. From the layer of dust on their uniform, black covers, Victoria guessed that nobody had touched them in a thousand years.

"These books are called dexologs. They're nearly indestructible, so don't be afraid to handle them," Athelea said. "Some of these dexes are quite complicated, so don't despair if you don't understand everything. If you familiarize yourself with the theory, you'll have a sound foundation for practice once you connect with your dexterity. You can look around the rest of the library if you get bored, but I expect we'll only be gone for a few hours."

Victoria nodded, thankful that Athelea had guessed her plans and essentially given her permission.

"You should be perfectly safe within the building, Victoria, but I will lock it for extra security while we're gone."

Victoria knew she was safer in the Grand Library than anywhere else in Atlantis, especially with Athelea's protections. "I won't leave the building," she promised. "Stay safe, both of you. Hope you find everything you're looking for."

Sarah waved goodbye, looking guilty, and she and Athelea headed downstairs and out of the library. Victoria watched them lock the door before she turned her attention to the books that Athelea had called dexologs. She opened the one on top, which looked thicker than the others, and found a tablet of Atlan stone, essentially an Atlantean coloring book for children. She felt tears of indignation sting her eyes. It was so unfair that she was doing this while Sarah went on adventures with Athelea.

Reminding herself that she'd used dexterity to color the maps she'd drawn in Atlantis, she dried her face after a minute and forced herself to focus on the dexolog. *Athelea left them for a reason,* she reminded herself. Atlan stone was supposed be the best conductor of dexterity, and she supposed this lesson was the best way to learn how to use hers. She read the instructions that some Atlantean had written thousands of years ago, and then tried the first task.

Turning the tablet a different color sounded simple,

but after nearly fifteen minutes, Victoria hadn't had any success. She read the instructions yet again, looking for any crucial information she might have missed. She wondered if she was supposed to be saying the words in ancient Atlantean language, but she hoped Athelea would have told her. She closed the dexolog, feeling defeated by what she understood should have been a simple task, especially because it wasn't keeping Atlantis safe. The nearby window had given her a view of the empty Plaza all morning, and she was getting frustrated seeing Atlantis so broken.

There must be information somewhere in the library about how the portals work or how to restore the dexes protecting the city, she thought. Leaving her coloring book behind, she explored the nearest bookshelves, hoping to stumble across answers by chance. To her surprise, most of the books were dexologs. Victoria skimmed over a few bookshelves before she headed upstairs, deciding she needed direction from the indexes. The top floor was the smallest in the library, containing only a few chairs and tables and shelves, one of which had books that looked worn with use. Opening one of these books, she confirmed that these were the indexes Athelea had mentioned. Finally feeling like she was doing something productive and useful, she brought a few books to the window and began her search.

After fifteen minutes, she hadn't found a single mention of portals or traveling within Atlantis. The lack of information made no sense to Victoria, and she hated that her search had reached a dead end so quickly. *I'll have to ask Athelea,* she decided. They couldn't risk leaving any potential route into Atlantis unexplored, or Caelan would exploit it. She returned downstairs and resigned herself to reading more dexologs by the window.

The proper dexologs were more interesting than Victoria had expected. Each included a summary of the dex, a technical description of how it worked, and information about how to invoke and revoke its effects. The dex for detecting lies seemed easier than she'd expected, and like any other dex, it was about understanding the energy behind an action. Working through the dexologs, Victoria had to admit that many of the dexes were useful for everyday tasks, though others were equally pointless and lazy. She could see easily where Atlanteans morality had been right and wrong.

What she didn't understand was why Athelea wanted to her to learn so many dexes when she still couldn't invoke even the simplest of them. Hoping she wasn't wasting effort and time, she finished reading the dexologs Athelea had chosen, and then searched for more. At the far end of the middle floor, she found one dexolog sticking halfway out of the shelf, seemingly waiting for her. She pulled it out, wondering whether Athelea had been the last person to read it.

"Darkness of Death," she said, reading the heading

of the page. Beneath it was a foreign word, which she assumed was the name of the dex. "*Desillumentia.*"

Without any warning, darkness consumed the Grand Library, as if the sun had burnt out and all the light in the world had disappeared.

Victoria managed to cover her mouth before she screamed, her heart racing in a mix of fear and elation. She'd invoked a proper dex at last. But after a few seconds of celebrating in the darkness, she began to realize she'd done something terribly wrong. She couldn't see anything. She reached forward and felt the bookshelf, reassuring her that she was still in the library, and she didn't bother looking at the text to see how to revoke the darkness. Slamming the dexolog shut, she stepped away from the shelves and visualized a fire glowing lightly on the palm of her hand. A second later, she could swear she smelled smoke, but she couldn't see or feel the source.

"At least the dexologs give accurate descriptions," she muttered. She closed her hands to extinguish the fire that probably didn't exist, reached for the bookshelf, and began to grope her way through the darkness, hoping she wasn't igniting anything in the process. She needed to leave the library, if it was possible to get through the locked doors. After a minute, she found the nearest staircase, thoroughly regretting having attempted dexes that Athelea hadn't recommended. When the steps ended at the ground floor, she groped her way through another group of tables, but instead of finding a door at the other end, she could only feel more bookshelves. She cursed under her breath.

As she paused to gather her bearings, she heard footsteps shuffling across the library floor. She froze, her heart racing, as she processed her options. She didn't need a dex to confirm she wasn't alone, and it didn't matter how the intruder had opened the door. *Maybe they invoked the darkness dex,* she thought. She couldn't tell if it was Athelea and Sarah approaching, but instinct warned her against saying anything. Either of them would have called out for her, but only someone with darker intentions would approach this way.

Caelan or Gryffin.

Victoria sank to her knees and silently crawled to the nearest table. Without moving the chairs, she hid herself the best she could and closed her eyes to listen. The footsteps slowed a few paces away from her, and she stayed perfectly still, not even daring to breathe. Her heartbeat seemed loud enough to announce her exact location, and the footsteps stopped directly in front of her, confirming her fears.

Chapter Nineteen
VISITORS

"Enough, darkness," a female voice muttered. Sunlight streamed into the library through the dome and windows, blinding Victoria with its brilliance. Athelea stood a few paces away with an apologetic expression on her face. Victoria would have collapsed in relief if she hadn't already been on the ground, and she felt slightly ridiculous now for having hidden.

Athelea extended a hand to help her up. "I see you have taken the liberty of exploring the Grand Library," Athelea said steadily, "And you finally invoked a dex. Congratulations are in order."

Victoria nodded, trying to calm her racing pulse. "I invoked the dex? It was an accident, so wasn't sure if it was someone else."

"You did invoke the dex, and I see you have also learned an important lesson about the potential dangers of dexterity?"

"Don't invoke a new dex without knowing how to revoke it?" Victoria sighed, embarrassed that she hadn't considered that herself earlier. She'd seen that type of information in all other dexologs, but she hadn't thought she would need it when she simply said the name of this dex.

Athelea offered a gentle smile. "Precisely. It is important to understand every modification of the dex you are working with before you use it. It is equally important to know how to invoke it and how to revoke it."

"I'll remember that," Victoria promised. "How did you break the darkness? Nothing I tried worked."

"I revoked whatever you had done to invoke the darkness," Athelea said after a moment of obvious deliberation. "I can override all your dexes. In the hierarchy which ensures dexterity is not misused, both royalty and elder blood relatives have the ability to trump most dexes."

"Are there any other rules I should know?"

Athelea nodded slowly. "Enough to fill an entire book. If we had more time, I would have asked you to read it, but until then, you can only learn them by mistakes and experience."

"Wonderful," Victoria groaned, looking at all the books around her. They seemed to glare back, promising to exceed her limits. "I'm never going to understand any of this."

Athelea smiled sympathetically. "You are at no more of a disadvantage than any Atlantean discovering her dexterity, except for when you attempt dexes you don't fully understand," she reassured her. Again, the slight smile crossed her lips, and Victoria felt she was missing a joke. But Athelea simply nodded in the direction of the staircase and began to walk. "Let's join Sarah outside. Follow me, and we'll tell you about our expedition."

They made their way through the books and tables to the front of the library, which Victoria had spectacularly overshot in the dark. Sarah was waiting on the Plaza steps and smiled in greeting. Her expression gave no information about whether her excursion with Athelea had been successful.

"How did your search go?" Victoria asked.

"The island you and Sarah visited was indeed the Isle of Time," Athelea said. There was a flicker of genuine excitement in her eyes. "Sarah showed me the Domain, but I couldn't find any way to enter the crypt you had mentioned. You must come with us next time, now we know that the island is perfectly safe."

"Really?" Victoria gasped. "Could we go now?"

Athelea glanced at the sky and frowned. "Unfortunately, it's too late to go back tonight. It will be dark in a few hours and the Night Rain will come, but we can visit in the day tomorrow."

Once again, Victoria couldn't argue with Athelea. She was annoyed that Sarah seemed to spend more time with Athelea than she did, even if their excursions were more dangerous than anything she did in Atlantis. *Athelea is sincerely trying to protect you,* she reminded herself as Athelea lit a candle in the Hall of Divinity. They continued to the palace from there, and after they had eaten another soup for dinner, Victoria had a feeling she knew what was next on Athelea's agenda.

"Shall we practice dexterity again?" Athelea asked. Victoria tried not to show her reluctance as she agreed, hoping her afternoon of studying would yield results. They left Sarah sketching on a bench in the Garden of the Gods just outside the Neutral Room, and Athelea sealed the doors of the Neutral Room shut behind Victoria.

After twenty minutes, Victoria found herself cursing her decision. Despite meditation and Athelea's tuition, she wasn't having any success fighting Athelea's dexterity. The room still felt suffocating, and every time Athelea gleamed more information about her personal life, Victoria felt more and more frustrated. After an hour, she had the worst headache of her life and felt ready to collapse. Without a word, she signaled that she was done.

"You can't excel at everything," Athelea reassured

her. "If you and I train for an hour or two every day, I'm sure you'll have mastered dexterity in no time."

"That's optimistic," Victoria muttered, feeling glum. "What can I do until then? I want to be useful to Atlantis."

Athelea's eyes lit up. "Of course," she said. "I don't know why I didn't think of it earlier, but there might be a way to strengthen your dexterity immediately. I cannot guarantee it will work, but it wouldn't hurt to try. If you wait with Sarah for a moment, I'll secure the palace, and we'll be on our way."

Sulking, Victoria followed Athelea outside. She felt an immediate sense of relief being out of the Neutral Room, but the sky had gotten dark while she'd been inside, and it felt like she'd wasted the entire day. Not even the sight of the Garden of the Gods or Sarah sketching cheered her up. Athelea excused herself to run her errands, and Sarah set her sketchbook down and looked at Victoria. "You look grumpy. What's the matter?" she asked.

"As if Athelea didn't tell you this afternoon," Victoria muttered before she could hold the words back. She stared around the Garden of the Gods, avoiding eye contact. Sarah deserved to know what it felt like.

"Right," Sarah said, appearing to hold back a sigh. "What the hell is that supposed to mean?"

"You know exactly what I mean." Receiving no response from Sarah after a few seconds, Victoria sighed.

"Honestly, Sarah, you and Athelea have been exploring Atlantis together these past few days, and I've either been unconscious or studying or preoccupied with other ways of supposedly saving Atlantis. If you haven't realized, I feel miserable and completely excluded."

Sarah looked at her with a dumbfounded expression for a few seconds before taking a seat next to her on the garden bench. "I'm sorry you feel that way," Sarah said cautiously, and very sincerely, "but you're being ridiculous. Athelea worries about you every second you're out of her sight. She's probably even worse than Tom, which I never thought was possible. You don't see it because you're not there, but she is so protective over you. She would love for you to do everything with us, but I can see she genuinely believes you have better things to do."

Victoria had never thought of it that way. "Why couldn't she just tell me that, instead of letting me get the wrong impression? I've felt awful."

Sarah shrugged. "I don't know, Vic. You should probably ask her yourself."

Victoria mused upon those words for a second, and suddenly, all her worries seemed petty. "I'm sorry. I know I've overreacted a bit, and there's no excuse," she said. "I'm lucky to have you as my best friend."

Sarah shook her head, stopping her. "Don't apologize. You're allowed to feel stressed. Just look where we are and what you're doing. You're trying to restore Atlantis. Nobody has ever had to deal with that."

Victoria rolled her eyes at the backhanded reassurance, wondering how exactly she was supposed to help Atlantis. Athelea returned a moment later, wearing a cloak over her dress and had another draped over her arm. "I'm ready to leave, if you are," she said, handing the cloak to Victoria. "Sarah, if you stay on the island, we'll only be gone an hour or so. My protective dexes will follow wherever you go."

Intrigued, Victoria fastened her cloak and followed Athelea to the main island. It wasn't long before she realized they were going into the Eternal Forest. Athelea took an unfamiliar path through the trees to a clearing at the top of a hill, the highest summit on this side of the island apart from Mount Theus. Athelea sat down on the grass and motioned for Victoria to join her. "Look up," she said.

Victoria did. She couldn't help but gasp, understanding exactly what was so special about this place. She'd never seen so many stars in her life, so close that she could swear she could touch any of them. All her frustration about struggling with dexterity and the others leaving her alone in Atlantis seemed unimportant when the universe was so big. "It's stunning," she whispered. She didn't know how else to describe it. "I've never seen anything like it."

Athelea smiled in a way that said she understood

exactly how Victoria felt. They watched the stars in silence for another minute before Athelea spoke. "As I said yesterday, I believe that you're struggling with dexterity because your energy is not entirely focused yet. You haven't been in Atlantis for very long, so that is only to be expected," Athelea said. "However, I believe we can expedite the process. Starlight is one of the most powerful forces in Atlantis. It should help refine your dexterity better than the Neutral Rooms did, and I hope that with a little more practice, you will be able to invoke dexes very soon. Now, if any of the stars permit it, you can take some of their starlight."

Victoria automatically glanced to the sky, her pulse racing. Athelea's words seemed impossible, but Atlantis was the only place where she could begin to imagine them being true. "Really? How?"

"Close your eyes and feel around the sky for a force that connects with you. When you feel it, open your eyes."

Closing her eyes, Victoria turned her thoughts to the sky and quickly found a force pulling at her consciousness, very gently at first. Looking up, had no difficulty finding the small but brilliant star amongst the millions of others. To her, it shone the brightest in the sky, and the gravitational force she'd felt tripled instantly.

And then, a sparkling little voice filled her head.

Atlanteana looks so pretty. She is beautiful. She

shines, too.

Stunned, Victoria turned to Athelea. "Did that star actually talk to me?"

"What do you think?" Athelea asked, smiling. "Stars are notorious for falling in love with Atlanteans. It doesn't happen to everybody, but it is wonderful to behold when it does."

Victoria could only stare, feeling like she'd lost her grasp on reality. Only the grass beneath her fingers linked her to everything she'd thought she knew about the world. "Stars fall in love? With humans?"

"Stars seek love and entertainment through contact with humans, especially Atlanteans," Athelea explained. "Watching over us, a star can spend centuries waiting for the right Atlantean, with whom it forms a bond of unconditional love. They often communicate with each other and form an incredibly close friendship for the life of the Atlantean. Philosophers have regarded it as another form of Forever Love."

It sounded wonderful and fantastical to Victoria, but it didn't make scientific sense. "How do they communicate? Stars are light years away from us."

"Nobody knows. The stars have many secrets they have chosen not to share."

It was so much to process. Victoria didn't know where to begin. "Can you hear this star?"

Athelea shook her head. "It's not my star. Many stars have spoken to me in the past because I'm Atlantean royalty, but I haven't listened to them since I was your age. Atlanteans are terribly vain, and too many compliments make everything worse. The stars do have unbelievable insight into life, though. That's probably what I miss most."

Victoria took a second to process that.

"You should ask the star its name?" Athelea prompted.

Her name, the star corrected. Victoria jumped, still surprised by the tiny voice in her head. *I'm Celeste, or Cel, and Atlanteana shines. She is so pretty. I love her.*

"Her name is Celeste, or Cel," Victoria told Athelea. She already understood exactly what Athelea had meant about Atlantean vanity. "Will the compliments ever stop?"

Athelea laughed. "Maybe, if you ask her enough, but don't waste your time." She became serious. "Now, ask Celeste if she would bequeath some of her light to you? Explain that you need it to learn dexterity, if she wasn't listening earlier."

Atlanteana already shines so brightly, but she can have all the starlight she wants. She is beautiful.

"Cel says yes," Victoria translated. Apparently, stars could hear everything.

"Perfect. Let's begin, then. Looking at her, try to pull some of her energy towards yourself, very gently," Athelea instructed. "Work slowly until you're more comfortable with the process."

Victoria tugged at the connection with her mind. A second later, she felt warmth coursing through her body. A faint stream of light formed between herself and the star a second later, glittering faintly, and when Victoria looked at her hand, her Sentence was glowing with starlight. The process continued for nearly a minute, and Victoria noticed a faint halo forming around her body. In the sky, Celeste flickered serenely.

"Carefully," Athelea reminded them.

Victoria took a breath of fresh evening air and tried to slow the speed of the transfer. For a second, this seemed to help, but then the stream of light began to flow more quickly. Victoria sensed something had gone very wrong. She pulled her hand back instinctively, but the light followed without breaking.

"I can't control it," she said, trying not to panic. Celeste was dimming quickly. "What do I do?"

"Relax," Athelea replied. "Celeste has everything under control. Ask her how she is doing."

Perfectly. Atlanteana is in control. She is so intelligent.

Victoria couldn't help but smile, enchanted by the little voice, until the star suddenly disappeared. Victoria swore under her breath. "Celeste?" she called, heart racing.

Silence. Victoria watched the last ray of starlight pass into her hand. *I've killed a star,* she thought with a sense of horror.

"Don't worry. Celeste is fine," Athelea said, touching her shoulder softly. Despite the reassurance, Victoria felt like she was going to cry. "She gave you too much of the energy she needs to shine. She'll warm up and glow again soon."

Very cold, Celeste agreed a moment later, *and dark.*

Victoria could hear her little voice shaking and felt a wave of guilt crash through her. The meadow suddenly seemed dark and cold, despite the mild night. "I'm so sorry," she whispered. She turned to Athelea. "How long?"

"Anywhere from a few minutes to a few years."

Victoria stared at the glowing imprint her hand had left in the grass, struck with a sense of hopelessness. She'd watched stars in fascination for years, and yet she knew nothing about this kind of starlight and the mysterious ways of Atlantis. She was sure a solution was obvious to Athelea, but she was Atlantean royalty.

"Since Celeste gave starlight to me," she ventured, inspired by the imprint of her hand on the grass, "could I give some back to her?"

Athelea nodded. "It wouldn't hurt to try."

"Same process in reverse?"

"Essentially. Celeste should be able to execute the

process flawlessly, since she is a star. You, however, must not lose focus. Now that she has donated her starlight to you, she can only take it back with your continual permission."

"Fair enough," Victoria agreed. "What next?"

"Ask her to take some of her starlight back."

No, Celeste interrupted. *Atlanteana is so pretty with my starlight. I don't want it.*

Victoria sighed. *Don't be difficult,* she scolded the star silently, though she wasn't sure whether Celeste could hear her thoughts. "She says I look pretty with it. She won't take it."

Athelea smirked. "Let her know how badly you want her to have her starlight back. She'll be far more inclined to do something if you explain how much it means to you."

That seemed logical. "Celeste," Victoria began, trying to put her desperation and apology into her voice, "please take some of your starlight back from me, or I will feel immensely guilty for making you go dark."

A thoughtful pause followed, then Victoria heard a cheerful reply. *Okay.*

Victoria nodded at Athelea.

Athelea smiled approvingly. "If you remember approximately where she is, you can continue."

Victoria reclined on the grass and lifted her hand to the sky, positioning Celeste somewhere between her fingers. Without Athelea saying, she instinctively knew what she had to do. After a few seconds, the starlight concentrated in her hands on her command and began to flow into the darkness in front of her. She watched the halo around her hands dim steadily for a minute, until a tiny sparkle reappeared in the midnight sky.

Much better. Warmer, Celeste said. Victoria heaved a sigh of relief and closed her eyes. *Atlanteana is lovely. I love her.*

"Love you, too," Victoria said, and to her surprise, she meant it. It felt like she and Celeste had been friends for years and understood each other perfectly. A second later, the first cloud of the night passed over the star. Victoria stared at the sky until Athelea stood up.

"The Night Rain will be here soon. We should go," Athelea said. She extended her hand and then seemed to reconsider. "I would help you up, but your body has so much starlight that touching you would cause extreme pain. You can talk to Celeste again tomorrow, though. She isn't going anywhere for a long time."

Victoria laughed. They walked to the Isle of the Gods together, and she marveled at how comfortable she felt with this woman, who had been a stranger only days ago. Athelea said goodbye outside the Royal Tower, and Victoria returned to her bedroom. To her surprise, Sarah was still out on the balcony, drinking tea and seeming engrossed with her latest art. She looked up at Victoria after a few moments and closed her sketchbook with a gasp. "Oh, my god, you're literally *glowing*. What have you been doing?"

Victoria smiled. Even if Atlantis was the most dangerous place she would ever visit, it was the most magical. "I talked to a star named Celeste."

Chapter Twenty
THE BURNT FEATHER

Victoria woke before Sarah, having had another night of restful sleep. She admired the sunrise over Atlantis from the balcony, and she was about to return inside when she suddenly noticed a charred, red feather at her feet. She stared at it for a second, and then stumbled to the nearby railing, feeling faint. She knew without any explanation that Caelan had left it as a warning.

He's going to burn Atlantis, she thought. She knew there was no logical reason to reach this conclusion from a burnt feather, but her intuition sensed this was exactly what it meant. *When was he here? When will he attack?* she wondered. She had so many questions. She carefully picked up the feather and, seeing that Sarah was still asleep, returned inside and hid it under her pillow.

Atlantis doesn't have birds, she realized as she slipped into the new dress Athelea had left overnight. *Caelan must have gotten the feather from somewhere else.* While it seemed to confirm her theory that it was a message from him, it reassured her slightly to think that Caelan ventured out of Atlantis.

In the end, she decided that her worries were too premature to mention the feather to Athelea or Sarah. They were meant to go to the Isle of Time today, and she refused to jeopardize their journey. Athelea arrived shortly after Sarah woke up, and breakfast proceeded as normal. Athelea led an excursion to the East Tower to collect a new batch of candles and perfume, and then left Sarah to sketch in the Garden of the Gods while she and Victoria went to the Neutral Room.

"I'd like for us to meditate for a few minutes," Athelea began. She sat down on the bench in the middle of the room, and gestured for Victoria to follow. "Close your eyes, sit quietly, and try to clear your mind."

Victoria obeyed, though she had too many questions to meditate properly. She sat, still and quiet, until she forgot that she was Atlantis, having the most impossible summer of her life. All she remembered was who she was.

"We're going to try something different today," Athelea said after some time. Victoria snapped back to reality with a nod, ignoring her headache from the room.

"This is another activity to encourage you to become more familiar with your dexterity, but you still won't have to invoke any dexes yourself. Now, if you were Caelan, what would you use if you wanted to destroy Atlantis?"

"Fire," Victoria said automatically.

"We can fight fire with water. Next?"

"Earthquake," Victoria asked, relief coursing through her veins at Athelea's response to her first answer.

Athelea laughed darkly. "Luckily, you have already learned how to fight those. Next?"

Victoria had to think now. "An army? Flooding Atlantis? Drowning us?"

Athelea nodded. "I suspect Caelan favors poison. It is readily available, easy to control, and often difficult to detect. Now, what I've planned for today isn't exactly a dex, but it will be a good test of your dexterity," Athelea said. She held out three shimmering vials, which Victoria could swear she'd produced from seemingly nowhere. "Can you tell me which of these are poisonous?"

Victoria faltered. "Should I know?"

"Take moment to feel their essences and you might."

Victoria picked up the first vial and held it for a second before she was struck with the feeling that she was losing the sense in her hand. It was more uncomfortable than painful, and she held on resolutely until Athelea took it back from her a moment later. She exchanged it for a second vial, which seemed to burn, and a third, which somehow felt frozen. Victoria glanced up warily.

"They're all poisonous."

"Yes, they are," Athelea agreed, producing a fourth vial. Reaching for it with a shaking hand, Victoria felt her headache worsen. The sensation was so much more painful than the previous three combined, physically preventing her body from getting too close. The pain spread to her hand as she made a final effort, and she stopped short in defeat. She was completely unable to touch it.

"Definitely poisonous."

Athelea nodded, smiling widely. "That was remarkable. Two drops of this liquid could have killed you in minutes, but no other poison leaves so faint a trace. Many Atlantean scholars have spent their lives learning to sense it, thereby gaining the ability to detect any amount or type of poison."

She waved her hands and the four vials disappeared.

Victoria blinked, looking back and forth between Athelea and where the vials had been. Even though dexterity looked like magic, Athelea seemed to have control over hers that Victoria sensed was beyond the ordinary. *She is brilliant at everything,* she mused, *even if she doesn't realize it herself.*

"You've done very well," Athelea said. "Don't be discouraged about dexterity, because your sense of your own is definitely growing. Let's collect Sarah and go the Isle of Time."

Victoria couldn't believe how quickly her day was improving. Her headache disappeared as they walked across the Garden of the Gods, and although she was still worried about what Caelan meant by the feather, it was easy to forget it all in the beautiful sunlight. Sarah packed her work away, and Athelea led them towards the island gates.

"Ladies, I'm going to show you how Healing works," Athelea said. She stopped by a bench near the pool and took a second to run her fingers through one of the fountains. Victoria was convinced that the water became clearer, but she wasn't sure if it was a dex or her imagination. "Around the world, the ability to heal immediately is unheard of, but in Atlantis, it is an assumed part of life, thanks to our dexterity. It makes us stronger and even more beautiful. We are rarely plagued with the inconvenience of cuts or bruises or scars."

While she spoke, she'd produced her dagger from her dress. Victoria caught another glimpse of the Sentence on Athelea's wrist and couldn't help but stare, noting that the writing looked different than her own Sentence. But a second later, as the dagger flashed in the sunlight, Victoria realized what was happening. She gasped in horror as Athelea ran the blade across her own palm. The longest second passed before the dagger clattered to the ground, and

Athelea's eyelids fluttered shut.

Victoria felt herself sway, and even Sarah swore behind her. "Athelea?" Victoria said. Something had gone incredibly wrong. She held out her hand, unsure of what else to do, and another second passed before Athelea slumped. Victoria lunged forward and caught her before she hit the ground.

"Athelea, what's wrong?" Victoria repeated.

"It's not healing," Athelea growled through clenched teeth.

Victoria leaned closer. "What? Why not?"

Athelea took an unsteady breath. "There's a power source that fuels dexterity. It must have stopped working."

Victoria felt her heart sink. "Was it Caelan?"

"No. He would never be strong enough to damage it. Atlantis is simply deteriorating."

Victoria refused to dwell on those words for now. Gently opening Athelea's fist, she saw a stream of red and flinched away. *She's probably never been hurt in her life,* she realized. She tore a strip of cloth off the bottom of her dress and wrapped it around Athelea's hand, looking away as soon as she had finished. Athelea smiled unspoken thanks, but Victoria could see she was still in immense pain.

"Can I fix the power supply?" Victoria pressed. "Is there anything I can do?"

"Possibly," Athelea said, after a pause. "The starlight

Celeste gave you should be enough to supply Atlantis for a while. When you reach the Castle, put your hands on the middle of the paving by the foot of the throne and let some of that energy flow back out. You shouldn't lose consciousness, but Sarah will be there to help you if you do."

"Shouldn't Sarah stay with you?"

"You'll need her more than I," Athelea said. She turned to Sarah. "You know your way out of the palace. Look after each other, and I'll wait right here."

Taking her dismissal, Victoria glanced at Sarah, and they started to run. Passing through the main gate and approaching the edge of the cliff, Sarah led the way onto the bridge with confidence, though the structure had been invisible since their first journey across it. They didn't stop running until they reached the Castle. Victoria raced through the old gate into the Keep, sank to her knees in front of the throne, and touched her palms to the stone.

Nothing happened.

"Why isn't it working?" she muttered. She trusted that Athelea had given her correct instructions, but something still didn't seem right.

"You're panicking," Sarah said over her shoulder. "Just concentrate and relax, and you'll be fine."

The physical contact with the stone wasn't enough, Victoria realized. She felt stupid for thinking it would be as simple as touching it. She tried to remember how the starlight had felt on her fingertips when she'd given it back to Celeste, the way it had burned with gentle force and illuminated everything around her, and her fingertips began to tingle. The starlight was waiting.

And then, a secondary instinct kicked in. Victoria realized the starlight wanted to obey her, and that she had guided it successfully before. This time should be no different. With a final push, her hand began to glow, and then, an explosion of light burst from her palms. The stream flowed into the stone, obeying her command. Victoria watched the stone slowly turn a vibrant silver, seeming to pulse with her donated energy. But when her vision flickered, she realized she was losing control. *Not again,* Victoria thought. She took a deep breath, but the air felt suffocating.

"How are you doing?" Sarah asked.

Victoria didn't respond, refusing to lose focus. Her vision was blurring badly, and all she could see now was the ribbon of light. The starlight continued to flow from her hand, and the ache grew into a fire that spread through her body. Victoria began to worry.

"Athelea didn't say when to stop," she gasped, suddenly remembering why she was here. She hoped this process was helping Athelea heal. The stream of light slowly began to fade, seeming to reassure her worries, until Victoria felt the connection extinguish. When she pulled away, a glowing imprint of her hand lingered on the stone. She closed her eyes and collapsed onto the ground, shaking.

"Deep breaths," Sarah said from next to her, engaging her consciousness. "You've done it."

Victoria nodded. A reassuring hand moved to her hair, and she eventually managed a few steady breaths. When she no longer felt faint, she opened her eyes. The bright blue sky and the buildings around her stayed where they were meant to be.

"Do you think it worked?" Sarah asked.

"Should have. I think I did it right."

Sarah smiled. "Everything looked good from my perspective. I've never seen anything like that starlight before."

"You should see it at night," Victoria mumbled. "It's even prettier then."

"I'm sure it is."

Victoria didn't care whether Sarah was sincere or simply agreeing for conversation. She wanted confirmation that Athelea was healing. And more than that, she wished that she didn't have to be in control of everything, if even for just one minute. She closed her eyes and tried to shut out the world, but a second later, the dreadful sound of stone grinding across stone filled the Castle's Keep.

"What was that?" Victoria asked, trying to remember

where she'd heard that sound before.

"The door to the library left of the throne just opened," Sarah said.

Victoria bolted to her feet. She felt a surge of energy as she walked across the Keep, and she knew she would feel like herself again in a few minutes. Through the open door, she could see a torch burning inside the small library, making the room seem warm and inviting. She hesitated, wondering what Atlantis was doing now. "Can you wait out here?" she asked Sarah. "If anything happens, get Athelea straightaway."

Sarah nodded, and Victoria stepped through the opening. To her relief, nobody else was in the room, and the stone doors stayed open behind her. Even though she'd only been here briefly before, she could tell that somebody had been here since her last visit. All the books were back in their shelves.

"Everything okay?" Sarah called.

"Athelea's cleaned up the books since the last time we were here," Victoria said. She noticed now that quite a few of the books were dexologs, and the only book in the entire library that wasn't in a shelf was lying open on the table. Victoria walked up to it, curious to see what Athelea had been reading. From the formation of lines and names across the page, she could tell it was a long and complicated family tree. She ran a finger along the soft parchment, recognizing the name at the very top. *Atlas.*

Victoria hesitated. She didn't want to pry too deeply into Athelea's personal life, but she was too intrigued to stop herself. *She would tell us anyway, if we asked.*

Beneath Atlas were many names Athelea hadn't mentioned. At the bottom, Victoria found Athelea's name linked with Tristan, whose name someone had handwritten as an apparent afterthought. *This might be the royal copy of the family tree,* Victoria mused. *Not many people knew they were married.* Beneath the line joining them together, a single word was written in an elegant script. It wasn't a date, like Victoria had expected, but rather a name that nearly made her pulse stop.

Not Gryffin.

Victoria.

Chapter Twenty-One
THE TRUTH

Victoria didn't say a single word during the journey back to the Isle of the Gods. She had been wrong about Gryffin. Lost in the storm of her emotions, growing from disbelief to confusion to anger, she ignored curious glances from Sarah, who had the intuition to not ask what was wrong. They met Athelea in the Garden of the Gods, and as soon as they confirmed that Athelea's hand had healed, Sarah excused herself to retrieve her notebook from their bedroom. Victoria hoped Sarah had the sense to take her time.

"You should have told me!" Victoria shouted at Athelea, blinking back tears, as soon as Sarah was out of sight. Anger and betrayal burned in her blood. "You left me for seventeen years without one word, and I've always wanted so badly to know my parents! You should have told me the second you saw me here in Atlantis, if you suspected for even a moment that I was your daughter!"

"Would you have believed me?" Athelea asked softly.

Victoria fell silent, knowing what the honest answer was. *Not immediately.* After so many years of believing her parents were dead, it was impossible to imagine any other truth. The more she thought about her relationship with Athelea, the more sense everything made, but she still didn't understand how it was possible. The myths said Atlantis had disappeared thousands of years ago. *I can't have been born so long ago,* Victoria thought. "What does it even matter now?" she returned, evading the answer. "You were probably never going to tell me, anyway."

Athelea flinched at the accusation. "Please sit down and listen to me, Victoria," she said, gesturing to the edge of the pool. After a second, Victoria reluctantly sat down, took off her sandals, and dipped her feet into the water. Now that she'd exorcised her initial anger, she felt slightly more willing to listen. "I knew who you were from the moment I saw you, but I wanted to tell you the truth when I thought you could handle it, and when I was ready to reveal it. I knew how difficult this conversation would be, and naturally, I was hesitant. I stopped telling my story early the other night because I didn't want to overwhelm you, but I see now that was a mistake."

"It was a mistake," Victoria retorted "I knew you were hiding something from me."

"Would you like me to finish the story now?" Athelea prompted. "You can be angry with me forever, but I only ask that you listen for a moment so I can tell you the full truth."

Victoria hesitated one last time. Even if this wasn't how she imagined learning about her parents, she had wanted to know the truth for years. She nodded, knowing she'd never be more ready.

"Do you want to wait until Sarah returns?"

Victoria shook her head. She needed more time to process this news before she believed it herself, let alone dared to tell anyone else. Athelea didn't question her decision, and Victoria took the opportunity to prompt the conversation. She had to hear the words directly from Athelea. "What happened after Tristan left?"

Athelea met her gaze steadily. "My mother was the first to realize I was pregnant with Tristan's child, and she became my support until the end. When my father finally found out the truth, it took him months to accept that I had so explicitly defied his wishes." She lowered her gaze hesitantly, and Victoria could only imagine the arguments that must have followed. "But I gave birth to a beautiful daughter, who is now sitting next to me. In the end, my father loved you even more than he loved Atlantis. He believed the prophecies that you would save the empire, and he was indebted to you until the very end. He repented for separating me from my Forever Love and amended the laws to support our marriage."

Victoria took a deep breath. Even if she hadn't wanted to believe Athelea, she could feel the truth in her blood. It was impossible to deny, however incredible it seemed, and she wondered how she hadn't realized it the second she met Athelea. The Garden briefly flashed out of focus, as her eyes flooded with tears, and she was glad she'd sat down.

"If Tristan had survived the war, I am sure you would have been the focus of his life," Athelea said. She took an unsteady breath, and her eyes overflowed with tears. "I loved you before I ever saw you, and saying goodbye to you during the Destruction, even for your own safety, nearly destroyed me. I had no idea if I would ever see you again, and I am eternally so very sorry it had to be that way. I missed your entire childhood and the chance to see you grow from a beautiful baby into an even more beautiful young woman."

"And we both know what happened after that," Victoria concluded. "Everything I actually know about."

"I was so relieved to see through your memories that Aiden and Andrea have cared for you like their own child, though you share no blood."

Victoria stopped waving her feet in the pool. "They are not related to me? I thought Andrea was my mother's sister."

"I believe your guardians are of Atlantean descent," Athelea said, "which we can confirm later, but they not related to you by blood. I had no family to look after you, but I wanted Atlanteans to raise you so you could maintain some sort connection with your heritage, should you ever return to Atlantis. The dex that I used to send you away guided you to an Atlantean family at a time and place the dex felt was best. I hope they've been the best family and provided the best home you could have wished for."

"They never spoke about it, but they must have known," Victoria said. "I mentioned Atlantis once after I discovered the mirror, and Andrea just walked away. I thought she was furious with me, but I didn't think to ask why."

"I cannot speak on their behalf," Athelea said, "but what I've told you is my complete and truthful story, and I have no more secrets to hide. I'm sorry if you feel I've delayed revealing the truth, but I'm sure you understand how difficult this is for me, too."

Victoria took a deep breath, sensing the importance of this moment. "I'm sorry I got upset with you, too," she said. "It's been a stressful week."

"You are perfectly within your rights to be upset," Athelea said with a smile that indicated all was forgiven. "Out of curiosity, how did you find out?"

Victoria laughed, realizing how unexpected her accusations must have been to Athelea. She relayed the events of the morning, still hardly believing that the woman sitting next to her was her mother.

"A few days before I came to Atlantis, I kept running into this boy in England," Victoria added, deciding that now was time to tell the truth herself. "His name was Gryffin. He had the Sentence on his wrist, and he stole the maps I had drawn of Atlantis. I was absolutely convinced he was your son, but I was terrified to ask you or mention him."

Athelea's eyes widened. "He had the Sentence?"

Victoria nodded. "And he seemed to be skilled at disappearing. I think he has dexterity."

"I don't know how he could be Atlantean, though he does seem to have the traits," Athelea admitted. She looked toward the Royal Tower and stood up, sighing. "Sarah is approaching now. Let's talk more about this boy later. Until then, if you have enough energy, we could still go to the Isle of Time today. It's only noon."

Victoria had nearly forgotten about their excursion. She still had so many questions for Athelea, but they could wait. The prospect of finally being able bring the Atlanteans back was more important. Sarah joined them a few minutes later, and the women made their way to the port on the main island, further down the coast from Shipwreck Beach, without delay.

Victoria had never been here before, but something about the calm harbor charmed her instantly. A wide, stone pier reached towards the horizon, and considering the current population of Atlantis, a surprising number of old boats were tied up along the docks. Some seemed large enough to hold an army, and others were simple rowboats. Victoria suspected they were all more advanced and powerful than they appeared.

"The boat we will use today is at the end of the pier," Athelea said. Victoria felt a pang of sadness as she imagined the port thousands of years ago, with the navy and merchants navigating their vessels through the busy harbor. Every time she thought about how much Atlantis and Athelea had lost, she felt a stronger need to make everything right. *Soon,* she reminded herself, *hopefully.*

At the end of the pier, Victoria saw a simple, wooden boat, like the one she and Sarah had used to travel to Atlantis. If anybody else had told her this would be their method of transport for the day, she would have been inclined to mention that there were many better ships nearby, but she trusted that Athelea had good reasons. Once they were situated, Athelea invoked a dex under her breath, and the boat gently lurched forward. It accumulated speed over the next few minutes, until it was out of the harbor and racing through open water faster than Victoria thought should have been physically possible. She exchanged a glance with Sarah, who didn't look surprised. Victoria remembered she had experienced this before.

"How exactly do these boats work?" Victoria asked.

"It's quite simple," Athelea said. "The boat uses a dex to pair to an Atlantean navigator, who then only has to think about the direction and speed of the journey. The boat does everything else, using some of the passengers' energy."

"I thought it might be something like that," Victoria said. "It explains why Sarah and I felt so exhausted during our journey here." When she looked up, Atlantis was already some distance away. In this summer sunshine, it was easy to forget that they were on a quest rather than a leisurely excursion. *Tom and Nick would love this,* Victoria thought, *but I would never want them to be here if Caelan is around.*

She found her thoughts drifting back to the burnt feather. *How did Caelan get into Atlantis?* she wondered. Without a way to keep him out, she needed to find a way to defend Atlantis. An army of Atlanteans seemed like the only way. *If the Lifeglasses are real, we might still have a hope.*

She snapped out of her daydream when the boat began to slow. They were approaching an island with rugged cliffs and golden beaches. It looked exactly like the island she and Sarah had visited a few days earlier, but they'd done the journey today in less than an hour.

"Is this the Isle of Time?" she asked in disbelief.

Athelea nodded.

"We definitely got the route to Atlantis wrong last time we were both here," Victoria said to Sarah, laughing humorlessly. "That was such a short journey."

"I'm sure it helps knowing how to operate the boat," Athelea said kindly. She tied the boat to the same pier Victoria and Sarah had used, and the three disembarked. Victoria looked around, wondering if she should finally tell Sarah and Athelea about the ghosts in the lake. Now that they were on the island, the omission felt like a mistake.

"Tell me, Victoria," Athelea said, making Victoria jump, "should we proceed directly to the Domain?"

Stop being so paranoid, Victoria scolded herself. *Wait until we know if the Lifeglasses are real.* Avoiding the path by the lake, she led the way to the Domain. Slowly, the sense that she wasn't supposed to be on the island increased as the temple came into view.

"Do you feel that, too?" Athelea said. "Sarah and I noticed it the last time we were here. Ancient Atlanteans invoked a dex to ward off intruders."

"That makes sense," Victoria said. "I felt it last time, too." They were on the Domain steps. Praying that the stone

256

wasn't still blocking the entry to the passageway, she knelt and got to work. The stone slid aside as if it had never been stuck, and Victoria stared down the gaping, black passage, too relieved to feel nervous anymore. Athelea invoked a dex, and torches that Victoria never would have seen burst into flame down the passageway.

Bloody practical dexes, Victoria grumbled inwardly. They were more useful than she wanted to admit.

"I can wait here," Sarah offered. "You need someone to keep guard."

Victoria sensed Sarah was giving her an opportunity to spend time with Athelea. She flashed Sarah a smile, knowing she understood the extent of her gratitude.

"I'll be right behind you," Athelea reassured Victoria. "Go ahead."

Refusing to get her hopes too high, Victoria held her breath and proceeded down the steps. When she reached the bottom, she couldn't quite believe what she'd not seen during her last venture here. It wasn't a funerary crypt, like Sarah had guessed. The enormous, circular room was filled from floor to ceiling with shelves of thousands of tiny hourglasses, glittering serenely in the light of ancient torches.

The Lifeglasses were real.

Chapter Twenty-Two
LIFEGLASSES

Victoria stared with a racing heart at the pile of glass and bright blue sand on the ground in the middle of the floor, exactly where she'd fallen on it a few days before. All the other hourglasses she could see were shelved neatly, frozen in various positions. She guessed that at least two were still moving somewhere in the room, and one of them was her own, but those weren't what she was here for. "Where should we start?" she asked Athelea.

Instead of responding, Athelea began to walk around the room. Victoria followed silently. Up close, she could see that each Lifeglass had a name engraved along its rim in beautiful script. Athelea searched through them, never touching any of them for more than a few seconds to read before she moved on to the next.

"They're sorted by family bloodline, and then by age, I believe," she said at last. "That makes everything quite straightforward."

Victoria nodded, even though there was little she could do with that information. "Are you looking for somebody specific?" she asked, though she suspected she already knew the answer. If she was Athelea, and if Tristan had a Lifeglass, she would be looking for his.

"Family members," Athelea replied simply. After a minute, she stopped walking to flip a Lifeglass over. "It's just a theory, but I suspect it might be easier to bring back an Atlantean with royal blood than common. That was my cousin's Lifeglass. She was my closest friend. I'm afraid the sand isn't moving yet."

The women fell into contemplative silence as they continued around the room. Victoria wondered whether Caelan knew about these hourglasses, and she instantly regretted where the thought led her. If there was one way he could truly ruin Atlantis, it was in this room. *He can never know,* she realized. It was time to be honest with Athelea about her last visit here, before it was too late.

"When I was exploring this island last week, I went into the lake," Victoria said. Athelea immediately looked up from the Lifeglasses, and Victoria took a deep breath. "When I got into the water, I was suddenly surrounded by hundreds of ghosts. They dragged me down to the bottom, and I nearly drowned. Do you think they were Atlantean souls?"

Athelea regarded Victoria with a gentle expression. "I'm sure it was a terrifying experience," she said. She didn't seem angry that Victoria had waited so long to share this information. "To me, that sounds like a dex to frighten intruders. They could not possibly be genuine Atlantean souls."

Victoria sighed. She never would have thought of dexterity, but it was the most obvious explanation. All the hope and fear she'd felt about the ghosts vanished, and the Lifeglasses were now the most promising way of bringing the Atlanteans back and restoring Atlantis. She followed Athelea in silence for a few more minutes, checking whether the Lifeglasses were showing any sign of life, and then returned outside to see if any Atlanteans were there. She found Sarah keeping watch over the monument, and her hopes faltered. The rest of the island was empty and still.

"The Lifeglasses are real," Victoria announced. Sarah gasped, though Victoria thought her excitement was premature. "They're all frozen, so we turned a few over anyway to see what happens."

"Are they moving now?"

Victoria shook her head. "Athelea's still working on it, if you want to see for yourself. I can wait here."

Sarah flashed a reassuring smile before she

proceeded down the steps. *Maybe the Atlanteans will come from the lake,* Victoria thought with a shiver, despite Athelea's earlier reassurance. She watched the water for any sign of color or movement, but after five minutes, nothing had happened. She jumped as Athelea and Sarah materialized through the doorway, neither seeming to have any news or be in any hurry.

"Where are they?" Victoria sighed. "How quickly will they come back?"

"That's an excellent question," Athelea agreed. "None of the books I've read have had any information on how the Lifeglasses work. It is possible that the Atlanteans have already appeared in Atlantis, and we only need to return to the mainland to meet them."

Victoria hesitated. While Athelea had a fair point, she wasn't convinced. "What if they arrive here after we leave?"

"We can come back tomorrow," Athelea said. Victoria sighed, but nobody seemed to notice. "If the Atlanteans were to appear today, they would probably be here already. There's no use waiting around when the process could potentially take time."

"A few days is too late," Victoria said, fighting off the horrible image of Atlantis burning. It was bad enough that Caelan wanted to burn Atlantis, but if he succeeded and the Atlanteans ever came back, they would have nothing left of their homes. After all the hope Athelea had placed in her, she would have failed everyone completely.

But words failed her, and she boarded the boat with Sarah and Athelea. The journey back to Atlantis seemed to last forever. Imagining an army of Atlanteans assembling on the main island, Victoria felt her anticipation grow as the main island came into sight. She had no doubt that Athelea could convince her people to fight against Caelan, and Atlantis would finally be safe. But docking the boat in an empty harbor, Victoria felt her heart fall. The city ahead radiated the same abandonment that Atlantis had known for millennia.

It was foolish to entertain hope, Victoria scolded herself. She numbly followed Athelea to the Hall of Divinity and waited while Athelea lit a candle, her mood worsening by the minute. If the Lifeglasses didn't work, she didn't know who or what could ever have the power to bring the Atlanteans back.

Nobody said a word on the walk to the palace. Victoria wondered whether it would be a good idea to mention the burnt feather now, but she could imagine the news would make Athelea even more overprotective and reckless. She sensed the others were already being careful not to mention the Atlanteans, and she especially didn't want them to be delicate with her about Caelan. *Athelea would never let me out of her sight if she found out,* Victoria decided. *This is my problem to deal with.* As the group of three walked up the Royal Tower, she resolved to find a solution herself.

"Now we wait," she sighed, sinking onto her bed. She desperately wanted a moment to herself to sulk and plan a new strategy, but when the others sat down too, she realized she wouldn't get that anytime soon.

"Now we wait," Athelea agreed with a grim smile. "Let's be patient. We've done everything we possibly could, so whatever happens, I don't want you to feel disappointed. We should congratulate ourselves for having discovered the Lifeglasses. Would either of you like wine?"

"Yes, please," Sarah and Victoria said in unison. Athelea laughed and distributed three generous glasses before moving to the balcony. The view of Atlantis made Victoria feel better instantly. From here, she could look out for both Atlanteans and smoke, or any other sign of activity. The sun was already getting low on the horizon and would set in a matter of hours. Time was running out.

"I could tell you more about Atlantean history," Athelea offered after a few minutes of pregnant silence.

Victoria glanced at Sarah, trying not to keep a neutral face. She wasn't sure she could handle any more revelations this week, though Athelea had promised she no longer had any secrets. Sarah, however, was already looking at Athelea with rapt attention, happily oblivious to Victoria's panic.

"*Atlantean* history," Athelea said with a laugh, but Victoria caught the discreet emphasis that Athelea had intended just for her. She relaxed, realizing that Athelea, too, wanted to keep the conversation neutral. "I would like to teach you real Atlantean history. I suspect that the rest of the world doesn't know the truth."

"What was Atlantis like in the end?" Sarah asked. "Was it as corrupt as the myths say?"

Athelea's expression darkened, and Victoria could see the pain she was trying to hide. "Yes. In the years before the Destruction, many Atlanteans wanted to revise the ancient laws," Athelea said. "However, they feared my father so much that nobody ever dared to suggest it. The Atlantean courts had really been under my father's power for years and never would have gone against him. Our people had lost faith in the monarchy and government, and I don't entirely blame them. Even though we had just won a war, the Atlanteans in power wanted more. They wouldn't rest until Atlantis was restored to its full glory."

"Who were the most famous or infamous Atlanteans?"

"When a demon supposedly killed King Atlas, the Atlanteans needed a new leader. The people felt his son wasn't suitable to reign, though he did take the throne eventually, and they didn't even consider his daughter.

Many generations later, Prince Adrias, King Atlas's descendent, and his beautiful wife were poised to take the throne when Adrias' younger brother, Caitas, murdered him and took the crown for himself. Conflict and instability continued to grow over the next few generations, and our society slowly deteriorated. At some point then, legend says, the Atlanteans received the Sentence. We have had it for generations since."

Athelea held out her right arm, where her Sentence was visible, and Sarah did likewise with her left. Victoria looked down at her own wrist with a new perspective. The black words under the frayed ribbon had become so familiar to her over the past week that she'd almost forgotten they were there. But they had become a part of her now. They were a link to the people of Atlantis, and she loved the Sentence even more for it. After a second, she untied the bow for the first time in a week and set the ribbon on the bed. It felt amazing to have the Sentence exposed, to no longer be ashamed or worried about it. "I never really understood what it meant," she admitted. "Will it ever go away?"

Athelea had been eyeing the ribbon with a proud smile but frowned now. "It is impossible to say. I'm sure Atlanteans have tried every possible method to remove their Sentences, but nothing has ever worked. I haven't researched it myself, but I expect we might finally be absolved and no longer have to carry the curse once Atlantis has a proper, righteous leader."

She glanced at Victoria and then at her own Sentence, her eyes watering with hope. But Victoria knew that after her failures today, she simply couldn't be right the person to help.

The women talked for another hour before Athelea finished her wine and departed. Victoria still felt too restless to sleep and instead listened to the wind and the rain pound on the windows. A bell tolled midnight in the distance, and Victoria wondered whether dexterity powered clocks around Atlantis. In the silence that followed, she could swear she heard footsteps across the room.

"Everything okay?" she asked, wondering for a fleeting moment if this presence was Sarah or an Atlantean. The footsteps continued, and a second later, Victoria found herself standing in the hallway outside her room, facing a shadowy figure she instantly recognized as Caelan. In the faint moonlight, they stared at each other for a few seconds. Victoria was torn between screaming for help and preparing to fight, although she knew she was in trouble whatever she did.

"I see you've discovered starlight. I knew you were very clever," Caelan said evenly.

Victoria detected a hint of admiration or jealousy in his voice. *He doesn't know about Athelea,* she realized, thankful she'd changed into one of her old shirts for the night. She shoved the thought out of her mind, suspecting Caelan wouldn't have been impressed or intimidated if knew how much Athelea had helped her since arriving in Atlantis. "Maybe I have," she replied, matching his steady tone. Behind her back, she felt for the wall and realized Caelan had already cornered her. She took a small step forward, and to her surprise, he took a full step back, increasing the distance between them. *So defensive.* She wondered if he'd overestimated her training and was expecting her to attack first. Pushing her luck, she smiled. "Do you feel threatened?"

"No," he said. Something in her instincts told her this was a lie, but she kept her expression blank, focusing on keeping her mind clear. Athelea's training would never be more important than now. "I'm giving you an ultimatum, Victoria. You have one day to leave Atlantis. If you are still here after sunset tomorrow, I will burn every atom of Atlantis to the ground. If you ever return, I swear I will kill you. The decision is yours to make, and you know the consequences perfectly."

Victoria stared at him, stunned. This threat was different from those he had made before. Hurting her because of a prophecy was one thing, but to destroy Atlantis made no sense. The land was defenseless and innocent. Before she could challenge Caelan, he took another step back and vanished into the shadows.

Even if he was afraid of her now, Victoria didn't need a dex to detect truth to know that he meant every word he had said.

Chapter Twenty-Three
ACHILLES HEEL

An hour later, Victoria was still wide awake. She had tried to sleep, but she felt sick with worry and paranoia. Every sound she heard outside the door or through the window made her jump, even if it was just the wind or rain. She had no idea where to find Athelea to let her know what was happening, or if she even wanted to have that conversation.

Realizing she wouldn't fall back to sleep, she decided she would brave the rain to try to talk to Celeste. She knew leaving her room could be a reckless idea, but she had nothing to lose in return for the star's insight. *Caelan already had his chance to say and do everything he wanted,* Victoria thought, pushing herself out of bed. He'd given her one day of truce, and even though she didn't want to trust him, she did. At least for today, she was safe on her own.

The palace was dark and quiet when Victoria left the Royal Tower. She ventured through the Garden of the Gods to see if she'd run into Athelea and ended up in a small, dark hallway she'd never seen before. In the middle of the hall was an alcove containing a large statue of a man. Victoria was certain she recognized his face from the portrait in the Grand Library. He wore what seemed to be traditional Atlantean robes, cradled a large book to his chest, and had a beautiful bird perched on his shoulder, its feathers carved with careful detail. He had a handsome, kind face and eyes that were full of knowledge and secrets. *It must be Atlas*, she mused. *But what is he hiding?*

And then she noticed the narrow passageway hidden in his shadow. Her curiosity flared as she realized there was just enough space in the alcove for her to squeeze around the statue and explore. She jumped onto the ledge and carefully made her way through the gap, her back pressed against the stone wall. Victoria felt her way along passage and found a set of steps going up. With some hesitation, she began her ascent.

As a faint light at the other end of the passage visible, Victoria realized it was leading to the roof of the palace, which hadn't been visible from any of the towers. The enormous terrace here had an unobstructed view of the sky and the Garden of the Gods. Its perimeter was paved with flat Atlan stone for walking, but the middle was overgrown with tall grass and wildflowers, looking like nobody had cared for it in decades. It was beautiful in an untamed way. Victoria could imagine the royals hosting their most exclusive, extravagant parties here on warm, summer nights and wondered if Athelea had ever been here.

And in the corner of the courtyard was a large, silver block that almost resembled a casket. Victoria approached it, intrigued yet aware that anything could be inside. The stone lid slid off easily, lighter in weight than Victoria had expected, to reveal a bundle of pristine blankets and pillows. Victoria smiled, her apprehensions vanishing. It had probably been centuries since anybody had been here, but she wasn't the first person to stargaze here. She spread out a blanket on the grass, tossed two pillows on top, and looked up.

The stars she could see between the clouds were so beautiful that the drizzle of rain didn't matter. Victoria found Celeste within seconds. The pull she felt towards the little star was weaker than before. *Probably because it's nearly morning,* Victoria thought. She let the warmth of the bond fill her for a few seconds, reassuring her that she knew what to do next.

"Celeste?" she whispered.

Silence. Victoria bit her lip. She felt ridiculous talking to herself, for expecting a star to listen to her from across the galaxy. It would be so easy to lose her grip on reality in Atlantis, but as she wondered what reality was, a little voice broke into her thoughts.

Why is Victoria so sad? a little voice asked.

Victoria opened her eyes, feeling the strength of that gravitational pull explode in a way she could never doubt. Celeste was glowing brighter than she'd been a minute ago. Victoria took a breath and let the entire story flood out.

Make Atlantis fireproof, Celeste suggested once Victoria had finished. Her tiny voice was more serious than Victoria had ever heard it, and it reassured her instantly. *Then he can't hurt Atlantis.*

Victoria thought it could have been a brilliant, simple solution, except for one problem. "I still can't invoke any proper dexes."

You can learn. You can learn very quickly. Or ask Athelea to help.

Another obvious yet flawed suggestion. Victoria shifted uncomfortably. "I can't tell her. She wouldn't let me out of her sight again, and we'd never get anything done. I'm so tired of people worrying about me."

Celeste was silent for a second. *Build an army and fight.*

It's true, Victoria thought, hoping Celeste couldn't hear her thoughts. *Stars are great listeners, but their feedback is less than helpful.* "There are no Atlanteans. We have tried to bring them back, but nothing has worked."

Not yet, Celeste said.

Victoria sat up, her heart racing. "What do you mean? Will they come back?"

Silence followed these words for too long. Victoria had a feeling she'd finally asked the right question. *Stars see nearly everything,* Celeste answered, *but we have many secrets, and there are many things we cannot tell the beautiful humans. I am sorry.*

Sensing an opportunity, Victoria raced for another question. She wanted an answer that Athelea couldn't give her, something that had been bothering her for a few days now. "How is Caelan getting into Atlantis? Athelea has put up defenses to keep Atlantis safe from intruders, but he's gotten right past them. I don't understand. Is he using a portal?"

It is neatly sunrise. We will talk very soon. I love you.

Victoria sighed. Nothing could ever be easy.

The first ray of sun appeared over the horizon, and the conversation ended. Victoria ran her fingers through the grass, wishing she could be the person Celeste thought she was. *Stars have it so easy,* she decided. *All they have to do is shine, and nothing can ever hurt them.*

And then, a horrible realization slowly dawned on her. Unless she found a way to fight Caelan, she would have to leave Atlantis much sooner than she'd hoped. As amazing as the experience was, she refused to put Athelea or Atlantis in danger by staying. There was simply no other solution. She had one day to leave, or she had to raise an army to fight.

She closed her eyes, suddenly feeling exhausted and overwhelmed with responsibility, and when she opened them again a few hours later, it was to a bright day. Victoria swore, never having intended to fall asleep on the roof. She raced back to her room, slowing only to look for signs of life in the Garden of the Gods, but the Atlanteans hadn't returned. She didn't hear worried voices when she reached her bedroom door, so she entered with the hope that her excursion had gone unnoticed.

Sarah was sketching in the balcony. She looked up as Victoria closed the door, her expression immediately conveying relief. "Morning," she said. Victoria could tell she was trying to sound conversational, but she didn't seem upset. "Where have you been?"

"Exploring," Victoria said, omitting the fact that she'd been out all night. "Please don't tell Athelea."

Sarah raised an eyebrow but resumed sketching without any question. Twenty minutes later, Athelea joined them, wearing another black dress and carrying the usual basket of beautiful fruit. Victoria had lost her appetite, but she made an effort to join the conversation and drink her tea, hoping it would keep her alert for the day. She would have to be on her best form to avoid raising suspicion. She relaxed slightly when breakfast finished and Athelea brought them to one of her workshops to collect candles to bring to the Hall of Divinity. The room smelled amazing, tempting her for a moment to forget her worries. She and Sarah exchanged glances when Athelea wasn't watching.

"Have you got any other exciting secrets to tell us, then?" Sarah asked when they returned to the Garden of the Gods. Victoria snapped back to reality, thinking for a second that Sarah had been talking to her. She reminded herself that they still didn't know anything about Caelan. Her paranoia would give her away soon if she wasn't careful.

"Not that I can think of at the moment," Athelea said. Victoria heaved a sigh of relief that nobody had noticed her paranoia. "But I thought we could make a quick excursion to the Isle of Time."

"You can go without me," Victoria suggested. "I should stay here to keep watch for Atlanteans."

"If that is what you want, Sarah and I can make the journey," Athelea said. "We won't be gone more than a few hours, which should be ample time for you to study dexologs or do whatever you wish while you wait."

Victoria felt a surge of disappointment. "I'm tired of all these dexes that don't seem to help anything. I've met Caelan a few times now and managed to escape only by luck. Atlantean magic had nothing to do with it," she said. And even if she had no intention of reading dexologs, the mere suggestion annoyed her.

"Victoria," Athelea said, interrupting her thoughts, "do not underestimate how important dexterity is. I appreciate that you still find it difficult, but you must persist. Atlantis would be a much more dangerous place without it."

"I won't stay behind if I can't roam around the main island," Victoria said. "I don't want to be locked in the Grand Library like last time."

Athelea sighed. "I suppose you can roam. You should spend your time how you see appropriate."

The others departed for the harbor, and Victoria took a few more minutes to admire the workshop. *Athelea does so much around Atlantis,* Victoria thought. She realized it more every day she was in Atlantis, and it made her proud that this woman was her mother. *It's amazing she has the time and energy to do everything she does.*

Victoria finished her tour of the tower and got to work on the main island. She checked on the Broken Portal, only to find it was still inactive, and then read a few dexologs in the Library to make Athelea happy. Every sound she heard filled her with hope that the Atlanteans had returned, until she realized it could equally be Caelan. *Would he really burn Atlantis?* Victoria wondered. *He wouldn't make an empty threat. There must be something holding him back from doing his worst damage.*

She eventually sat down on the grass in the Plaza to wait. She had a feeling that if the Atlanteans did return on this island, it would be in this magical place. After a while, she found her thoughts wondering to what the truth about her heritage meant. Aiden and Andrea had walked in this Plaza once but had never told her about Atlantis. Apart from their recent argument, Aiden and Andrea had been the best family she could have asked for, but she didn't know how their relationship would be the same after such astounding deception. She could understand why they hadn't told her the truth, but the revelation that even one of her parents was still alive filled her with a sense of being unwanted.

Athelea had valid reasons to send you away, she reminded herself. *There's no point dwelling on the past.*

Sarah and Athelea found her in the Plaza an hour later. Victoria could tell from their expressions that the Isle of Time had been deserted, and they took a boat out to sea after lunch without any mention of their excursion. Victoria sulked while Sarah taught Athelea how to fish. She would have to think of a solution soon if the Atlanteans didn't return, or Atlantis would be burning in hours.

Caelan could come back any time.

"It's been a while since we practiced dexterity, Victoria," Athelea said when they returned the boat to the harbor. They had caught quite a few beautiful fish, but

Victoria wasn't any closer to deciding how to fight Caelan. She couldn't do anything without the Atlanteans. "Shall we try again in a Neutral Room?"

Victoria agreed to practice dexterity, and she and Athelea left Sarah in the Grand Library to draw. Victoria attempted to focus her thoughts while she and Athelea walked back to the Isle of the Gods, though she knew she would be doing meditation exercises in a few minutes regardless. They passed through the palace gate in silence, and as she stepped into the Garden of the Gods, she felt herself swoon. She held up her hand, stopping without a word.

Athelea looked at her in alarm. "Is everything alright?"

Victoria shook her head. Closing her eyes, she fought off another wave of nausea. For a moment, she thought she'd gotten too much sun out on the boat, but a horrible feeling was overwhelming her, radiating from the middle of the Garden of the Gods. As she forced herself to walk closer to the middle of the courtyard, her discomfort grew even stronger, and when she was a few steps away from a large circle of Atlan stone filled with water, she understood exactly what had happened. It was a well. "Something about the Garden doesn't feel right," she said, turning to Athelea. "I think the water is poisoned."

Chapter Twenty-Four
POISON

Athelea stopped dead in her tracks. Victoria could see this news had surprised her. "Don't you feel it, too?" Victoria asked.

Athelea shook her head. "I don't understand. This is the water we drink. It was fine this morning." She waved her hand, and a moment passed before the water turned the color of fresh blood. Victoria exchanged a dark glance with Athelea, feeling sick. "There is enough poison in the water to kill a herd of elephants. It's no wonder you sensed it."

Victoria shuddered. "What kind of poison is it?"

"I don't recognize it. I do not believe, however, that it originated in Atlantis."

Victoria felt an unexpected surge of relief push through her nausea. "Does that mean Caelan isn't staying in

Atlantis?"

"The evidence would suggest so."

Victoria felt her heart soar. Along with the burnt feather, the evidence did seem to prove that Caelan wasn't hiding in Atlantis. "Can you fix the water?"

"I can treat it easily enough," Athelea said. "It depends how the water has been poisoned. I should be able to make an antidote or, as royalty, can overrule practically any dex in Atlantis. It may not take effect immediately, but we will have drinkable water by the evening. You should probably sit down. This might take a minute, and you look rather faint."

Victoria took a seat on the nearest bench without being asked again. Athelea leaned over the well and began to invoke a dex. When she stood up a minute later, frowning, Victoria couldn't see any difference in the water, though that was hardly indicative of progress. She still felt too sick to function properly.

"That was a generic dex for water purification," Athelea explained, "but it doesn't appear to have worked. I believe the poison is combined with a dex that makes it difficult to purify. Fortunately, whoever made it seems unaware that I have the power to revoke any dex. If you would allow me a moment, I will look for an antidote in the Garden."

Victoria nodded meekly. The longer she was near the

well, the worse she felt. Athelea disappeared for a few minutes and returned holding a handful of flowers that Victoria didn't recognize. She threw them into the water and began to walk around the pool, repeating a new dex under her breath. Victoria felt a shiver run through her body. Whatever this dex was, she could feel it was incredibly powerful.

With each circuit Athelea walked around the pool, the water became less red, until it was finally back to its beautiful shade of blue that mirrored the sky. The flowers disappeared in a burst of smoke, and Victoria instantly felt normal again. "That should be it," Athelea said, returning to Victoria with a smug smile. "At least you detected the poison before it was too late. Shall we proceed?"

Victoria didn't know how Athelea could be so calm, but she followed Athelea through the Garden, regretting that she'd agreed to practice dexes. It seemed like playing a silly game in the middle of a battlefield. *We might not have known about the water if I hadn't agreed,* she reminded herself. *Maybe Caelan won't come back now.*

The glimmer of hope lasted until she returned to the Neutral Room. She hated how the room made her feel disconnected, like she was missing an important part of her unconscious of which she was never usually aware. She suspected that the Atlan fire was interfering, too, even if Athelea said it was there to help. The familiar headache returned within a few seconds, and Victoria would have rather turned around and walked back into the Garden of the Gods.

"You remember the process of blocking your mind from the other day, I'm sure," Athelea said after she had led Victoria through a series of meditation exercises. "With your permission, we will try that again. The best way for you to learn is through practice."

Victoria took a deep breath. She'd known that coming to Atlantis wouldn't exactly be a holiday in the sun, but this was much more difficult than she'd expected. She closed her eyes, trying not to think of all the civilized places she could have visited instead, but with a gentle breeze on her face, her thoughts returned to the Neutral Room. She could never escape Atlantis. Feeling the full force of Athelea touching her thoughts, her resistance collapsed, and she thought of Tom. The summer before, they'd spent long nights talking in the garden, and she had never wanted it to end. Everything seemed so different now.

"I can't do it," she sighed after a few more unsuccessful attempts at blocking her mind. "I just can't do any of this dexterity stuff. I'm trying so hard, but you're still able to read me like a book."

Athelea frowned sympathetically. Victoria didn't think it was much consolation. "I can tell you're anxious about the poison, and you're letting those thoughts overpower your concentration. Don't say you can't, though. You detected the poison, and you must believe that you'll discover the rest of your dexterity soon."

"Of course I'm worried about the poison. If I hadn't discovered it in the well, we would have drunk the water and died," she snapped. "Caelan's efforts to harm us and Atlantis are becoming more successful every day, and it terrifies me that he might one day succeed. I might discover dexterity eventually, but it won't be soon enough." Pushing her loose hair away from her face, she took a deep breath. *You've got to find your dexterity,* she thought. She was just about to suggest another attempt at the dex when she suddenly realized something.

"You said the other day that royals often have a natural affinity with dexterity," she said, "but I can't even manage a stupid dex coloring book. I've gotten starlight from Celeste, and even that hasn't helped. Is something wrong with me?"

Athelea sat down on the bench and gestured for Victoria to join her. "Nothing is wrong with you," she said gently. Victoria couldn't hear any doubt in her words. "As I have been saying these past few days, you haven't been in Atlantis for very long. Your body is unaccustomed to this new energy, even with the starlight to help. Like anything, it takes time to learn dexes. I am terribly sorry if the coloring book offended you, but at least the poison confirmed without a doubt that you have dexterity. Not every Atlantean does. You just need to find it."

"Could we stop for now, please? I'm not up for training at the moment."

"Of course. You must be terribly homesick," Athelea ventured.

Victoria nodded. For half a second, the thought of Tom's proposal to take a gap year together seemed to suffocate her, but she remembered that she wasn't the first generation to experience forbidden love. "It's difficult being away from Tom. We've never been apart this long."

"I can tell you miss him," Athelea said softly.

"Terribly," Victoria said. "He asked me to go to university with him, or take a gap year together."

Athelea smiled at her with sparkling eyes. "And what did you tell him?"

"I had to say no," Victoria said flatly. She didn't want to talk about this right now, and she could feel her mood sinking even lower, but she knew Athelea understood the situation better than Aiden and Andrea had. "The decision wasn't mine to make. Aiden said they wouldn't pay my tuition if I go with Tom. They're worried he'll be a distraction from my education."

Athelea swore under her breath. "That is such an obsolete, Atlantean way of thinking. Nobody should tell how to live your life. Especially if you love Tom as much as

I sense, they should know better."

"Tell that to them," she muttered. "Apparently, I'm too young to think for myself."

"I'm so sorry," Athelea said. "You love him very much."

"More than anybody in the world."

Athelea buried her face in her hands. "Please forgive me. My decision to send you away has had so many consequences I had not anticipated. I can no longer talk to your guardians, but when you see them again, inform them that I personally consent to your whatever plans you make for your education or future. Accept my apology for all the pain that my lack of foresight has caused you."

Victoria wasn't sure Aiden and Andrea would be convinced. It was still so strange to think that they were Atlantean. "Will they know who you are?"

Athelea laughed with dangerous softness. "They should still be familiar with Atlantean history, unless they've completely forgotten who they are. You should talk to them when you get home. Your time here will have given a new depth to your relationship."

Victoria felt her heart soar with gratitude to Athelea while it simultaneously broke. She was gathering the parts of her future together, when it had seemed so impossible only a week ago. Tom would be at her side, and her relationship with her family would recover, but it would mean leaving Athelea someday. "Thank you so much," she whispered.

"You're welcome," Athelea said with a smile. "There are special mirrors in Atlantis which allow the viewer to Watch something or someone else. I can't guarantee it'll work, but you might find it reassuring to Watch Tom."

Victoria gaped at Athelea, who clearly hadn't realized the potential of this dex. "Could we see Caelan?"

"*Watch* him," Athelea corrected, not showing the surprise Victoria expected at the suggestion. "I hadn't considered that possibility, but I know nothing about him, so I doubt I'd be able to Watch him regardless. You might have more success, if you'd like to try."

"Yes, please," Victoria said. She wished Athelea had mentioned this days ago, but the possibility of being able to monitor Caelan mitigated her annoyance. She would be able to see if he intended to burn Atlantis.

"Follow me," Athelea said. Victoria stood up, happy to leave the oppressive air of the Neutral Room behind. Sarah had walked to the Isle of the Gods while they'd been there. They said hello quickly, and Athelea and Victoria continued through the Garden to the Royal Tower, up a single flight of steps, and into a small room that was nearly empty, except for basic bedroom furniture.

"I remember the dex," Athelea said, closing the door

behind her. She picked up a handheld mirror from the table and spoke a few words Victoria didn't understand before handing it over. Victoria couldn't see what was so special about it. Apart from its beautiful frame, it looked just like an ordinary mirror she would have in England.

"Try your best to imagine where Caelan is. When you're ready, look into the mirror," Athelea said. "It would probably be easier if you had something of his to connect you, but we must work with what we have."

Victoria stared deep into the mirror, wanting nothing more than to see Caelan, but the mirror only showed her own reflection. She sighed, trying to ignore how ridiculous she felt trusting in Atlantean magic. *Watching would have been far too simple a way to learn if Caelan is going to start a fire.*

"I can leave you alone for a moment, if I'm distracting you," Athelea offered. "I'll invoke a dex on the room to keep you safe and wait with Sarah in the Garden."

Victoria shrugged, genuinely indifferent, and Athelea left the room without another word. Victoria tried to think of a place she knew better, just to see if the dex on the mirror worked. When she held up the mirror, she no longer saw her reflection, but rather a perfect image of her new bedroom in England. For a moment, the scene was how exactly how she'd left it last week.

And then, Tom entered her room.

287

He was wearing dark jeans and the light blue shirt that Victoria loved, and there was sadness in his eyes as he surveyed the room. In one hand, he held a large envelope that probably contained her copy of a university prospectus. He set the envelope on her desk, looked at the door and, after a moment's hesitation, carefully ruffled through the other papers on the desk. He glanced around the room, and then at the mirror, and Victoria suddenly felt as if he could see her in the reflection. They both sighed at the same time, and Victoria stopped Watching with a gasp.

What was Tom looking for?

With an aching heart, Victoria tried to think of what Tom could have found on her desk. Most of the documents and booklets there were from universities, but she knew he already had copies of his own. She'd hidden her journal in the top drawer of her desk, but if Tom found it, he would know everything about the orb, the Sentence, the mirror, and her visits about Atlantis. *Tom would never touch my journal,* she reminded herself. To read her most personal thoughts would be a complete invasion of her trust and privacy, but it occurred to her that there was something even worse he could find.

The maps.

And she knew, even if she hadn't Watched it, that Tom was coming to Atlantis.

Victoria set the mirror down and raced out of the

room to find Athelea. *The mirror in my room didn't look like a portal. Tom could never physically manage the journey on his own. Sarah and I barely managed with the help of the portal and the boat,* she thought. *Even if he found a way, he would be walking into danger.* She could imagine nothing worse than Tom and Caelan fighting each other.

"I think Tom is coming to Atlantis," she gasped when she found Sarah and Athelea drinking wine by the pool in the Garden, "I Watched him find maps in my room."

"Really? That's great news," Athelea said, a smile lighting her face. "It would be wonderful to meet him, and you must be incredibly excited to see him again."

"No, I don't want him to come to Atlantis!" Victoria wanted to shake Athelea. It was clear that she didn't understand the severity of the situation, though Sarah at least looked concerned. "He could be in danger."

Finally seeming to understand, Athelea set her glass down and gave Victoria her full attention. "Did you ever tell him about Atlantis?"

For the first time since having that fateful dream, Victoria felt a massive wave of relief that she'd never said a word to Tom about Atlantis. The truth was their only secret. "No, never."

"Then why would he would come to Atlantis?" Athelea pressed gently.

"Because he loves me," Victoria sighed. It should

have been obvious to the others. "I'm sure he's worried because I left home so suddenly and haven't responded to any of his texts for days. Now he feels like he has to be a hero and rescue me."

Athelea folded her hands and looked at Victoria. "Don't worry," she said, sounding calmer than Victoria felt. "Even if Tom wanted to look for you, he has no way to get here and no knowledge of where Atlantis is."

"I tried to draw the maps I'd seen in my visits," Victoria sighed, wishing she'd destroyed the evidence before she left. "Every attempt came out wrong, but Tom wouldn't know that if he found them. He could get lost following my stupid scribbles. He could die, or Caelan could find him."

"You told him you were looking at universities with me," Sarah reminded her. "I can't see any reason why he would think otherwise."

Victoria prayed Sarah was right, but she couldn't ignore her instinct that Tom would set off to find her the instant he knew where she really was. Athelea poured a third glass of wine, seeming intent on getting Victoria to relax. At sunset, Athelea led an excursion to light another candle in the Hall of Divinity before the Night Rain started, but even that didn't help. "You can Watch Tom again tomorrow, if that reassures you," she said when they returned to the palace. "I can see you're distressed, but he will be fine."

Victoria nodded. Now that she had a future with Tom, she could only pray that he never found out about Atlantis, or their future might never happen.

Chapter Twenty-Five
TRAPPED

Despite everyone's reassurances and distractions, Victoria felt on edge for the rest of the evening. As the sky became dark, she became aware that Caelan could return any minute to set fire to Atlantis. She didn't enjoy the wonderful meal Athelea made, or the stories Athelea told about Atlantis, as much as she wanted. Midnight approached without incident, and Victoria wondered what was delaying Caelan. Once Athelea had gone to sleep, sleep, she braved the Night Rain and ventured to the palace rooftop to talk to Celeste.

Hello, Celeste chimed. Her voice was barely audible. *How are you this evening?*

Victoria sighed. "I'm worried that Tom is coming to Atlantis. I'll watch him in the morning if Athelea and Sarah go to the Isle of Time again to look for Atlanteans."

You don't sound very happy.

"I want them to look," Victoria said. "I do want the Atlanteans back, and Sarah and Athelea are doing what they have to. But I still feel like I'm not personally doing enough to help." She paused, and took a deep breath. "Did you know Athelea is my mother?"

Celeste was silent for a second. *Yes.*

Victoria had already guessed as much, but she was more hurt than angry that Celeste had withheld this information. "Why didn't you tell me?"

Some things you must learn on you own. We stars watch and listen, but we never interfere.

"I suppose," Victoria sighed. "Do you think I should tell Sarah?"

I do not think it would do any harm. She is your very best friend.

Victoria smiled. Stars never gave direct answers. "I don't know if I'm ready to tell her yet."

Sarah can help you. You do not have to face every obstacle in life by yourself.

"Everybody says that," Victoria complained. Celeste was right, though. She hated keeping secrets from Sarah, and there was no reason why she couldn't tell her about Athelea. She'd grown to accept the truth over the past few days, and sharing it with others now seemed the natural progression.

"Why did Athelea send me away, Cel?" Victoria asked. It was one of the few questions that had bothered over the past few days, but voicing it for the first time eased the sense of abandonment she'd been entertaining. "I always assumed my parents had died when I was young, since Aiden and Andrea never told me otherwise. I shouldn't feel unwanted, but I am hurt by the fact that Athelea gave me up."

I think you should ask Athelea herself, the star replied. Her voice was even fainter than before.

Victoria sighed. "Can you tell me about Tristan? What was he like?" she pressed, deciding she could push her luck a little further. She wasn't surprised that the star remained silent, and a minute passed before she spoke again, more to herself than anyone. "What would Tom say if he was here?"

Celeste was silent.

Victoria sighed. Tom would absolutely adore Atlantis, but it would also upset him more than anyone that the island was abandoned and in such poor condition. He would think Athelea was amazing because she was Victoria's mother, and he would try to fix the island and make everything better. The thought made Victoria smile, though she could feel her heart breaking. In so many ways, it was a curse and blessing that he didn't know. Feeling exhausted and slightly reassured, she returned to her bedroom and finally allowed herself to sleep.

There was still no sign of fire in Atlantis when she woke up.

"I think you and Sarah should go back to the Isle of Time today," Victoria said to Athelea after breakfast. She'd only slept a few hours and had barely been able to eat because of her nerves. She couldn't wait much longer. Every minute they waited put her more on edge that Tom had left England and was heading into terrible danger. She needed to Watch him again. "The Atlanteans aren't on any of these main islands. I really think someone should check the Isle of Time, just in case, but I should probably study more dexes."

"Are you sure?" Athelea asked.

Victoria nodded, trying not to show how desperate she was for time for her own agenda.

Athelea hesitated. "Very well."

Victoria waited a few minutes after the others had left before she setting off for the room where she'd Watched Tom before. The door was still unlocked, and the mirror was where she'd left it on the table. She heaved a sigh of relief. Hoping the dex Athelea had invoked on the mirror still worked, she stared into her reflection and prayed to the stars she would be able to Watch Tom again.

A second later, her reflection morphed into an unexpectedly bright scene. Tom was in a park that Victoria knew was just around the corner from his home. He typed a message on his phone before he resumed reading the prospectus at his side. Victoria was sure that back in England, her phone was chiming. She heaved a sigh of relief as she put the mirror down. Athelea had been right. Tom was still in England, and he didn't seem to have any plans to leave.

With relief obliterating her fears, she ventured to the Reflector, then the Grand Library. She tried the coloring dex again to no avail, though failure didn't upset her anymore, and contented herself with studying dexologs. *Sarah and Athelea must be back by now,* she thought in the late afternoon. The day felt long without activity and conversation. She returned to the palace and checked the bedroom while she was at this end of Atlantis. There was a note on the table that hadn't been there this morning. Victoria picked it up, annoyed that the others hadn't found her directly. *Meet me at the port when you get this,* it said.

Victoria tossed the note onto the table and headed back to the main island. She hoped Athelea and Sarah would be waiting for her with good news, or maybe even an invitation to go back to the Isle of Time. But their boat wasn't at Shipwreck Beach or the harbor. *They probably docked somewhere else and went to the Grand Library to look for me,* Victoria realized.

She strolled down the pier while she waited, deciding

it would be best to stay in one place until the others found her. The sun was getting lower on the horizon, and Victoria sat down at the edge of the dock to enjoy the view, wondering if any of the old Atlanteans would ever do the same. The dock creaked behind her, and before Victoria turned around, a pair of hands put pressure on her shoulders, keeping her in place.

"Oh, my stars, you scared me," she gasped. "I didn't hear you coming."

"I would be surprised if you had," a male voice said, and Victoria immediately understood. Sarah and Athelea weren't coming. They probably weren't even on the island. The note had been a trap, and she'd fallen for it without any hesitation.

"Caelan."

"I believe, Victoria, that it has been more than one day since I last spoke to you. I permitted you more time that I had intended, yet you are still in Atlantis. How very reckless. I had hoped better of you."

Victoria bit her lip to keep it from trembling. "I'm not afraid anymore," she lied. She tried to remember whether Athelea had invoked a dex on her that would keep her safe, though the fact that Caelan had already touched her didn't bode well. "I'm stronger now. I can fight back."

Caelan released her, and she took the opportunity to face him while she could. It only took her a second to realize he'd trapped her on the pier, with no way to escape. "And yet I know Atlantis infinitely better than you do," he returned. Victoria didn't doubt him. "I'm going to turn it against you. You will watch hopelessly while the city burns, and you will soon forget why you ever came to Atlantis."

And then he's going to drown you, she thought, a sense of dread filling her. There was no other reason for him to bring her to the harbor. It seemed so simple. Whether or not he knew, Sarah and Athelea probably wouldn't be back for another hour. Even though they would probably realize the truth eventually, there would be no witnesses, nobody to stop the fires from spreading, and everything would look like an accident.

Caelan took a hold of her again and began to march her further down the pier. The end wasn't far away now. Victoria took a deep breath, trying to stay calm. The water would be deep here, and she wouldn't have a chance of survival if he tried to drown her. But to her surprise, Caelan stopped a few seconds later, next to a smaller ship with black sails.

"After you," he said, gesturing to the plank.

Victoria hesitated, trying to understand his plan. Drowning was unlikely if he was putting her on a ship. *He's going to lock me up and take me somewhere,* she realized. She was going to end up in another prison and waste away in a slow death. Between that and drowning, she was sure that whatever he had planned was worse.

"I'm waiting," he reminded her.

Victoria sighed and stepped onto the ship. Caelan led her to the steps in the middle of the deck and marched her downstairs to the heart of the ship. "This boat will be out of Atlantean waters by midnight," he said. He stopped in a large, empty room lit only by portholes, and Victoria felt her body lock involuntarily under the influence of some horrible dex that Caelan had invoked. "By then, Atlantis will have burnt to the ground, destroyed forever. I am sorry to say that everything you have done and everything you have learned has been in vain."

I'm going to die here, Victoria realized. Caelan released his grasp on her to open a small door she hadn't noticed next to him, and she found herself taking a few involuntary steps through it, her body feeling disgustingly like a puppet that only Caelan could control. Despite the fog in her thoughts, she understood what the threat in his words meant. He closed the door before she could resist any of his dexes, leaving her in complete darkness.

"Goodbye, Victoria. I'm truly sorry it had to end this way."

The lock clicked into position. Caelan's footsteps faded as he returned to the upper deck, and then they silenced completely. After a minute, Victoria felt her body relax as the dex keeping her petrified seemed to loosen.

Caelan's leaving, Victoria thought. When she regained full control of her body, she was able to panic.

Her prison was a cupboard. She could only take half a step in any direction before finding herself against a wall. There was no handle on the inside of the door, and a simple push against it confirmed that Caelan had locked it properly. Victoria felt a stab of annoyance that she hadn't mastered an unlocking dex for emergencies like this. *Those dexes are actually useful,* she reprimanded herself. After hitting the door a few times, she sat down and began to cry. Atlantis was going to burn. There was nothing she could do but pray that Sarah and Athelea would either return with an army, or return quickly enough to fight the fire themselves.

An hour seemed to pass, even though Victoria knew from her watch that it had been barley half that time. She regretted not telling Sarah and Athelea about Caelan's previous visit. She imagined he'd already started his crusade in the heart of the city, where he could wreak the most havoc in the least time. The Night Rain wouldn't fall for hours, if Caelan hadn't put a dex on his fire to keep it burning. If Sarah and Athelea brought their boat directly back to the main island from the Isle of Time, they might stand a chance of minimizing the damage.

He could have put me in a burning building instead of here, she suddenly realized. *Why didn't he?* The question occupied her until a much worse thought occurred to her.

When Sarah and Athelea failed to find her, they would never know she hadn't met that horrible fate. They probably wouldn't even notice that a ship was missing, let alone think she'd been on it. And unless they found her by chance, it seemed unlikely that there would be a way of tracking her. *Caelan must have known about Sarah,* she reminded herself. *He would take precautions.* It didn't feel like he'd put a dex on the ship to make it move out of the harbor faster, but she had no way to know for sure.

Another hour seemed to pass.

"Victoria?" a voice called in the distance. Victoria froze, wondering if she'd imagined it. The sound was muted through all the wood of the ship, but Victoria would have recognized the voice anywhere. Sarah didn't sound terribly far away. "Are you here?"

Victoria felt her heart soar. "I'm on the ship with black masts!" she shouted. She began pounding on the door. "I can't get out!"

A few seconds passed with no response. "Victoria?" Sarah repeated. "Can you hear me?"

Any hope Victoria had felt vanished. The ship was too far away from the pier by now, its layers of wood too thick for Sarah to hear her from the pier. Victoria held her breath, listening carefully for what Sarah would do next. She hoped that the lone ship floating in the harbor would be enough to raise suspicion. She heard a splash a second later and hoped that Sarah had jumped into the water.

Please come to the ship, she prayed.

Half a minute passed before the splashing stopped. Victoria hoped Sarah had been swimming closer, and a few seconds later, she heard light footsteps on the deck above. Her heart soared.

"I'm downstairs!" Victoria shouted, pounding on the door. She had a terrible feeling that Caelan had made the room soundproof with a dex, expecting that someone would look for her. She could hear footsteps going down the stairs now, and Sarah finally stopped in front of the door. Holding her breath, Victoria listened to as a key the lock and click. The door swung open without any further warning, and Victoria launched herself into Sarah's arms.

"Sarah," she gasped, "I'm so glad you're here."

Sarah was soaked from swimming to the ship, and she'd never looked more worried. "Are you okay?"

Victoria shook her head. "Caelan was here," she said. "He's going to burn Atlantis to the ground. "We need to go."

Sarah sighed and helped Victoria walk up the stairs to the deck. The boat hadn't drifted quite some distance from the pier, but not too far to swim back. "Look at Atlantis. Do you see smoke anywhere?"

Victoria shook her head. The sky was clear apart from a few early clouds, and she couldn't see smoke or any sign of fire.

"Then we can take two minutes for you to calm down," Sarah said. "The ship is drifting, though. Let's swim back to shore and talk there. If we leave the ship for now, Athelea can get it later."

"Or leave it," Victoria muttered, standing up. "Then Caelan will think I've gone."

"We can see what Athelea thinks is best," Sarah said. She dove overboard, and Victoria followed. The water was beautifully warm, and setting foot onto the beach, Victoria felt a sense of calm begin to return. She sat down next to Sarah on the sand, shaking. She had so many questions.

"Are the Atlanteans back?"

"We didn't see anyone at the Isle of Time."

Victoria swore. She wasn't going to have an army to fight Caelan. "Same here. How did you unlock the door?"

"This key," Sarah said, touching her necklace. On it was the key that Victoria had found on the ship at Shipwreck Beach. "I looked around the palace when you and Athelea were busy the other day, and from what I could see, it opens a lot of locks. Maybe every lock."

"It must be a dex," Victoria said, feeling relieved she'd let Sarah keep the key. "How did you know where to find me?"

"You left a note on the table in our room. I found it."

Victoria shook her head. "Caelan left that for me. I

fell for it, too."

"Anybody would have," Sarah said, giving her another hug. "I'm just glad it showed me where to find you. What did he want this time?"

Victoria knew she could no longer withhold the truth. "He came to the Royal Tower a few nights ago when you were sleeping and told me he would burn Atlantis to the ground if we were still around."

Sarah stared at Victoria with an indignant expression. "You should have told us straightaway!" she said. "He's dangerous, but I'm sure Athelea could have helped!"

"I didn't want you to worry," Victoria muttered. Saying it now, she could hear how weak her excuse was. "Athelea is too protective sometimes. She'd never let me do anything she thought was remotely dangerous."

"We should find her and tell her what's happened. We can fight Caelan. There's three of us, and only one of him."

You don't understand, Victoria wanted to say. *He's too strong.* But there was no point hiding what she was thinking now. In the last hour, everything had changed. "Sarah," she said, "I don't want to stay in Atlantis."

"What?" Sarah asked. Her emerald eyes were wide with surprise. "Why not?"

Victoria took a deep breath and let a handful of sand

run through her fingers before she spoke. "I feel like I've been causing problems for Atlantis ever since we arrived here. I have no idea how to bring the Atlanteans back, and I can't use dexterity to fix anything. I want to leave before anything goes seriously wrong because of me."

Sarah shook her head. "We'll talk to Athelea. I'm sure she'd disagree that you're causing problems, but I can see you're shaken by what's just happened."

"Of course I am," Victoria snapped. She could hear the edge of hysteria in her own voice. "Caelan's trying to kill me."

Victoria felt tears stream down her face as the enormous pressure of the past few weeks overwhelmed her. Athelea expected so much of her, Caelan was trying to destroy her, and she still couldn't understand why Atlantis had wanted her here so badly. Looking around at the empty harbor, she felt like her dream adventure in Atlantis had turned into a nightmare.

"Come here," Sarah said, enveloping her in another hug. "You know you always have me and Athelea to help you."

"What about Tom?" Victoria sniffled. "I need him, too."

"I'm sure he'd love to be with you and protect you and see all the sites," Sarah agreed, "but you can see him as soon as we get back to England."

"Soon," Victoria sighed. "I feel incomplete without him." She thought of her dream of Tom in Atlantis. It seemed so long ago, but it had only been a week. So much had happened since then, and she'd made up her mind about what to do next. Watching him hadn't helped how much she missed him. With or without Sarah, whether or not the Atlanteans came back, she was going home at the first opportunity possible.

Chapter Twenty-Six
FIRE

"Victoria? Are you okay?"

Athelea had found them at the port only a few minutes later. The alarm and immediacy of the question made Victoria wonder if her emotions were written across her face, or whether Athelea had noticed the ship floating away in the harbor.

Victoria shook her head. "Caelan was in Atlantis again," she said. Athelea gasped, looking pale, and Sarah nodded in encouragement. "He locked me on a ship, set it loose, and said he was going to burn Atlantis to the ground."

"This key unlocked the door," Sarah interjected. "Lucky I had it."

"Lucky indeed," Athelea said, looking pale. "Are you okay, Victoria?"

Victoria nodded.

"Thank the stars. Did Caelan say where he was going next?"

Victoria shook her head before looking towards the city. There was still no sign of fire, but she knew it was only a matter of time. "Probably wherever he can cause the most damage. I reckon he'll go somewhere in the city, probably the Plaza."

"We must make sure Atlantis is safe, then," Athelea said. She muttered something under her breath, and Victoria felt a sense of warmth wrap around her body like a blanket. She stopped shaking after a few seconds and felt a peacefulness that she knew wasn't originating in her own body. It was the most wonderful dex she'd experienced yet. Athelea flashed an encouraging smile and then nodded towards the city. "If you're feeling well enough, let's continue. I'll bring the ship back into the harbor later."

Despite the reassurance of Athelea's dex, Victoria felt her anxiety grow as they walked towards the city. As much as she wanted to run, she wanted to find Caelan and fight him. Even though they were unprepared and he probably wasn't in Atlantis anymore, the possibility of ending his offense on Atlantis was irresistible. If he was no longer a threat, she could leave Atlantis with a clear conscience.

"Still no smoke," Sarah said, interrupting her

thoughts as they reached the edge of the Eternal Forest.

Victoria frowned. "Doesn't mean there isn't a fire," she replied. She knew Caelan was finished with empty threats, and the others would realize it soon enough. There would be a fire somewhere in Atlantis, and she hoped they found it before it was too late.

Athelea turned onto a smaller path through the Eternal Forest, instead of continuing to the city as Victoria expected. Sarah shot Victoria a questioning look, to which Victoria could only shrug. Athelea obviously had somewhere she wanted to go, and that was good enough to follow.

"Athelea, where are we going?" Victoria said when they began to climb an unfamiliar path up Mount Theus for a few minutes.

"The watchtower," Athelea said. Victoria instantly understood, remembering the sentry she'd seen in her first dream of Atlantis. He'd been watching over Atlantis from the side of Mount Theus and had seen the wave before anybody else on the island. When they reached the stone outpost a minute later, the detour had been worth it. She could see the entire city from here, sprawling across the land between herself and the sea, and Athelea had been right. There was no smoke in sight.

"There," Sarah said after a moment, pointing towards the city, "by the Library."

Looking towards the Plaza, Victoria saw what Sarah meant. The entrance to the building was glowing with a flickering light. The other buildings blocked her view of the Plaza itself, but Victoria knew a fire was burning there. "What do we do?" she asked.

Athelea was already whispering something under her breath, her hands clasped in front of her face. A second later, a tiny cloud formed between her palms. Victoria glimpsed misty raindrops falling onto her Sentence before Athelea blew the dex forward. The cloud grew larger and the rain heavier as it drifted towards the city. When it finally stopped over the Plaza, a downpour was visible, and the glow on the library slowly disappeared.

It was a very powerful dex. Victoria smiled at Athelea.

"Let's go to the Plaza, ladies," Athelea said. "I can't guarantee that the dex worked perfectly, and it might not have been an ordinary fire, either."

"What if Caelan's there?" Sarah asked. Victoria could tell she was more shaken by recent events than she'd admitted.

"I'll send a dex ahead to detect human presences," Athelea replied simply. "We won't be unprepared."

Athelea invoked a dex, and five minutes later, the women were standing in the Plaza. Victoria could hear Athelea's rain hiss as it extinguished the fire. Most of the grass on the Plaza had been burnt, but there was no sign of Caelan. *That doesn't mean he's gone forever,* Victoria thought.

"Arrogance," Athelea muttered, burying her face in her hands. She looked exhausted. "He believes his plans are perfect, and he is confident they will never fail. He expected a single, ordinary fire to destroy all of Atlantis because he had locked you away. He never considered how your friends or your skills could deter him. Someday, this will be his downfall."

"Do you think we're safe?" Victoria asked.

"Caelan will not come back to Atlantis tonight."

"How do you know?"

"Arrogance. He didn't expect anyone to find you on the ship, and he trusted his pathetic fire to destroy Atlantis," Athelea repeated. "It was not enhanced with a single dex, and I believe he will allow it a few days to run its full course through the city before he returns to survey his work."

"What should we do if he comes back? Will your protective dexes work?"

"We fight," Athelea said simply. She began to pace around the edge of the Plaza, and Victoria and Sarah followed. "We fight with everything we have. And until then, we prepare. From now on, we must always be one step ahead of him."

A few days ago, Victoria would have been thrilled at

the suggestion, but the time for fighting Caelan had passed. "I don't want to stay here," she said.

Athelea stopped pacing. "I'm sorry?"

Victoria knew Athelea had heard her. Sarah fidgeted uncomfortably between them. "I want to leave Atlantis," she said. "Today."

Athelea closed her eyes, and a long silence punctuated the moment. Victoria suddenly felt like she was about to face a jury for a crime she hadn't committed.

"Atlantis needs you, Victoria," Athelea said. *Atlantis is killing me,* Victoria thought reflexively, looking around the burnt Plaza, but she knew better than to say it. "On its behalf, I must ask one more favor of you."

Victoria exchanged wary glances with Sarah. "What is it?"

Now Athelea hesitated. "I need you to help me. I see now that Atlantis is too full of history, too full of valuable information and important places, to leave unguarded. I have made a terrible mistake in not securing it more thoroughly sooner, and my carelessness nearly destroyed everything. But I know you're stronger than me and will be able to help more than I ever could."

"How long will it take?" Victoria asked, ignoring the flattery. She couldn't let compliments get to her head.

"A few days at the most. But if you want to leave after we have worked tomorrow, I will let you go."

Victoria shuddered. *One day is still too long.* She was glad that Athelea had finally had her epiphany about protecting Atlantis, but it was too late. She and Sarah needed to leave now.

"I know you don't want to stay in Atlantis any longer, but all I ask of you is a little more time," Athelea persisted. She sat down on the steps of the Grand Library, looking defeated. "I will stay at your side every second until you leave, if you are worried about your safety. I promise on my own life that Caelan will never touch you or Sarah again. Why don't we go to the Hall of Divinity while you consider it?"

Victoria let Athelea lead the way, needing time to muse over the situation. *There is so little I can do to help Atlantis that we haven't already tried,* she thought while Athelea lit another candle. The routine had become so familiar during her time in Atlantis, and she would miss it, but Athelea's prayers weren't enough. She glanced at Sarah, reluctant to decide on her own, and received a noncommittal shrug in response.

"What about Sarah?" Victoria asked when Athelea had finished her prayer.

"She will be able to help us, too," Athelea said. "She can lock every door and window with her key."

Sarah nodded in approval, touching the key on her necklace.

"What exactly will you and I have to do?" Victoria pressed.

"The procedure is quite simple. I want to secure all the important places in Atlantis in such a way that only we can enter. Sarah and I were late to come back today because I sealed the Domain to protect the Lifeglasses. It took less than an hour, and we can use the same process on buildings around the city."

"Would we use dexes?"

Athelea nodded. She sent the candle floating towards the others overhead. "Yes. I have a protective dex that worked nicely on the Domain."

"But I can't invoke dexes," Victoria sighed. They were both wasting precious time by returning to this argument. "You've got too much faith in my ability to do the impossible."

"You can learn," Athelea said. She sounded dangerously close to begging now. "Please stay. Even one more day is enough to protect the most important buildings in Atlantis with a basic dex."

Victoria felt like they were rapidly undoing the progress they'd made towards compromising. "Are you sure Caelan won't come back?"

Athelea nodded earnestly. "I have a suspicion that Caelan won't return for a few days. He will give the fire plenty of time to burn Atlantis first, and more importantly, he doesn't think anything will have stopped it. This is our only chance to truly save Atlantis."

Victoria glanced at Sarah and received a nod of encouragement. *Atlantis is going to kill me someday,* Victoria thought begrudgingly, *but it needs me.* With a sigh, she thought again of the beautiful, restored incarnation of Atlantis she'd dreamed about after leaving the Isle of Time. If she gave up on Atlantis now, she would lose that vision forever.

"A few more days," Victoria finally agreed. "But after that, or if I can't invoke dexes soon, Sarah and I are both going home."

Athelea smiled, though tears had begun to well in her beautiful silver eyes. "I understand your sacrifice, and a few more days is all I can ask of you. Thank you."

It means a lot to her that we're staying, Victoria realized. It was her chance to do something meaningful at last. Returning to the Isle of the Gods, Athelea secured every lock on the main gate for the first time that week and invoked an extra dex for security. Victoria was sure it would only allow them an extra minute if Caelan did visit, but it was better than anything she could offer. She ate in somber silence with the others in the Garden and began to make plans for the rest of her time in Atlantis. "I want to try to Watch Gryffin," she decided as the sun began to set. "If he's dangerous or with Caelan, I want to know."

"I can sketch in the Tower," Sarah suggested. "I don't want to get in your way."

"Very well," Athelea said. She led Victoria to the room with the mirror for Watching, and Sarah proceeded to the top of the tower. "I'll stand guard on the steps to keep an eye on the Garden. The dex on the mirror should still work. Take your time."

Victoria closed the door behind herself and walked to the mirror, praying this attempt would work. She wanted insight into who the handsome boy with the Sentence was. A second later, her reflection turned into the scene of a beach she didn't recognize.

A cloaked figure sat on a bench at the end of a stone pier, his back to Victoria. A grid of shimmering bars surrounded him, the same style of prison that had contained Victoria on the Isle of Time, and he was brushing his long, brunette hair aimlessly with his fingers. He didn't seem to mind his situation or be in any hurry to get out. Victoria felt her heart race. Although she couldn't see his face, she knew it was Gryffin.

He lowered his hood and then, so slightly that Victoria barely noticed, he made a movement in his shoulders that was barely more than a breath. The bars around him crumbled to the ground in a million glittering pieces, and he stood up. As he turned around, Victoria noticed the unmistakable smirk on his lips.

He had dust over his entire body and shadows of stubble on his jaw, but his beautiful, angular face was unmistakable beneath it all. Only his mane of hair, so similar Athelea's, had misled Victoria. She felt a fleeting sense of smugness once she'd recovered from the shock. After all the warnings he'd given her, he was the one who had gotten into trouble. *He should have listened to his own advice,* she thought. But as she silently laughed to herself, she suddenly understood what she hadn't before.

He was looking for Atlantis, too.

When he finished stretching in the sun, Gryffin began to walk towards the sea. There was grace and nobility in his stride that Victoria hadn't noticed before, and she watched in fascination. He paused in front of the water for a second and then stepped in. After a few more strides, the surface of the water remained under his bare feet. Victoria gasped, barely believing what she was seeing. He was walking on water.

Without warning, Gryffin stopped walking and looked over his shoulder. Victoria lowered the mirror, but it was too late. His silver eyes glared into hers. He had seen her somehow, and the anger in his expression said enough. She had made a terrible mistake in deciding to search for Atlantis.

She stopped Watching him and called for Athelea.

"Who is Gryffin, if he's not your son?" Victoria

asked. "He's got the Sentence on his wrist, and I'm sure it's not a tattoo. I'm pretty sure he used dexterity to disappear the first time I met him, and he was walking on water when I Watched him. Everything suggests that Atlantean, but I don't see how it's possible."

Athelea shook her head. "I feel inclined to follow your thoughts. It seems unlikely that someone born outside of Atlantis so long after the Destruction could have dexterity, but you must trust your instinct."

"What should we do about him?"

"Gryffin doesn't appear to pose any threat to Atlantis. As far as I am aware, he has no knowledge of its location and no means to get here if he did."

"Apart from a mirror to the Reflector."

Athelea nodded. "What did he say about Atlantis?"

"He said it's dangerous and warned me to stay away." A silence followed, and Victoria suspected she and Athelea had the same thought. Either he genuinely meant it, or he was trying to keep me away so he could have Atlantis to himself."

"Do you suspect he has some connection to Caelan?"

Victoria shook her head. "If they know about each other, they're not working together. I doubt Gryffin knows where Atlantis is, and even if he did, he's not got any way of getting here."

"We should not worry about him for now," Athelea

suggested. "Caelan will get him first if he gets too near to Atlantis."

Victoria wondered why she hadn't realized that sooner. Feeling slightly more reassured about the situation, she followed Athelea to the Neutral Room. Now, all that mattered was her time remaining in Atlantis. "I want to learn how to make objects fireproof," Victoria said after a few meditation exercises.

"The dex is *inflamana*," Athelea said. "One of its many counterparts is *reflamana*, to allow the object to burn again, but don't worry about that right now."

Victoria nodded. After working so hard that week to protect her own thoughts from intrusion, it felt strange yet wonderful to be protecting objects instead. She tried for nearly half an hour to invoke the new dex on blank sheets of paper, but with each unsuccessful attempt, her optimism dwindled. She and Athelea had burned through a sizable stack of paper, but as Athelea held a new sheet up, the pile didn't seem to be getting any smaller.

"*Inflamana*," Victoria said.

Athelea snapped her fingers, and a bright fire consumed the parchment in her hand in a matter of seconds.

Victoria sighed. Athelea produced a fresh sheet of paper and held it up in the air. "*Inflamana*," Victoria repeated.

Athelea snapped her fingers, and the paper burst into

fire.

"This is never going to work," Victoria sighed. "What am I doing wrong?"

"It will never work if you have that attitude," Athelea said, sounding maternal, though her tone was firm. Victoria resisted the urge to laugh, her determination only fueled by her frustration. "You must believe in the dex and desire to invoke it. The energy won't move if you don't care enough to move it."

Victoria raised her eyebrows, surprised. Athelea had never talked to her that way that before. For a brief second, the lonely woman who hid her emotions behind her beauty disappeared, and Victoria saw a true commander, fierce and determined to save her country.

She took a breath, provoked by the insinuation that she didn't care. She would not let the paper burn again. Atlantis would never burn again. "*Inflamana*," she growled.

Athelea snapped her fingers, and the fire sprung up around the parchment.

But this time, the paper didn't burn. The dex had finally worked.

Chapter Twenty-Seven
FORTA

"I stayed up until sunrise practicing dexes," Victoria told Sarah over breakfast on the balcony the next morning. It was a beautiful, warm day, and for the first time since arriving in Atlantis, the possibility of restoring the island was real. She couldn't wait to begin. "I've definitely got the hang of it now. I don't know why it took so long to master dexterity."

"That's bloody great news," Sarah said, helping herself to juice and fruit. "Does that mean we are going to protect Atlantis today?"

"I hope so," Victoria said. Despite her long night of studying, her excitement meant that she didn't feel tired. She forced herself to eat a good meal, suspecting she would need the energy later. "Athelea left a note asking us to eat and get ready without her. She will probably be here soon and give us a plan. The note is definitely from her."

"It's strange not having her around," Sarah mused. "I really like her."

"There is something you should know about her," Victoria said. She took a deep breath and hesitated, suddenly nervous for her big revelation.

Sarah looked up from her juice. "What's that?"

"Athelea is my biological mother."

A long moment passed. Victoria could tell words had failed Sarah and decided to help. "The other day, when we were in the Castle library, I found the royal family tree open on the table. It said Athelea is my mother."

Understanding dawned in Sarah's eyes. "That's why you two argued?"

Victoria nodded. "I didn't tell you sooner because I barely believed it myself. It seemed so impossible, but I've had time to think about it since I talked to Athelea, and most of it makes sense now. It's just a shock to learn the truth after all these years."

"I understand," Sarah said, and the balcony fell silent. Victoria stared at the city across the sea, wondering when Athelea would return. After a minute, Sarah turned to Victoria. "It's kind of funny," she said. "You and Athelea are so similar. Same hair, same eyes, same fiery stubbornness. I should have seen it sooner."

"To be fair, neither of us was expecting I would find my mother in Atlantis."

"True," Sarah agreed. "Do you have any idea how old she is? And what about you? Atlantis has been a myth for thousands of years, but you're seventeen and she only looks a few years older."

Victoria shrugged. "Atlantis must have invoked some sort of dex on her to keep her frozen in time. Even Athelea doesn't know how it works, but we could probably ask her. I'm sure she wouldn't mind."

"Rather you than me," Sarah said. But when Athelea arrived twenty minutes later, they left for the main island without much delay. They stopped to lock the gate to the Isle of the Gods, and Victoria told Athelea about her conversation with Sarah as they walked through the city. She wasn't surprised that the first building they visited was the Grand Library. Inside, Athelea led them across the floor to the furthest row of shelves on the ground level.

"This dex should be pretty straightforward," she began, addressing Victoria directly. "All you have to do is place your hands on the wall every few paces and invoke the dex. Meanwhile, Sarah can lock the windows and internal doors with her key and sketch in her free time. When we're finished inside, we'll move on to the outside, and then on to the next building."

"What's the dex?" Victoria asked.

"It's *forta*," Athelea said. "It's a generic fortification dex."

Victoria nodded, instantly liking that word. It sounded strong and hopeful, which was exactly what Atlantis needed. "Should we do every floor?" she asked.

Athelea shook her head. "If we just protect the ground floor, the Atlan stone should transmit it throughout the rest of the building. The foundations are the most vulnerable, anyway."

With a reassuring smile, she turned towards the wall and ran her hands along the stones between the bookshelves. "*Forta*," she murmured, and pure white light burst from her fingertips, illuminating the stones she touched. The light then trickled up to the ceiling and down to the floor in a thick stream before it began to fade. Repeating the dex every few seconds, Athelea walked along the wall, the trail of light following in her wake like a wave.

Victoria hoped the dex was as easy as it looked. Taking a deep breath, she walked to the point where Athelea had started and brought her hand to the unmarked wall. She imagined her fingertips bursting with the immense strength to fortify stone, and she said the dex when she felt ready. A gentle warmth like starlight filled her hand a second later, and her own sapphire dexterity burst from her fingers.

Behind her, Sarah gasped in amazement. Even Victoria felt a surge of relief that she'd managed a dex outside of a Neutral Room when it mattered, and she couldn't understand how it had taken her so long to find her dexterity. *It seems so simple now,* the thought. Her dex trickled up and down the wall more tentatively than Athelea's, but it eventually reached the ceiling and floor. Feeling rather pleased, Victoria began to work her way around the building. Sarah followed her for a minute before locking windows and doors, then sat down to sketch.

"Could Caelan ever undo these dexes?" she asked quietly after a few minutes.

Victoria felt her concentration and confidence falter, and Athelea's carefree laughter from across the room surprised her. "Never," she said. Victoria could hear the triumphant smile in her voice. "The royal Atlantean blood that runs through our veins places our dexes at the very top of the dexterity hierarchy. There is no way Caelan could ever interfere with our work."

Despite her distaste for this system when they'd discussed it previously, Victoria didn't feel it was so unfair. Nothing else was protecting Atlantis from Caelan. With Athelea, she invoked the fortification dex upon the outside of the Grand Library before moving on to the Hall of Divinity, and then down the street to a building Victoria had never paid much attention to before. It looked more severe and less elaborate from the outside than its neighbors, and Victoria was surprised to find a grand reception room when she entered through the massive wooden doors. Stepping through a smaller set of doors into one of the most commanding rooms she'd seen in Atlantis, she sensed that the building had once been incredibly important.

"This is the Courthouse," Athelea said. Victoria could imagine a judge sitting at the enormous podium at the front of the room and the rest of the court listening in rapt silence from their rows of smaller tables, the room demanding absolute respect. Behind the judge's desk, Victoria noticed a single door.

"What's through that?" she asked.

"That is the judge's office," Athelea said. She crossed the courtroom and opened the door. Peering into a small room, Victoria was surprised to see that one entire wall was a window. Through it, she could see that a passageway linked this room to one in the next building. The desk in the middle of the room was covered with a thick layer of dust, and the other walls were lined with shelves of documents.

"Are these all the court records ever made?"

Athelea shook her head. "These are the unsettled cases. All the older, settled cases are in the Hall of Verdicts next door, and most other legal records are in their own building, the Hall of Records, across the street."

Nothing could have prepared Victoria for the size of the archives when they entered the beautiful building across the street. It was nearly the same size as the Courthouse, but instead of housing benches and tables, the Hall of Records contained hundreds of shelves that reached from floor to ceiling. Each shelf housed scrolls that someone had rolled tightly and tied with ribbon, making the inside of the building looked like a paper honeycomb. "Wow," Victoria breathed. "These are all the civil records? How many Atlanteans were there?"

Athelea nodded. "These are the government copies of birth, death, and marriage certificates. The number of Atlanteans ever born must have been recorded somewhere, but I do not know where or what the number is. All the military records are in the military district, and all the settled legal records are next to the courthouse, in the Hall of Verdicts. The three buildings are nearly identical in design and function."

"There are so many great buildings here," Sarah interrupted. "Could I draw this one, too, once I've locked everything?"

Athelea looked around. "That should be fine. I don't believe you need to check Victoria's dexes any longer. She seems to be doing beautifully."

Flushing at the compliment, Victoria walked to one of the walls, and Athelea went to the opposite. They worked their way around the room while Sarah sketched, and Victoria felt another wave of satisfaction with her decision to stay in Atlantis. The dex seemed simpler every time she used it, and it no longer felt like work. She was enjoying seeing the most special places in Atlantis. *Caelan's attempts to scare us away have backfired,* she thought smugly. *Atlantis is stronger than it has been in centuries. Athelea would never have been able to do it all on her own.*

"Would any of Aiden and Andrea's family records be here?" she wondered when she'd finished invoking her share of dexes.

"Possibly," Athelea said. "If they kept their Atlantean surname, we could look for them."

"It's Etsema," Victoria said. "I've never met anyone in England with the surname."

Athelea's eyes sparkled with delight. "The Etsema family was one of the oldest and most powerful in Atlantis. I have a feeling you might be in luck."

She walked through the Hall of Records and stopped in front of one of the many honeycomb shelves. After a second, she pulled out a roll of paper and gently untied the ribbon which bound it. "Aiden and Andrea were married in Atlantis," she said, handing the paper to Victoria. "They must have used powerful dexterity to leave Atlantis days before the Destruction."

Victoria didn't bother to look at the dates, torn between hurt and wonder. Aiden and Andrea had walked through the streets of Atlantis and had probably lived in one of the houses or apartments she'd passed in the city. "There is so much I don't know about them. I wonder if they are Forever Loves."

"It's very possible," Athelea said. "The disposition for Forever Love tends to be strong in the ancient families."

"They must be," Sarah interrupted. "There's something in the way they look at each other. They always seem so happy together, and they're never apart."

Athelea nodded in agreement. Victoria looked at the certificate more closely, wondering what it all meant. "Did they live in the city?"

"The Etsema family had an island off the coast of Atlantis. This record says Aiden and Andrea lived in their own house there."

"And now they live in the city in England," Victoria said, handing. "I can't believe they never told me anything."

Lost in her thoughts, she followed Athelea to the Hall of Verdicts, which was nearly identical to the Hall of Records. "There's no way Athelea could have done this on her own," Victoria whispered to Sarah as they fortified the exterior of the building. "I'm so glad we stayed to help."

When they finished fortifying the Hall of Verdicts half an hour later, Victoria expected to move on to another building, but Athelea stopped in the middle of the street. "Let's take a break, ladies," she said. She suddenly looked exhausted. "We've worked hard today, and we deserve to relax. Let's go to the spa."

Victoria felt her heart soar at the word. *Spa*. That idea was the same across the centuries, everywhere in the world. She had missed pampering herself, and she was sure that even Sarah could be persuaded. It had been too long since she'd taken a moment to relax properly.

Athelea led them in a brisk walk back to the palace. She stopped at one of her workshops to grab shampoos and soaps, then continued to West Tower and through an archway into an enormous conservatory. Victoria could imagine the room had been a place of leisure in its prime, filled with amazing plants and places to lounge. She could still smell cinnamon and vanilla in the air, and she exchanged an excited glance with Sarah. The scent grew stronger as they crossed the room to a staircase leading underground. Athelea lit a torch, and they began their descent under the palace.

The wonderful scent grew stronger with every step, until they reached the room at the bottom of the staircase. Looking around, Victoria could hardly believe what she was seeing. They were standing in a massive underground spa, which had enormous, steaming pools. The wonderful scent of spices filled the humid air, and candles and torches flickered serenely around the cave.

"This is the royal spa. It uses various dexes to heat the water, create the streams, light the torches, and scent the air," Athelea said, procuring a few towels from the chest by the window. Victoria thought she looked slightly uneasy, which didn't make sense in such a tranquil room. *She's had a difficult day,* she thought. *Seeing Atlantis like this must be especially difficult for her.*

"Legend says that King Atlas wanted a place where he could relax without any interference from the outside world, so he designed this very spa," Athelea continued. "Within these walls, all other dexes are effectively useless, eliminating distractions and the possibility of attacks from the outside. Eventually, all the spas in Atlantis adopted this tradition, and spas became an essential part of Atlantean life."

Victoria couldn't think of a better place to relax. She stripped down to the swimsuit under her dress and joined the others in the water, which she now realized was the source of that beautiful scent. The temperature was perfect. She wished Athelea had brought them here days ago, when she'd really needed to unwind, and now that she had a minute, she found herself reflecting on what she'd learned about Aiden and Andrea. If somebody had told her a week ago that she would be in Atlantis with her mother, she never would have believed it.

"Athelea," Victoria began, "there's one thing I still don't understand about my past."

Athelea regarded her with a gentle expression as she

decanted into the water a sparkling liquid from one of the glass bottles around the spa. Bubbles sprang up, smelling like cinnamon. "What's that?"

"Why did you send me away?"

Athelea flushed a deep rose color that the steam couldn't hide. "I had no other choice," she said. The sadness in her silver eyes said this was the truth. "In the days before the Destruction, many scholars came to visit me. They warned me of an ancient prophecy and advised me send you away, for your safety and that of Atlantis. When news of these secret meetings became public, the citizens plead with me to allow you to stay, believing you would protect and restore Atlantis to its former splendor. In the end, I had to make the most difficult decision of my life. To save you, not just from the Destruction, but from these people who had such high expectations of us, I had to send you away."

"Why?" Victoria pressed. "Because of a prophecy? What did the it say?"

"It said Atlantis would survive only if I sent you away."

Victoria played with a handful of bubbles while she thought. Even if she was in the most fantastical world, facing problems beyond her wildest dreams, she couldn't possibly be the savior of Atlantis. Having an Atlantean princess for her mother didn't change the fact that she was a normal teenager. But she could see how much the decision had hurt Athelea and the conviction she must have had to follow her heart.

"I probably would have done the same in your position," she admitted. The confirmation that Athelea had always loved made the prophecies unimportant and filled a void that had been in her life for longer than she could remember. She blinked a few times, thankful that her face was already wet, and finally looked at Athelea. In the dim light, they exchanged smiles filled with understanding that words couldn't convey. Whatever had happened in the past, they'd formed an unbreakable bond now that they would only ever share with each other.

"The problem is that most Atlanteans citizens believed you could lead the empire in a new direction after generations of corruption. Society seemed to collapse when they heard rumors that I had spoken about sending you away," Athelea continued. "They called me selfish, blamed me for conspiring to forge an alliance between the royals and scholars. On the last night before the Destruction, the military finally returned from the War, and from the celebration rose an unprecedented riot. The next afternoon, a Guard must have discovered the wave in the distance, because the alarm sounded. I'm sure that most Atlanteans raced for shelter throughout the city, but it was already too late. I had failed to listen to my own people, whose lives I was responsible for, and I lost you anyway."

Tears were streaming down her face.

Victoria couldn't believe that Athelea still had these misconceptions after all this time. "You can't blame yourself," she said. "The Atlanteans might have been upset with your decision and rioted, but they didn't cause the wave. You certainly didn't cause the wave, either."

"I shouldn't have survived it, either," Athelea interrupted. The bleakness in her voice surprised Victoria. She had suspected that Athelea might have felt guilt over being the only survivor of the Destruction, but hearing it sent a wave of shock and sadness through her body. *She still hasn't forgiven herself.*

"Atlantis wouldn't have any hope if you weren't here," Sarah said. "You must see that."

Athelea looked up with an expression of gratitude. "That's very kind," she said. Without another word on the Destruction, she reached for her bottles of lotions and bath salts and spent a few minutes explaining how she'd made each of them. *There is nothing my mother can't do,* Victoria thought, filled with a sense of pride. *She just needs to be easier on herself. Nobody has reminded her of her worth since the Destruction.*

"Athelea, Victoria and I were wondering something the other night," Sarah said cryptically after a minute, but Victoria already knew what was coming. "Please don't take offense, but how old you are? In our myths, Atlantis disappeared thousands of years ago, but you still look so young."

Athelea laughed. "Thank you. Unfortunately, I can't give you an exact answer. The Destruction was so long ago that I have lost count of how many years have passed since then. It happened the week of my twenty-sixth birthday. Physically, I don't believe I have aged since then, but I am not entirely sure how old to consider myself. I believe that there is some deep magic keeping me and Atlantis frozen in time. I've never heard of a dex like it, but Atlantis must have done something unprecedented to protect itself."

Victoria opened her eyes to exchange a dark glance with Sarah, thankful the lighting was so dark. In a sense, Athelea was trapped in time in her own body. *Will I become older than her someday?* Victoria wondered. The thought made her feel uneasy.

"Before I forget," Athelea said, "I want to make sure you aren't worrying about Tom anymore. Would you like to Watch him again?"

"I don't need to," Victoria admitted, debating how much she should reveal about what she'd done. "I Watched him yesterday morning when you and Sarah were at the Isle of Time."

"I should have guessed," Athelea said, flashing a smile. "I'm so glad to hear he's safe."

My mum is incredible, Victoria thought. Their

conversation ended there, and the women stayed at the spa for another hour. Back in the Royal Tower, Athelea prepared dinner and opened another bottle of wine. The women spent an hour enjoying the late afternoon on the balcony before Victoria began to feel restless. She didn't have long left in Atlantis, and she wanted to make a difference while she was still here.

"I'd like to do more tonight," Victoria said when their wine bottle was nearly empty. She still felt hot after the spa, and the humid Atlantean evening wasn't helping. "I could use some fresh air, and I don't really feel like drinking." She had a feeling Athelea would be receptive to drinking while they worked, but she decided against mentioning it. Protecting Atlantis properly was more important.

When they finished their bottle of wine, Athelea led them to the city. She stopped in front of the Reflector and pushed the gate open, her dex indicating that nobody else was around. Victoria took a deep breath before she stepped inside. This building was so much larger than the others they'd visited today, but she was sure she had enough dexterity to protect it. By reflex, she glanced at the Broken Portal. In the light of the torches around the room, its reflection of the building still looked dull.

"Always worth checking," Sarah said under her breath.

Without another word, the women got to work. "Is there any way Caelan can use these portals to get in and out of Atlantis?" Victoria asked for the last time when Sarah started sketching.

Across the room, Athelea shook her head. "I Watched the Reflector a few days ago, when you expressed your concerns about him," she said. "Nobody but us has been in or out of the building in years, and once we are done fortifying it, nobody but us can use it in the future."

She should have done this years ago, Victoria thought, but there was no use blaming her for past mistakes. The work they were doing now was more important. "Thank you for looking," she said. The sun was beginning to set by the time they finished the exterior of the Reflector. Athelea led them on a walk out of the city and into a walled section at the east of the island that Victoria hadn't noticed from the watchtower.

"Welcome to the military district, ladies," Athelea said. Numerous buildings surrounded a massive field, where Victoria assumed soldiers had trained. At the far end of the complex was what Victoria assumed was a gym and spa, and she recognized another building as a Neutral Room. The building closest to them looked identical to the Hall of Records, though Victoria sensed more of a corporate atmosphere when they entered using Sarah's key. From Athelea's distant expression, she instantly understood why they were here. "This is the military's legal house, and behind it are the barracks where the military lived and trained. Conscription and registration, mutiny, provisions, deaths, and battles are all recorded and archived here."

Victoria exchanged a glance with Sarah when Athelea wasn't looking, wondering if she had the same question. "Could I see Tristan's records?" Victoria asked.

Athelea nodded and led them to a shelf at the far end of the building without a word. Victoria had a feeling Athelea had been here many times before. She found a file without any hesitation and handed it to Victoria gently. Victoria was surprised to find that the top page was a generic death announcement. She read every word in a mixture of fascination and unexpected grief. She turned to the next page with a shaking hand and was surprised to find his signature at the bottom of a contract, confirming his acceptance of military duty on the night he'd been married.

This man who lived and died thousands of years ago is my father, she thought, her eyes stinging with tears. *This is this closest I'll ever get to him.* She closed the file and handed it back to Athelea without reading more. She fully understood why they needed to protect this building. More than anywhere else in Atlantis, this room housed the memories of the most brave, heroic Atlanteans who would probably never return.

"Let's get this building fortified," Victoria choked

out.

The process only took fifteen minutes, but Victoria felt more exhausted and warm when she finished. She could only imagine how Athelea felt, and even Sarah had fallen into a somber silence as she alternated between locking windows and sketching. The dex had gotten easier with practice over the course of the day, but she didn't know how much longer she could continue.

"We've fortified the most important buildings, ladies," Athelea said after they had admired their work. She looked shaken, and Victoria could tell the day had worn on her emotions. "It'll be dark soon, and I need time to think about what we can do next. Let's have some more wine and relax. Thank you for your help."

The next second, she leaned in and hugged Victoria. Victoria returned the embrace, sharing her sense of accomplishment. It felt right that they'd protected Atlantis together, and even if this was all they accomplished before she returned home, it had been worth staying. Caelan had lost his crusade.

Chapter Twenty-Eight
LOVESICK

Victoria felt feverish when she woke up. *It must be the heat of the spa,* she thought. The room was still dark with night, and she knew she should to go back to sleep. But when she'd nearly drifted off, a burst of light filled her eyelids. She bolted up, able to recognize that glow anywhere.

The orb had returned.

Victoria grabbed her cloak and rolled out of bed, ignoring her cold sweats. The orb drifted across the room, and Victoria followed it off the Isle of the Gods and to the ancient castle on the main island. The cool air and Night Rain felt amazing against her skin. The orb stopped before the throne so suddenly that Victoria nearly walked into it, and she could tell it wanted something from her. She reached for the orb, but instead of recoiling from her like it usually did, it allowed her to approach.

I know what you want from me, she thought. She could feel the orb's wishes running through her blood. With a final stretch, she clasped the orb in her palms. It didn't struggle, but she knew from the feel of its amazing power that it was there. Guided by a sense she couldn't explain, she knelt and pushed the orb into the stone at the foot of the throne. The orb vanished with a magnificent burst of light, leaving her hands empty.

Shivering in the nighttime silence, Victoria stood up, wondering what the orb would do next.

The effort of staying on her feet became exhausting after within seconds, and Victoria could no longer lie to herself. She had a fever, and she felt worse with every breath she took. She looked at the throne after so many days of resisting its call. She was sure it had become more symbolic than functional since the palace had become the seat of power. *Athelea wouldn't be offended,* she convinced herself, and she took a seat. A second later, she felt an agonizing flash of heat in her right wrist, and when she looked down, she nearly swooned.

The Sentence looked faded.

Victoria felt a wave of emotions crash over her. *Is the curse lifting?* she wondered. She stared at her wrist, wondering if it would fade any further. She quickly summoned a flame into her hand and was relieved to see that her dexterity still worked. And then she remembered what the message she'd received from Atlantis so long ago had said. *The Sentence will be your key to Atlantis.*

I will want to return someday, she thought. She had to interpret the message literally. *I can't leave forever.*

Fighting a wave of nausea, she closed her eyes and willed the Sentence to stay. She loved having it on her body, loved how it made her feel connected to the Atlanteans who still weren't here. Heat flashed through her wrist a second later, and when she opened her eyes, the words were as dark on her skin as they'd ever been.

Her heart soared. She waited a few minutes, but the orb didn't return, and she continued to feel even more unwell. Accepting that she wouldn't get an answer, she resolved to ask Athelea in the morning and stumbled back to the palace through the rain. She woke up to a bright, warm day only when Athelea opened the curtains for breakfast.

Victoria pulled the duvet over her eyes to stop the room from spinning. The thought of food made her feel sick. A second later, she felt someone sit on her bed, and a cold hand moved to her forehead.

"You're burning up," Sarah said. "Are you alright?"

"I feel awful," Victoria admitted. "What's wrong with me?"

A new set of hands moved to her forehead. "Give me a moment to think," Athelea said, sounding stressed. "I'm not a doctor, but let me use a few basic dexes to see if I can determine what's wrong."

She invoked a dex that seemed to be a ball of light. It floated around Victoria for a moment, and then disappeared. Athelea frowned. "Nothing seems to be wrong, apart from your fever."

"Something is wrong," Victoria insisted.

Athelea began to pace around the room. Sarah looked on nervously, and Victoria buried herself further into her duvet, suddenly feeling chill. "Do you believe Tom is your soulmate?" Athelea asked eventually.

Victoria emerged from her covers for air. "I would do anything for him. He is the best person I know, and he completes me and makes me a better person."

"Is there any chance that he could be your Forever Love?"

"He is my soulmate," Victoria whispered, opening her eyes. "I don't know how I could love anyone more."

Athelea exchanged a glance with Sarah that Victoria couldn't decipher. Sarah nodded, and Athelea was silent for what felt like an hour before she sat down on Victoria's bed.

"I'm sorry, Victoria. Being away from your Forever Love is killing you."

Victoria and Sarah both stared at Athelea. "What do you mean?" Victoria asked.

"I should have seen it earlier, in your memories. Tom

must be your Forever Love. Being away from him is making you dangerously Lovesick."

"It makes sense," Sarah interjected. "How I've seen it, you two have always been so sure of your relationship. You do make each other better people, and you're never apart from each other for more than a few days."

"How can we fix it?" Victoria whispered.

"I suffered very similar symptoms when Tristan left me. The healers were able to cure me with advanced medical dexes, but those secrets disappeared with them. There is nothing I can do, no dex I can invoke, to help you feel better.

Silence filled the room. "What does that mean?" Sarah said eventually. Victoria didn't have the courage to ask the question herself.

"You must return to England."

Victoria felt a wave of dizziness wash over her. "We still haven't protected Atlantis," she said.

"That's the fever talking," Sarah said, sitting next to Victoria. "We've protected all the buildings, Vic. They're all secure now."

"It's not good enough," Victoria said. The others would never understand. "Caelan can still get in."

"But he cannot do any harm," Athelea said.

Victoria would have argued, but a thought suddenly occurred to her. "Is Tom okay?"

"If you are Forever Loves, he will feel the effects of separation eventually. Being out of Atlantis will probably make it easier. What does your intuition say?" Athelea said.

Victoria closed her eyes and searched her heart for the answer. "I think he's safe still. He seemed fine when I Watched him the other day, and he's always been stronger than me."

"You must still return to England," Athelea said. "Your symptoms should improve as you get closer to Tom. When you are reunited with him, you will have returned to normal. The journey will not be easy, but you will have Sarah with you to help."

"My Sentence faded a bit last night," Victoria said, suddenly remembering. "Does that mean anything?"

Athelea and Sarah looked at their wrists simultaneously, and Athelea gasped. This news seemed to be even more important news to her than Lovesickness. Her eyes flooded with tears, which Victoria didn't know how to interpret.

"My Sentence is lighter, too. You've changed the curse," Athelea whispered. "How did you do it?"

"My Sentence is completely gone," Sarah said. Everyone turned to look at her, then back to Victoria.

"It probably went when mine did," Victoria said. "Athelea, I put the orb into the ground at the foot of the throne, and then I felt a flash of heat through my wrist when

I sat down."

"Do you feel well enough to show me exactly where you put the orb?" Athelea asked.

Victoria nodded. "If you think it's important."

"I can pack," Sarah offered. "We should leave as soon as possible."

"That would be helpful," Athelea said. "If I don't see you before you leave, Sarah, I want to say that you can keep your drawings of Atlantis. I trust they mean a great deal to you, and that you will continue keep Atlantis an absolute secret even though you have the proof."

"I will," Sarah said, leaning in to hug Athelea. "Thank you so much. It's been lovely getting to know you."

With that, they parted. Athelea helped Victoria walk to the city, taking the shortcut through the Eternal Forest. In the meadow where she'd first met Athelea, Victoria began to feel faint. "I need to sit down," she said. Athelea guided her to the stone bench without any question, and Victoria reclined. The meadow faded in and out of focus until she managed to take a few deep breaths. Athelea sighed next to her, obviously worried.

"Victoria, would you promise me something?" she said. "Whatever happens when you return to England, you must *never* speak of Atlantis to anybody, unless you trust that person with your life," Athelea said. "Do you understand?"

"Yes, I do," Victoria replied, remembering how difficult it had been to convince Sarah that Atlantis was real. She had a feeling that Tom and Nick probably would believe her more readily, but she wasn't in any hurry to test her suspicions. "I've only ever told Sarah. There's only a few people who would believe me, anyway."

"Never underestimate the power of friendship," Athelea reminded her, seeming to read her thoughts. "Keep your friends close, and they will never let you down."

Victoria smiled at the flash of maternal advice. "I always have. They mean the world to me."

"I'm glad," Athelea said. Victoria had a feeling she was working through topics to discuss before they parted, making up for the time they'd never spent together. "If you want me to, I can bring a boat to Shipwreck Beach while you get Sarah, if you're feeling well enough. I will put a dex on it to calm the nearby waters like your boat before, but it will probably drain some of your energy, so remember to rest occasionally."

"I can get Sarah," Victoria said.

"The boat will know exactly where to bring you," Athelea continued. "You should probably leave soon if you want to have a full day of travel today. And help yourself to food from the palace. You haven't got a dex to sustain you this journey, and Lovesickness won't help your strength."

"That would be really helpful," Victoria said. She

wondered if the orb would return to make another portal, but if it didn't, the boat would still have saved them from swimming. *Otherwise I would die of Lovesickness here.* "Thank you again, for everything, Athelea. We couldn't have survived here without you."

"It's the least I can do," Athelea said, standing up finally. "Thank you for everything you have done."

Victoria tried to convince herself that she was only imagining the sadness she heard in those words. She felt guilty for leaving Athelea behind in such an empty, quiet land, but even stronger frustration that Athelea seemed to be content with this. Even the hope that the Atlanteans would return someday wasn't a good enough excuse.

"Come with us," Victoria said. "Live in England with me and Aiden and Andrea. You would love it."

Athelea shook her head. "It is my responsibility to watch over Atlantis while it is defenseless. I belong here as its guardian, and you must follow your own destiny. You must have the life you deserve, a freedom I could never have myself."

Victoria felt her heart breaking, but the tears in Athelea's eyes prevented her from arguing. Nothing in the world, not even the pain of losing her daughter again, could make her leave Atlantis.

When Victoria regained enough strength to walk, she and Athelea finished the journey to the Castle. Victoria showed Athelea where she'd put the orb into the stone, then sat on the old throne while Athelea silently examined the surrounding stones. Victoria couldn't see anything unusual about the Keep in the light of day, and she wondered where the orb was now.

"What exactly is the orb?" she asked.

Athelea shook her head. "Ever since you first told me about the orb, I always thought it sounded like one of the gifts that King Atlas received from the gods. Legend says it was what granted Atlantean dexterity, though some scholars say it is the soul of Atlantis. Until now, I had thought both theories are myths, but I don't know what to believe."

"It felt powerful," Victoria said. Neither of Athelea's theories seemed likely to her, but she couldn't believe that the orb was simply a ball of light. "It's guided me so much on my journey here. It seems more probable that it's the soul of Atlantis, but how can a place have a soul?"

"The gods lived here once," Athelea said. "Anything is possible. Regardless, I should bring the orb to the palace. I can guard it there."

Victoria nodded weakly, thankful that Athelea wanted to take responsibility. Athelea invoked a dex to lift the stone out of the ground and used her other arm to support Victoria. Passing through the heart of the city, Victoria took the opportunity to soak up her surroundings one last time. She tried to memorize the way each building looked, the way the cobbled street felt under her feet, and the silence and emptiness that filled the air. There was still so much she could have learned, so many secrets in Atlantis that she hadn't discovered, and her memories would never be enough.

In the Plaza, she automatically glanced at the Reflector. Her journey with Atlantis has started here, and she'd never imagined she'd never see it again. An inexplicable energy surged through her without warning as she neared the front door.

"Wait," she begged Athelea. Even without seeing it, she knew something was happening to the Broken Portal. She ran the rest of the distance, knowing it could only be good news, but nothing could have prepared her for what she found inside. The Broken Portal was emitting a faint white halo that made all the other mirrors in the Reflector seem dull. Athelea gasped next to her, her eyes full of the awe and curiosity Victoria felt.

"What's going on?" Victoria whispered. She ran her hands gently along the top of the frame and watched in fascination as her fingers left a glowing imprint. "It's warm," she noted.

Before Athelea could answer, a blinding light burst from the stone. A sparkling vapor began to cascade down the mirror, making her reflection ripple surreally. Whatever it was, the vapor didn't look or feel dangerous. After a moment of deliberation, Victoria lowered her hand to touch the glass. She couldn't feel the vapor, but she could see it flowing across her fingers, trickling over her palm and her Sentence.

And the next second, the vapor disappeared, like her skin had absorbed it.

"Don't move, Victoria," Athelea instructed. "Are you okay?"

A sweet fragrance of flowers and spices suddenly struck Victoria and rendered her speechless. The scent bore traces of the past, reminders of the present, and promises of the future. Victoria could feel the failures, triumphs, and secrets of Atlanteans surround her, and she could feel Atlantis become a part of her more than it already was. She swayed for a second but stayed on her feet with Athelea's support.

"Are you okay?" Athelea asked repeated. She seemed completely unaffected by whatever the Broken Portal was emitting.

"I think so," Victoria said. She stared at the mirror, perplexed. There didn't seem to be anything dangerous hidden behind the seductive, luxurious scent. She ran her finger through the vapor again, even more cautious and intrigued this time, and attempted to touch the mirror. Her fingers tingled for a second before her palm went numb, warning her to move away, but she couldn't. When the mysterious force of the portal finally released her, the senses returned to her hand, and the fog around her consciousness lifted. Fascinated, she watched the vapor shimmer on her skin before it disappeared, leaving her hands completely dry.

"Athelea," she demanded, "what's happening?"

Athelea lifted her hand to the waterfall. From what Victoria could see, the vapor simply ran over her skin. "It has probably gone into to your bloodstream," Athelea said. Victoria didn't understand how she could announce that so calmly. "But it won't harm you. You sensed that there wasn't anything dangerous in it, and there isn't. I don't understand why my own skin hasn't absorbed it, though."

Victoria looked closer at her hand, appraising it for damage. The idea of having anything foreign in her blood was unappealing, but at least Athelea wasn't worried. "What is it?"

"I may be completely wrong, but I believe this may be the foundation for a portal."

Even with a fever, Victoria could comprehend what this meant. "A portal for travel in Atlantis?"

"Exactly."

Victoria felt her heart race, imagining the possibilities. This was the second sign of real progress she'd seen in Atlantis since she'd arrived here, if not the first real change to happen since the Destruction. She wished Athelea would let excitement overcome her maternal worry. "Have

352

you got any idea where this one goes?"

"Unfortunately not. The other side doesn't appear to have formed yet. It could be anywhere in Atlantis, and it could take years."

Victoria stared at the portal in wonder. Atlantis was healing. The process was bound to be slow, but this portal had to be a sign that Atlantis was finally healing. She simultaneously felt more and less guilty about leaving, knowing that Atlantis would be okay, though she was bitterly disappointed that she would miss all the amazing changes that were sure to come. "Could you keep an eye on this for me?" she asked. "Just in case it leads outside of Atlantis."

"Of course." After a few minutes, they set off. Fifteen minutes later, they reached the palace gates. Victoria stopped for a moment, shivering although the morning was already warm. She suspected it was a combination of her fever and her growing apprehension at the journey ahead.

"If you can manage to get Sarah, I'll prepare the boat for you," Athelea said as she unlocked the gate. "It will be waiting for you at Shipwreck Beach when you get there."

Victoria nodded, her throat suddenly tight. She was struck with the impression that this was their last goodbye, and she had to take her chance. "Thank you for everything, Athelea. This has been the most amazing experience. I'll really miss you and Atlantis."

"You deserve the thanks, Victoria," Athelea said. "You have been so brave and done so much for Atlantis. I will keep searching for the Atlanteans, and if they ever return, I will find a way to let you know."

"Stay safe until then," Victoria choked out. "Please take care of yourself, and don't fight Caelan if you ever see him."

"I will stay safe, and you, too. You have a wonderful future ahead of you."

Victoria realized neither of them were going to say the word, but a second later, she found herself in Athelea's arms. Their unspoken goodbye lingered in their embrace, and after a long second, they parted. With a final smile, Athelea turned around, and Victoria turned to the palace.

You got what you want, Caelan, Victoria thought, her heart breaking. *I'm leaving everything behind, including the most amazing mother anyone could ask for.*

And a tear slid down her cheek.

Returning to her bedroom, she found that Sarah had made their beds and collected their belongings in a small pile in the middle of the room. Victoria used a dex to transform her cloak into another bag and turned her attention to packing.

"Goodbyes are horrible," Sarah said.

Victoria nodded and put away Sarah's notebooks and the clothes they'd brought to Atlantis. Apart from a few dresses Athelea had made, there was so little they would be taking back. She added all the food from the table, knowing they would need it for the journey ahead since they no longer had a dex to help them.

"I'm going to miss this place, too, you know," Sarah said softly. "But at least we have the memories to take back. They're not going anywhere, are they?"

But what does Athelea have? Victoria wondered. She knew nothing could make up for the lost years and memories, but she wanted to give Athelea something to remember her by. When Sarah wasn't looking, she reached into her bag for the tatty pink ribbon that had been on her wrist for so long after she'd first gotten her Sentence. The words *mene mene tekel upharsin* still shone brightly on her skin, and she never wanted to hide them again, no matter what Aiden or Andrea might think.

And, blinking back tears, she let the ribbon flutter onto the bed. *I hope you can forgive me for leaving, someday,* Victoria thought. It felt right to leave this reminder of her past behind for Athelea, especially now that she was facing the future, and Athelea would know what it signified. She stood up, knowing she'd done everything she could for Atlantis and would never really feel ready to leave. She could only pray that the Atlanteans would return soon to keep Athelea company.

She and Sarah left the Isle of the Gods. Victoria felt

a nervous flutter in her stomach as they approached Shipwreck Beach. The city was still empty, and she struggled to believe this was the last time she would see it. A wooden boat was on the sand, but Athelea was nowhere in sight. Victoria felt a wave of sadness as the truth hit her. "That was goodbye," she said. She could feel Atlantis begging her to stay with everything it had, but her raging fever was impossible to ignore.

"We have to go home."

Victoria nodded. She tossed the bag of clothes and sketchbooks to the bottom of the boat, hoping she hadn't forgotten anything. Looking to the pier, she shuddered as she saw that the ship in which Caelan had imprisoned her was there, reminding her that leaving was the right decision. "There's one more thing I'd like to do," she said to Sarah, suddenly realizing what was preventing her from leaving Atlantis with a clear conscience. "Could you wait here? I'll be back in a sec."

Sarah nodded, and Victoria grabbed a spare sheet of paper from the bag and made her way onto the pier. Boarding the ship with black masts, she had no way of telling if Caelan had been here since she'd escaped, but she would have to take the risk. She made her way through the empty cabin and down to the hold, knowing it was the first place Caelan would eventually search for her. When she reached the small closet that had been her prison, she found her pen and paper and scrawled a note that was still perfectly legible in the dim light.

You will never destroy Atlantis, she wrote. *I promise.*

And she pricked her fingertip on the pin from her dress, smeared the resulting drop of blood along the bottom of the paper like a signature, and slid it through the crack under the door. She walked to the boat with tears in her eyes, though she couldn't help but smile.

Atlantis would be safe, hidden forever.

THE END

Dear Reader,

Thank you for taking the time to read my first full-length novel. It's been a long time in the making, and I'm so excited to be sharing my work with readers all around the world at last.

If you enjoyed *The Last Atlanteans* as much as I enjoyed writing it, please leave a review on your local Amazon site or share with friends. For updates on future works, I'm currently on Facebook and Twitter (links below) and would love to get to know my readers better. At the end of the day, I just want to thank you for reading. My writing wouldn't be here without you!

Best wishes,
Katrina Ryan

About the Author

Katrina has been writing for as long as she can remember. She lived in Scottsdale, Arizona, until she moved to the UK for university. She studied creative writing as an undergraduate, graduated from Durham University with a MA in English, and interned with various London publishers before focusing on her own writing. She has a passion for languages, travelling, and Harry Potter and still lives in the UK with her husband and cat.

Contact Katrina

Facebook: facebook.com/TheLastAtlanteans
Twitter: @LastAtlanteans
Instagram: @LastAtlanteans
#TheLastAtlanteans

Also by Katrina Ryan
The Rise of Atlantis

Printed in Great Britain
by Amazon

76415883R00220